THE SECRET BROKER

A LUCA VOSS NOVEL

THE SECRET BROKER

SIMON CRANE

QUARTET

First published in 2016 by Quartet Books Limited
A member of the Namara Group
27 Goodge Street, London W1T 2LD
Copyright © Simon Crane 2016
The right of Simon Crane
to be identified as the author of this work
has been asserted by him in accordance with the
Copyright, Designs and Patents Act, 1988.

A catalogue record for this book
is available from the British Library
ISBN 978 0 7043 7411 9

Typeset by Josh Bryson
Printed and bound in Great Britain by
T J International Ltd, Padstow, Cornwall

This is a work of fiction. All characters are fictitious.
Any resemblance to actual events, locales or persons,
living or dead, is entirely coincidental.

Dedicated to Chantal Crane

Nothing strengthens authority so much as silence.
Leonardo da Vinci

1
North Pacific,
650 kilometres South-East of Japan

The craggy-faced Japanese captain of the cargo ship cursed himself for agreeing to make the trip. His craft, *Shisupiritto*, was a feeder-class freight ship able to carry just under two hundred and fifty full-size shipping containers. It was a minnow compared to the largest bulk carriers that could carry fifteen times as much, but at over one hundred metres long, it had served him and his crew well as they delivered rice—humanitarian aid—to the people of North Korea on behalf of the United Nations.

To the concern of his crew, the captain had taken on six undeclared passengers before travelling down to South Korea where they had filled half its capacity with cargo bound for Los Angeles. Many of the crew had been with the captain for over a decade but none of them had ever before known him to pull a stunt like this. They knew it was illegal, his strict insistence on silence confirming that, but it was something worse still: it was dangerous, as if somehow the gods might punish them. The storm circling around them seemed confirmation of this to several of the more superstitious members of the crew. Even rational men adopted strange beliefs after enough time at sea.

The captain squeezed his eyes shut with remorse. *What was I thinking?* Then he cursed himself again. He knew what he was thinking, he was thinking of the money. After a lifetime in the Japanese Navy and the Merchant Navy, any hope of a comfortable retirement had evaporated when his pension had been all but wiped out during the last recession. He had already worked ten years longer than he had planned, but this one act could guarantee security for his wife—and his mistress. But the doubts still lingered. *How did they find me? How did they know I would say yes? Who were they?* These, along with dozens of other self-critical questions, tossed about in his mind until the storm cut through and grabbed his attention.

Shīsupiritto was being battered by twenty-metre-high waves, lifted out of the security of the waters only to dive perilously back down, plunging the bow into yet another monstrous wave. Despite the ship's seven thousand tonnes it was no match for the furious sea and every rivet that held the freight carrier together seemed to groan as the ship slapped down onto the water. There was no escape.

In weather like this, the captain had three priorities, which he never tired of dictating: 'Keep the engines running, keep the engines running, keep the engines running.' The task was in the hands of two brothers from Japan's north island of Hokkaido who monitored the banks of dials and workstations in the engine room with practised eyes, scouting for any problems. For now, they had no concerns—the 4,825-kilowatt diesel engines were made for these conditions and worse.

The rest was up to the captain, and this proved harder. Rain coming in at a 45-degree angle had tested the mettle of crew members who earlier had braved the slippery sub-decks as they ran around every last chain to reassure the captain that each was secured and would stay that way as they entered the storm. Now these crew members were with the captain on the bridge, swapping jokes to shore up each other's courage. After an hour of this, though, their masks slipped, all conversation dying in an instant. A wave taller than the ship crashed across the bow, washing along the tops of the four-storey-high block of containers before pouring away to reveal the ship once again. Those who didn't hear the metallic snap of the chains saw the effects—a row of containers at the bow suddenly began to spill over—and the first stack fell off the ship and into the ocean.

The captain fought down the fear that swelled inside him as he looked through the rain-soaked windscreens, doubting whether his nerves could take it on top of the burden of his cargo. It was then the Shinto-worshipping ex-Navy officer felt the presence of his ancestors pointing their fingers at him, as if they had arranged the tempest as an earthly punishment for his act of greed. He shook his head to banish the phantoms then began cursing anew as he attempted to turn the ship into the prevailing waves.

Isamu, the youngest of the crew, had cast a glance first at the unshackled cargo at the far end of the deck then back at his captain. 'We could still save the bottom ones,' he said.

'I will not lose a member of my crew because of some stupid cargo,' the captain replied.

There was silence as another wave, larger than the last, consumed the bow, rolling along the top of the containers and onto the bridge. Its dissipating energy was not enough to threaten the stormproof windows, but it was still an unnerving sight for all who witnessed it.

Then an unexpected change occurred.

As the ship turned in on the waves with aching slowness, the weather that had rolled in out of nowhere seemed to lose its anger. The day remained almost night-dark, but the wind dropped from a storm to a strong gale in a matter of seconds. The rain slowed from torrential to driving. The seas settled from mountains to hills. Without saying so, the crew all thought of the captain's earlier promise that they were catching the edge of the storm. As ever, he had been proved right, a fact confirmed by a lethal mass of heavy clouds passing by on their starboard side. Their worst fears had failed to materialise. With the lifting of the weather, their hearts dared to lift too. This is why they sailed with Captain Tokuji, they reminded themselves; his grizzled face with its wispy beard and ever-present cigarette had a pessimistic temperament to match, but nobody knew the sea better. And for this, they thanked the stars and their ancestors.

Then the navigation officer turned his head away from the screens in front of him, doubtful of his own words as he scratched his chin with a biro. 'Captain. Something's approaching. Fast.'

The captain's heart leapt into his mouth, his worst fears taunting him. 'What is it?'

'It's too fast for a boat—it must be a plane.'

The captain looked out at the endless clouds leading down to the horizon. 'Probably a commercial flight.'

The young navigation officer twirled a pen around his fingers as he continued to stare at his screens. 'We're in the middle of the Pacific, Captain, and this thing is coming directly towards us—from the north.'

The captain's stomach tightened to the point of nausea. *It can't be a coincidence.* Then, like everybody else, he looked out of the port windows to see a large twin-prop plane emerging from the clouds and heading their way.

'What the hell is it doing?' he muttered.

A burly crew member, built entirely of muscle and nautical tattoos, pulled a disbelieving face. 'It looks like it's going to buzz us. Look how it's coming in.'

But the young Isamu shook his head. 'It's coming in to land.'

'*Land?*' The captain was almost angry at the insanity of it. 'What are you talking about?'

4

Isamu respectfully pointed at the aircraft. 'I'm talking about that, Captain.'

One by one, they all saw it. It was a helicopter, but instead of a top-mounted propeller, it had wings, like a plane, with rotor blades that were switching from their forward position to a vertical position.

Isamu answered the question hanging unanswered. 'It's an Osprey, the military use them. Maybe it needs help?'

The captain shook his head sceptically, his nerves rattled at the various scenarios his guilty conscience was suggesting in his mind. 'No helicopter could reach us from land, we're too far out. Where has it come from?'

The navigation officer looked at his console uncertainly. 'Should I try to contact it?'

The captain dropped his long-extinguished cigarette to the floor and squashed it under foot.

'No. Contact the US Coast Guard. Tell them—'

The flash from the helicopter was bright enough to erase all other thoughts. It took a few seconds for the captain and crew to register that all the electronics on the bridge had gone dead; that every screen, light and communication device had been shut down in an instant.

The tattooed crew member was moving quickly along the bridge control console, looking for signs of life in any of the equipment. 'What's happening?' he asked.

Isamu had joined the crew from university. He had broken his parents' hearts by honouring their desire to see him graduate but then ending his obedience and realising his dream of the sea. Still, his studies in physics were not in vain and they leapt to his mind now.

'It's an EMP device, electromagnetic pulse. It's a bomb of sorts—that flash from the helicopter must have been an explosion; anything that's stopped working will have had its inside fried to shit.'

5

The other crew members who had ribbed 'Einstein' since his arrival three years earlier listened dumbly, aware that he knew exactly what he was talking about.

Voices rose with concern as the engines down below painfully whirred to a halt. The captain pulled out his phone and saw it was switched off. Not as he had left it. He pressed the power button, but there was nothing.

Then, as one, everyone had a new concern: the seven-thousand-tonne vessel was adrift alongside a hurricane that could turn back towards them at any moment. The consequences were unthinkable and a fearful silence descended.

They all knew they were at the mercy of the helicopter's occupants as it swooped in faster than anybody believed to be safe, pulling up treacherously late and buffeting the bridge with the *thud thud thud* of its blades before hovering briefly, rotating 180 degrees, and landing on a flat row of containers. With its rear facing them, a large loading bay began to yawn open.

The ten men present looked on silently before Isamu pointed in alarm at what was coming out of the bowels of the craft.

The captain nodded fatalistically. 'I see it.' He reached into a cupboard below the steering controls, rapidly dialled open a safe and pulled out an automatic pistol.

The men were as hardy and tested as any group could be, but the sight of their captain arming himself for the first time ever filled each of them with a rising dread and a certainty that taking on the illegal cargo had been a big mistake.

The captain looked out at the helicopter with its slowing propellers and then at the six men in black SWAT gear, Uzi sub-machine guns held across their fronts, walking down the ramp. There was a short man in front of them, his hands behind his back, his full-length leather coat whipping about his legs in the winds of the dying storm. The captain shoved the pistol into the top of his jeans and covered it with his pullover, his all-weather coat completely hiding any bulk it might suggest.

He gave his men a sharp look that brooked no opposition. 'I'll do the talking.'

The newly arrived squad of armed men were rendered anonymous by the visors on their dark riot helmets. Their leader wore a cloth wrapped around his face like a curiously stylish bank robber. From his boots to his combat trousers, his full-length leather jacket to his hair, everything on his person was black. Even the reflective police-style sunglasses that stared lifelessly into the captain's eyes stuck to the theme.

The captain went to speak but the leader of the new arrivals spoke over him.

'You have passengers on board.' It was said loudly, in the crew's native Japanese, though with a mainland accent.

The captain knew it was not posed as a question and his chest tightened at this impossible complication, the man who thought himself irreligious once again regretting the fact he had not remembered his ancestors before taking on the passengers. He cast a careful glance at Isamu—loyalty the young crewman's greatest strength and weakness. Then he choked as he struggled to find any words. In part, because it was his ship, his authority being questioned in front of his entire crew for the first time, but mostly because seven men stood before him and he had a gun in the front of his jeans with nine bullets.

He dared to calculate whether he could pull out his gun and either shoot the intruders in succession or at least hold their ringleader at gunpoint. But then, another thought: *who the hell were they? Would he be shooting Americans, Japanese, Chinese, North Koreans, or another nationality? Were they the border police? Were they pirates?*

Then a doubt about the handgun: was the safety catch on? He hadn't checked. What if he pulled the trigger, nothing happened, and he was left helpless as six guns turned on him?

'No. This is a freight ship. We have no passengers.' It was Isamu who said this, his nerves buckling at the sight of his hesitant captain.

The leader of the armed men gave what seemed a thoughtful nod, then brought his hand out from behind him, pointed a large semi-automatic pistol at Isamu and pulled the trigger.

If the murderer saw the back of Isamu's head explode over two of the other crew members before his lifeless body slumped backwards, if he heard the swiftly muffled cries of the crew itself, he gave no indication of it. Instead, he calmly addressed the captain once again.

'You have passengers on board.'

The captain wanted to form a lie, his mouth working silently for a moment before he resigned himself to the inevitable, shame mixing with fear, fear mixing with horror.

'Yes, yes we do.'

'Bring them here now. All six of them.'

The captain, torn by remorse, turned to four of his crew and indicated they do as instructed. As they all but ran back towards the bridge, the intruder spoke again.

'Now show me where their cargo is.'

Halfway along the deck was an alleyway dividing two blocks of shipping containers. Standing between them, four storeys of containers on either side, were the newly arrived gunmen, the captain, and the crew. Also present were six American passengers. Five of them were terrified, the two women and youngest male fighting to hold back tears. Only a late middle-aged man eyed them calmly. He was wearing a dark blue baseball cap emblazoned with USS *Missouri BB-63* and a battleship.

8

The leather-coat-wearing intruder waved his gun about. 'Which container?'

He was met with silence. Half-defiant, half-uncertain.

He raised his gun at the captain without drama. 'I only need one of you alive to answer my questions.'

The eldest of the two female Americans yelped in alarm. 'JVXZ something. That one there, I think.' She felt no guilt at pointing to a nearby container at the bottom of the stack.

One of the crew sliced through the lock on the container door with a large pair of bolt cutters. Another unlocked the door and after seeking permission from his boss, which came in the form of a nod, he swung both doors open. For the first time since the helicopter had landed everybody present forgot they were on board a ship helplessly adrift in the sea. For now, everybody was staring at a neat wall of cardboard boxes.

The captain knew nothing about this container or its contents, not even that it might be connected to his illegal passengers, but he knew the rules of the sea.

'I forbid you to interfere with this ship's cargo.'

The spray from a tall wave showered the group as the militia leader, his hands behind his back, turned to the captain.

'Did they really pay you enough to take a bullet for this?' He gestured with his gun to the illegal passengers and the open container.

The captain looked shame-facedly at his feet.

Without being asked, two of the militiamen stepped forward and with a certainty borne of knowledge thumped at the boxes with the stocks of their Uzis creating a kind of archway that led into the container. One militiaman walked into the darkness to emerge a few seconds later with a large metal briefcase, which he took directly to his leader.

9

As the militia leader crouched down and unclasped the case the passenger with the USS *Missouri* baseball cap took a step forward.

'You can't—'

But any other words were lost as the stock of an Uzi made violent contact with the base of his skull causing him to crash to the deck.

The leader seemed to take no interest in the altercation and instead lifted up the lid of the briefcase to reveal a foam-lined interior with a dozen glass jars with different dark-coloured substances inside. He inspected one that was full of grey powder, reading its handwritten label. Then he addressed the five passengers who were still standing.

'Kanggye, that's in North Korea, isn't it? Now, why would six American geologists have mineral samples from there?'

The passengers' terrified silence confessed their guilt in a way words never could. The young man started to cry. One of the women took his hand and squeezed it tight.

The militia leader took off his sunglasses and an unpleasant smile filled his bright green eyes.

'Don't rush to answer—you're coming with us.'

The prone body of the oldest geologist, his USS *Missouri* baseball cap resting on his chest, had been lifted onto the Osprey helicopter. Behind him, the remaining five passengers were herded on at gunpoint. After the armed men, their leader was the last to board, watched by the ship's helpless and shaken crew. He stood at the bottom of the loading bay and looked about the scene: Isamu dead on the row of containers, the ship adrift in the choppy waters, the behemoth of storm clouds off to the south. Then he addressed the crew in Japanese.

'Sorry about the electronics. We'll send out an SOS for you. In a while. Enjoy the sea.'

The Osprey started to rise as he walked up the loading bay ramp, the door closing mechanically as he entered. The departing helicopter was watched aghast by captain and crew as they were left to the mercy of the Pacific Ocean.

2

Costa Alegre, West Coast of Mexico

JJ was in her element. She didn't even care that the car she was driving was borrowed, after all, everything else felt as though it had been borrowed; the paradise-like weather of blue skies and sun, the British racing green Bentley convertible she was steering along the idyllic coastline, even the time she was spending with Luca. Luca, the first man to have made her come back for more. Luca, the only man she had ever allowed in, however guarded she remained. Only, right now, Luca was nowhere to be seen.

'Where *are* you?'

'There's a straight stretch of road coming up, take her down to sixty kilometres per hour.'

Luca's voice was coming through the car phone speakers but try as she might the twenty-eight-year-old Chinese woman couldn't see him anywhere.

'Are you on a motorbike? Baby, where are you?'

She searched the rear-view mirror, the road up ahead, to the left, and to the right, but she was undeniably alone on the endless stretch of coastline highway. She took the car down to sixty as instructed and looked about once again.

'OK, I get it, you're messing with me. Ha-ha, Mr Voss. You win.'

Out of nowhere, her companion landed on the seats behind her with as graceful a thump as was possible, releasing his parachute so it whipped away behind him.

JJ screamed, lost control, veering the Bentley into the opposite lane. After regaining control and bringing it back, she started to laugh while looking behind her to see Luca's serenely smiling visage staring back. She reached over her shoulder and slapped at him with a hand.

'You bastard. *You crazy bastard.*'

Ignoring her flailing hand, Luca leaned forward and lightly hopped into the front passenger seat, delivering her a questioning smile as he did so.

'Well, you told me to drop by when I was finished.'

The Swiss man looked at his Chinese companion who was laughing incredulously between moments of anger, her jet-black hair flowing down over her shoulders somehow perfect, like everything about her. Despite a childhood spent in a Shanghai slum, JJ's adoption by British parents meant that her English was near perfect. She had mentioned a Ukrainian grandmother once and there was definitely a Eurasian element to her, the bone structure slightly longer, fuller. Luca had to admit to himself that with her athletic body, megawatt smile and eyes that invited a world of pleasure, she was probably as good as it got. This made the purpose of their brief time away all the harder for him; it was an opportunity to spoil her before breaking the news that he was off to Japan for six months and that this would be a good time to end their affair.

JJ's laughter had subsided and she looked out at the coastline trailing past them as they blasted along the Mexican highway. When she turned back, her look was almost critical.

'You could have killed yourself back there.'

Luca gave an almost imperceptible shrug. 'Maybe that was the point.'

As Luca looked at the road ahead, JJ studied his face for a smile to undo what he had just said but found nothing.

Luca's property on Mexico's Pacific coast looked like a flying saucer sitting on stilts leaning over the clifftop. The effect was

13

a space age house floating above the blue sea that lapped at the blonde beach below. The interior was a similar story. White living spaces blurred into each other with minimal dividing walls as they wrapped around a central hub. Windows ran unbroken around the entire single floor, but for the odd discreet doorway onto a patio affording spectacular views across the Pacific.

To one side in a lounge area hung a black punchbag with red Cantonese writing running down it. JJ had flicked off her shoes on entering the house and made straight for it where she then proceeded to assault it with a series of skilful Wing Chun kicks and punches, which saw her leap off the ground before landing in a crouch, only to relaunch herself at her target.

Luca had wandered over to the kitchen bar to fix them a cocktail, all the while watching JJ with a mixture of admiration and curiosity. He had noticed since meeting her a few months before that when she was processing information, or when trying to clarify an issue in her mind, she would work it out of her system in one of two ways. Either she would practice her martial arts until she was so spent that she had to shower to cool down or—

JJ stopped abruptly and looked at her lover almost irritated, then began a long-legged stride towards him. 'Shall we move to the bedroom or what?'

Luca grinned mischievously as he handed her a drink in a tall glass. 'Tell me more about the what.'

JJ eyed him over a mouthful of the drink before lifting her head with a satisfied gasp. After a pause that was part pleasure at the rehydration, part making him wait, a twinkle came to her eye. '*What...* would you like?' Then the taste of the cocktail came back to her and she found herself pausing to enjoy it. 'What's this you've made me?'

Luca pulled a nonchalant face as he listed the ingredients. 'Gin, elderflower, cucumber, tonic, with four shakes of orange bitters. Would you prefer a coke?'

She smiled at his faux snobby dig and began to move around the bar with feline grace, all but purring as she undid the few buttons of her red silk shirt, which opened to barely cover her two modest but beautifully curved breasts.

JJ looked up at her lover; the chocolate-drop eyes that seemed to see right through her, the long sandy hair in which she always longed to bury her face, the handsome, chiselled face, arrogant but without vanity, and that body he zealously exercised as if on some kind of mission he would not reveal. She loved it all. What worried her was whether she was in love with the man, because love meant weakness.

She shook the glass in her hand, gave it a little rattle to hear the cubes inside it click. 'Remind me, Mr Voss. What happened the other night when you ran an ice cube around my nipple? Got all hard, didn't it?'

Luca matched her smile. It was then that his Swiss smart-watch announced the arrival of a text message.

This stopped JJ in her tracks. In the five months she had known him that watch had never made a sound. His mobile phone had rung, but only occasionally. He'd even had conversations in front of her, though not many. But the smart-watch? Never. Not once.

He looked down at it and read the message: 'Switch on BBC News.'

JJ saw the seriousness with which he greeted the text. 'Who sent that?'

His look was not accompanied by words but she knew what it meant. *I don't want to say*.

As they stood in the middle of the lounge area, the television in front of them, there were three headline stories on the news. One, which was part way through when they tuned in, told the story of a cargo ship found adrift three thousand kilometres off the coast of Japan. The next concerned a

North Korean weapons test that saw a missile provocatively cross the skies over the southern tip of Japan before landing harmlessly in the sea three hundred kilometres to its east. But it was the third and final headline that had Luca gripped as the newsreader spoke over an accompanying map of three borders at North Korea's north-eastern point.

'...a diplomatic row has broken out between North Korea, China, and Russia over responsibility for an unidentified body found at their joint border on the edge of the small Russian town of Khasan. For more, we're joined by our East Asia correspondent John Sudworth...'

'What?' asked JJ.

Luca's response had unnerved JJ and he seemed not to notice her question as he looked slowly about himself, the news hitting him hard.

'Franz...' he muttered to himself.

'Luca, what's wrong, please?'

'I think I know who that man was.'

'Who?'

But before he could answer the smartwatch trilled again. As Luca read it, JJ hesitantly tried to lighten the mood.

'So what is it telling us to watch this time, South Park? Because I can watch that all—'

'Get out.'

'Luca, I was just kidding—'

'Not you—*us*.'

Luca held his watch out so JJ could see the message: 'Get out.'

'What does that mean?'

'It means—'

And before she could say another word he had grabbed her by the upper arm and was frogmarching her firmly out of the room.

'My shoes.'

But Luca ignored her. He scooped up the keys from a stone bowl near the front door, flung it open, and left it that way as he continued marching JJ to the car.

'I'll drive.'

Instead of joining him in the open-top Bentley, JJ collected herself and, though partly embarrassed at her own truculence, folded her arms. 'What the hell makes you think you can treat me that way?'

Luca's look was one of such ferocity that it left her a little breathless until he bit down on his own excited anger.

'I apologise. But, either way, I'm leaving in three seconds.'

JJ couldn't deny that she felt more strongly about him than any man she had ever known, but she had seen her adopted mother pushed about by her father and swore never to go down that path.

'Well, then you're going to have to…'

Luca glared at her. '*What?*'

JJ couldn't meet his eye. Hurt, insulted, and disappointed, she stared out past the insane flying saucer of a house to the sea. But then, a moment later, she leapt over the door into the passenger seat, Luca flooring the accelerator before she'd even made contact with her seat. The car reached one hundred kilometres per hour before the end of the short drive where it fishtailed onto the highway, just in time for both of them to see two missiles slam into the building behind them, obliterating it into rubble and flames as a jet fighter roared overhead at five hundred kilometres per hour.

Luca stopped the car to take in the scene of destruction that had been his property seconds before.

JJ looked from it to her lover, confusion mixed with bewilderment and adrenaline.

'Who the—' She shook her head in disbelief. 'Who sent that text?'

★　　★　　★

Luca had handled it badly and he knew it. When JJ had needed him to talk, to explain the wrecking ball that had just crashed through their world, he hadn't said a word. He had remained mute knowing that he was making a bad situation worse.

JJ couldn't begin to understand what had just happened to them. She hadn't asked any more questions as Luca drove them to the nearby harbour. Hadn't demanded to know who would do that to them as they motored the 143-foot-long Wally yacht out into the bay. Hadn't insisted on learning who could do that to them as she complied with his taciturn requests for assistance in getting the sailing under way as they headed out into the Pacific Ocean. What she knew now was that the playboy with whom she had spent an increasing amount of time of late was more of a mystery than she had imagined. In learning something about the nature of his enemies, she knew less about Luca than ever before.

After two hours of sailing, the sun began to set on their port side as they tracked the Mexican coast north. JJ had been sitting in a small horseshoe of sofas at the stern waiting to know her own mind, or for the man she realised she knew almost nothing about to give an indication of whether he was going to open up or stay as closed as a clam. Then, for the briefest of moments, she wondered if he posed a threat to her. *Who had she let into her life? If killers were lined up against him, did that make him a killer too? Did he run with his own type?*

But no, she decided that whatever he was, he wasn't a threat, he was an enigma; which was a pity, because the past few years had taught her to deal with threats. In the underground world of gambling she had needed more than Lady Luck to survive.

Such were her meandering thoughts that she only noticed Luca had disappeared when he emerged from the cabin holding a couple of gin and tonics—the yacht on autopilot. He seated himself opposite JJ, her graceful high-cheekboned face basking in the dying warmth of the day's sun. Slowly she looked at him, saw the patient but expectant look on his face, and knew he was ready to talk. At the sight of this she felt her tension ease slightly, only realising now how uptight the whole affair had made her feel, how distant she may have seemed herself.

'Two gin and tonics for you but nothing for me, where did you learn to woo a lady?'

Luca allowed a contrite smile to grow on one side of his face as he proffered her one of the glasses. She took it and they fell into an easy silence, both sipping from their drinks as they pondered the setting sun across the water.

Then they both spoke at the same moment.

'You know…'

'I should have…'

JJ let go a heavy sigh but gave Luca the floor, not interested in lecturing him. Just yet.

'We're in the middle of something.'

JJ waited for more but nothing came. 'We?'

'I'm… I'm in the middle of something.'

'You don't say.' She took another sip from her drink and waited again, but was met with an apologetic silence. She considered him, tanned and attractive, and curiously impeccable in his white shirt, loose white trousers, and boat shoes. Then she almost did a double take when she remembered that he hadn't been dressed like that when they arrived at the boat. He must have changed for their evening together. She almost sighed again as she realised that without ever announcing it, he had what her adoptive mother would have called 'an indefinable air of class' about him. He accepted her for what she was, but quietly lived by his own rules. Rules that, to her irritation, she found very attractive.

She looked around the yacht in the gently fading light. It was a sleek craft finished with teak decking. Taking it all in, JJ felt the glorious throwback to some imagined *La Dolce Vita* era, like they might be about to glide into port in 1950s Rome. The boat was, she realised, also something else. It was expensive. Very expensive. Just like the clifftop house. Just like the car—just like all the cars he'd driven her around in during their globetrotting. Politeness had stopped her probing before, but now, with the insanity back at the house, she felt all social niceties were up for review.

'Luca, where do you get the money for all this?'

Her companion pushed his sandy hair out of his eyes and pulled a non-committal face. 'From my work.'

The hesitation wasn't lost on her, but she chose to let it slide. 'I've known you, what, almost six months? You've never talked about your work. I thought…'

'Thought what?'

'I thought you didn't work.'

Luca pulled a face that told her he found that an unattractive proposition. 'Independently wealthy, you mean?'

'Something like that.'

'No. No, not at all. It's not that I don't work, it's just that…'

'Just what?'

'Just that it's all borrowed, that's all.' Something about his own words seemed briefly to hold an infinite sadness for Luca that he tried, and failed, to hide from JJ.

'Borrowed?'

'Maybe not borrowed. Maybe—I don't know; think of it as loaned to me. As a down payment for…' Rather than finishing the sentence he sighed, the matter weighing heavily on his mind.

'Down payment for what, Luca?'

He looked at her and it was clear to JJ that it was more than just a burden to her companion, it was a secret. Then, to break the tension, or dismiss the matter, he visibly relaxed.

'For a service I may have to perform. Or maybe not.' He shrugged, finished his drink, and saw that she had done the same. 'Another one?'

As he made his way down into the cabin JJ tried to get her head round his cagey explanation of the luxury lifestyle he enjoyed, a lifestyle he happily shared with her without explaining how he could afford it. Something was eating at her, something that had bothered her from day one and only now was bubbling up to the surface. *That was it.* She suddenly understood what was wrong. He had never been showy about anything, had never worn the proprietorial grin of the playboy showing off his playthings, not when he picked her up in a six-figure sports car, or flew her to a casino by helicopter. He wasn't lying. He *didn't* own any of it.

'What service? What job would you have to do that would pay this much up front?'

Luca was re-emerging with the drinks. He paused on the top step, looked out at the ball of fire that was the sun melting into the horizon, a pink hue framing his lover. Then he stepped round one of the yacht's large wooden wheels towards the bench at the rear and sat down.

JJ watched him carefully before sliding over, lifting up her drink and moving to sit herself sideways on his lap. Her face was inches from his as she scoured his eyes for clues. 'Herr Voss, are you a spy?'

For a brief moment, Luca fought a smile but lost the battle. 'Who for?'

'The Swiss. Maybe that's how they avoid all the wars, with spies everywhere?'

'Well, if I *was* a spy I couldn't exactly tell *you*, could I? How do I know *you're* not a spy?'

JJ bit her lip suggestively. 'Like one of those Mata Hari types, sent to screw the information out of the enemy?'

'Delicately put as ever.'

She looked sternly at him but could not hide the smile in her eyes. She put both their drinks aside, then, with gymnastic grace, lifted a leg clean over his head, bringing it down so that she sat astride him. She went to speak, but was interrupted.

'You know JJ, you've never told me what you do.'

Luca felt a tiny pang of guilt at asking the question, not needing to hear the answer, but interested in her version of it. He had been handed a dossier a week after meeting her, knew about her string of expulsions from England's finest schools, her moonlighting work at London casinos, her being banned from all of them for an unexplained stretch of winning. Luca didn't doubt this was down to pure skill after the pain he saw her inflict on the Strip during their weekend in Vegas recently.

'Don't change the subject, Herr Voss. Whatever it is I do, people don't try to blow me up for it.'

A moment of seriousness had arrived out of nowhere, and the playfulness seemed to have gone as she looked at him with a kind intensity that demanded answers. Luca leaned his head back to get a better look, studying her face for clues.

'Why aren't you crying?'

She looked at him askew. 'What do you mean?'

'Somebody tried to kill us. Ninety-nine out of a hundred women would be putting as much distance between themselves and me as they could right now, but you're still here. Why?'

JJ hesitated. An answer came to mind. *Because I've got nowhere else to go.* But something stopped her from saying it. Maybe it was too serious or maybe it was too flippant.

Instead, she leaned forward and kissed him slowly. As his hands moved up her back she felt the near-shudder his hands always inspired in her. She knew why she had not said it: it was too honest.

3
Northern Myanmar,
50 kilometres North of Myitkyina

The Mongolian man stared out from the upper deck of the 240-foot mega-yacht *Charon*, at the lush, verdant world around him. Raised on the edge of the Gobi Desert the sight that met him could almost have been of a Martian planet, so removed was it from the land he had grown up in. The jungle stretched as far as the eye could see, its trees rising up into low mountains to the west, rendering the air thick with a humidity that could be escaped by retreating into the yacht's enormous cabin. Gone was the full-length leather coat, the black combat wear; he wore light linen clothes, grey from head to foot, his style Western with a nod to his Mongol culture in the discreetly tailored patterns. Butakhan allowed himself a smile at the thought of the name of the country: no longer Burma, but Myanmar. Asserting its roots. Asia rising. Asia shifting from underneath the American jackboot, America having no idea what was coming. Proud of his role in it, excited by it.

Down below, the boat itself was moored to a rudimentary jetty by a track. Along the jetty, being marched at gunpoint, were the six American geologists. Even in the last forty-eight hours, they had shrunk visibly, their spirits reduced by their captivity. They had undoubtedly been disoriented by the distance travelled, the alien landscape into which they had now been dropped and the bleak uncertainty of their future. A group of soldiers standing by an ex-army truck were waiting to transport them into the jungle. A stocky militiaman in army fatigues unlatched a rear panel on the truck to allow access for the passengers. The metallic slam earned a chorus of shrieks from birds and nearby monkeys, the trees trembling for a brief moment as primates escaped them and green and yellow parrots took flight.

A woman's hand gently squeezed the Mongolian man's shoulder. He looked at its owner, a creature more exotic than anything found in these backwaters. Her name was Scarlett and she wore a short, white sheer dress on top of a white bikini. More Miami than Myanmar, but he had no complaints. He liked to see her curves. He liked the world to see the curves of his woman.

She was a thirty-year-old Californian who could have passed for a blonde bombshell from the golden age of Hollywood. Everything about Scarlett was just a little bit too much: the hair too platinum, the make-up a shade too bright, the clothes a touch too revealing. Scarlett the Harlot he called her. In his mind, she was Marilyn Monroe and Jane Mansfield rolled into one. She was just how he liked a woman and she worked hard to make him happy. Quiet and respectful when the black dogs took his moods, fun and sassy at functions, wild and without limits in the bedroom. She had, she told him, run away from a dirt-poor and brutal childhood and was happy to go where the wind took her. He liked her company. With the long scar on his face, he called her the beauty to his beast. She made his world more colourful. Still, the short man noted of his taller partner, there was something hidden away in there, something he didn't quite get. 'Women,' he often mused. 'The eternal mystery.'

'Where have you been?'

Scarlett gave him a playful wide-eyed look that said mind your own business. 'We ladies have to work hard to look this good. Especially in this heat.'

The Mongolian man sipped on the iced tea she had bought him, refreshed by the coolness of the crushed ice. He looked down without emotion at the Americans being manhandled onto the back of the truck.

Scarlett forced herself to look relaxed; scenes such as these were something she knew she would never get used to.

'What will happen to them?' she asked.

He glanced at her before looking back over his prisoners with a critical scowl and patriarchal manner. 'They will make me money. Or they will die.'

'*Please.*' The youngest American male was resisting pathetically as he was being lifted onto the back of the truck.

Scarlett winced at the sight and hoped to God that the message she had sent from her bedroom five minutes earlier had been received.

4
Ticino, Switzerland

The sight of the Swiss chateau never failed to stir Luca's spirit. It was the closest thing to home he had ever known, nestled into the side of an Alpine mountain on the shores of Lake Luzzone on a rocky islet jutting into the water, accessed by a long stone bridge of many arches. The chateau's three exposed sides were sheer blocks topped by squat pyramids for roofs, the towers themselves peppered with high windows, the medieval castle built unquestionably for defensive purposes originally. At some time in the eighteenth century vanity or wealth, or both, saw some softening touches: circular towers added to the two front corners; large Gothic windows inserted into the south-facing wall. And, whether by accident or design, vines had been allowed to grow up and around the rock walls of the castle such that it was rendered almost invisible to passers-by on the far side of the lake.

As Luca drove his British racing green Bentley Continental Zagato in a wide arc around the lake on the road that led to the chateau, he remembered being brought here as a seven-year-old to be told the news that changed things forever. His parents had died in a plane crash in Mozambique. The news was broken in a curiously matter-of-fact fashion by Stefan Hesse, the tall, skeletal-faced, white-haired General Counsel to the Families. Teutonic in manner as well as breeding, curt without being unkind, perhaps it was everything else he had to explain to Luca that day that made the tragic news almost a side story to the main affair. *Or perhaps he was just useless with people*, Luca mused darkly to himself as he slowed his car at the rise of the stone bridge that led to the castle itself. One thing he had to admit, however, was that as much as the revelations of that day seemed hard to take, putting them into practice—living nowhere for more than six months for the rest of his childhood—had been harder still.

A small wooden hatch within the castle's huge door was opened by a young Swiss servant in a sober black uniform, her hair tightly and neatly packed on top of her head. She greeted Luca with a smile that was part welcome, part concern.

'Herr Voss, Herr Hesse is in the library.'

A casual visitor would have been surprised that such a well-defended castle would be opened by such a defenceless woman, but then a casual visitor would not have noticed that their presence had been tracked from the moment they drove onto the castle's long driveway.

Luca crossed through a large medieval courtyard of cobbled stones surrounded by low buildings with warped slate roofs. From here, he walked deep into the far side of the castle itself, down long corridors of arched stone pillars where, as a child, he had imagined knights and foot soldiers waiting to leap out to attack errant travellers. He walked past the understated stone entrance down into the bowels of the castle, with its dungeons rumoured to be the largest of any chateau in the country, impenetrable courtesy of their position in the bedrock of the island itself. They had been given over to an altogether different purpose in the twenty-first century, one that even Luca had never seen.

Eventually he arrived at a studded door and knocked firmly. After a long pause, a stern voice beckoned him from within.

Luca entered a room as tall as the castle with its own keep dug into the mountainside. Its five levels wrapped round a central atrium, each floor packed with shelves that ached with books going back as far as any text in existence. A clever use of discreet windows allowed in more light than could ever have been anticipated and Luca recalled his early visits where he had been encouraged to explore, to discover the joys of the books therein, told to report what he found. He was able to tell of ancient religious texts, the notebooks of Sir Isaac Newton, of the sketchbooks of Leonardo da Vinci, but he held back his best discovery: the network of wooden staircases, so plentiful as to almost form a work by M. C. Escher, the dozen windows, sunk into the walls, letting light into every floor and gallery. It remained his favourite room anywhere, a place where his rudely interrupted boyhood had been replaced with the rigors of academia, his education taken to the highest level by necessity.

As he walked slowly to the centre of the floor around a cluster of monkish desks Luca smiled at the memory of his brief time at a local boarding school. He had written an essay citing an Aristotelian text that his schoolmaster insisted did not exist. Luca, in his naive wisdom, had therefore brought it to show to the master at the beginning of the next term—such was the quality and profundity of the library's collection. The attention it created locally got him into as much trouble as he could remember; withdrawal from the school the least of it. He learned that later the Vatican had initiated a relationship with the castle that saw their two libraries swapping books to great mutual benefit. Eventually he had taken some comfort from that.

'Ho there. I'll be right with you.' The voice of the septuagenarian Stefan Hesse rang down from above, his tall body striding along the third floor.

Luca waited until this man with the vitality of someone twenty years his junior made his way down to greet him. They shook hands, and the General Counsel surprised Luca by putting a familial hand on his shoulder.

'You got my message.'

Luca raised his eyebrows with more than a touch of irony. 'Evidently, I saw the news about the body found on the Korean–Russian border. Has something happened to Franz?'

The eyes in Hesse's skeletal face seemed to want to read whatever he could in Luca's before speaking, as if looking for a clue to something. 'Not just Franz, Raoul as well.'

Luca was rocked by Hesse's words. 'But that only leaves—'

The tall man nodded his head of thin, white hair. 'You.'

Luca and Herr Hesse were sitting in tall leather armchairs in front of an enormous stone fireplace. A decanter of 1963 Taylor's Port and two glasses were on a small table between them. Courtesy of an education in wine that would qualify him as a world-class sommelier, Luca was familiar with the drink's array of spices and nuttiness, though for once, such niceties were not to be dwelt on.

'What do we know about Franz?'

The old man stared into his drink for such a long time that Luca wondered if he was going to answer the question. Finally he shook his head slowly. 'Dumped on a riverbank on the Russian side. All his fingers removed.'

Luca unconsciously leaned forward at the revelation. 'Why would they? Were they trying to hide his identity?'

Hesse again shook his head. 'No. His teeth were not touched. You know how one goes with the other these days.'

'Was it torture?'

Hesse met the eye of his younger associate. 'We don't think so. They were removed after he died.'

The younger man sensed that the General Counsel was holding something back, his manner too careful. A long look between them eventually made Hesse scowl apologetically.

'But there was torture also. Extreme. I don't want to discuss it. I think he may have talked.'

Luca gave a dismissive wave of his hand. 'Everybody talks.' He knew it to be true, it was a myth that people held out. Everybody had a personal breaking point and it was lower than most people imagined. Even those who knew nothing would make something up to appease their tormentors. Luca had been trained, not to survive torture, but to manipulate his captors as best he could, a skill he hadn't called on yet. He pulled his mind back to the task, and ran over the new revelation, drawing a blank on every obvious answer. Was it a message to the Families? Maybe. 'Has anybody contacted us about it?'

'No. We only found out the little we know because of friendly sources in the Russian border guard.'

A thousand questions leapt into Luca's mind to do with the nature of Franz's mission, but they would have to wait. 'What happened to Raoul?'

'His body was dumped outside a police station in Manila. Shot through the head. Nothing else.'

The old man considered the younger man across from him, his hands clasped between his knees in thought. Even through his smart casual clothes, the tailored blazer and trousers, Luca's lithe form was hinted at, his animal instincts, honed over years of training ever present. Luca was a man of action itching to do something about their predicament. Maybe too hotheaded, Hesse mused, but then maybe the alternative was less desirable. Of the three men who had been at his disposal Luca was by far the least experienced, by far the least prepared, and yet of the three he was the most like a—Hesse had to reach back into his mother tongue for the appropriate word—*Krieger*. A warrior.

31

'So how did they know where to find us all? None of us know each other's whereabouts.'

And now Herr Hesse surprised Luca by emptying his glass of vintage port in one go. He refilled himself and offered more to Luca who accepted watchfully. The old man sat back in his chair and seemed uncharacteristically tired, the events, whatever they were, of the last two days catching up with him. He supped on his drink then closed his eyes in such repose as to make Luca entertain the notion that he might have drifted off to sleep.

'I told Franz where you all were.'

'You told him? But that's against—'

'Protocol. I know.' Hesse opened his eyes and looked directly at Luca, pride and shame present on his face. 'He said there was something he wanted to discuss with you both.'

'What?'

'He didn't tell me. But as soon as I heard about the body at the border I contacted you and moments later I learned about Raoul's fate and, well, you know the rest.'

Luca didn't want to look at his one-time mentor, a man whose tutelage he had perhaps outgrown. Hesse had broken a protocol that was there to protect everybody and, in doing so, had cost one of them their lives, almost cost him his own. It was a lot to take in and he had to fight the urge to follow suit by downing his own port.

'I'm going to resign.'

Luca visibly flinched. 'What? You can't.'

'I can and I must.'

'Herr Hesse you have been the Families' General Counsel almost since I was born.'

The old man smiled ruefully. 'The youngest ever appointee and the longest serving since the seventeenth century. But that is vanity. Perhaps this mistake is a sign that I am not the right man anymore.'

'No, no, just... Your line has fulfilled this role since the beginning. It's the wrong time to go. We need continuity. The Families will forgive a mistake—they have to.'

'If I'm making mistakes then what is the point in my being the General Counsel, Luca?'

If Luca had been prone to demonstrating jaw-dropping amazement, this was when it would have happened. Never in the thirty-five years he had known Herr Stefan Hesse had he called him by his first name. There was a vulnerability to it that surprised Luca. He felt sorry—that was it—he felt sorry for his former mentor and master.

When Luca didn't answer, Herr Hesse seemed to chide himself for going off course with his moment of self-pity. 'Voss, a Japanese cargo ship was found drifting in the Pacific two days ago.'

'I saw, it was on the news.'

Hesse nodded sagely. 'What wasn't on the news was that it had been attacked. Somebody had knocked out all its electronics then hijacked its cargo.'

'What was its cargo?'

'Six geologists from Pennsylvania State University.'

The General Counsel pulled out a photograph from his old-fashioned jacket and handed it to the young man. It showed a group photo of the geologists on the university campus smiling, their eldest member wearing his ever-present USS *Missouri* baseball cap.

'What were they doing travelling on a cargo ship? Incognito, I presume?'

Hesse sighed, impressed by his former pupil's astuteness. 'They were collecting rare earth samples from within North Korea.'

'OK. Ignoring the UN sanctions—why?'

'The US is planning for a post-Kim Il Sung world and assessing the value of the resources there.'

Luca nodded unimpressed. 'If it's worth it to them they'll invade, is that it?'

Hesse smiled humourlessly. 'They believe that regime-change will come from within. We have information that certain members of their military are looking to overthrow their glorious leader, and Washington wants to see how quickly they can get the economy back up on its feet.'

Luca gave Hesse a sceptical look. 'What's this got to do with us?'

'Franz was the point man. He smuggled them in and out. They're not spies these people, they're just ordinary scientists.'

Luca sniffed sceptically. 'They became spies the moment they entered North Korea.' He returned to the photo. 'So I need to pick up the trail immediately.'

'Not you, Voss.'

The young man looked up slowly at the General Counsel. 'What do you mean?'

'You're not ready.'

'I am ready.'

'Luca—'

And this time the use of his first name irritated him. 'I've trained for this all my life.'

'You haven't finished your training.'

'I've almost finished my training.' Luca felt stupid saying it because it sounded adolescent. The riposte was obvious and swift.

'You haven't learned how to assassinate someone.'

'I can—I can kill somebody. If I have to.'

Hesse smiled sadly at him and when he spoke, it was almost with an apologetic air of resignation. 'You are many remarkable things, Herr Voss, but a killer is not one of them. You are not ready to be the Broker.'

Silence had followed the General Counsel's last remark. His was the last word. Eventually he spoke again, striking a conciliatory tone.

'The truth is that we don't need a Broker right now. We need somebody to investigate Franz's death and to report back to the Families.'

'I'll do that.'

'No, you should go to Japan, finish your training.'

'You don't think I'm ready to even ask questions?'

Herr Hesse paused at the steely look that met him, privately admiring the mettle of its owner. 'Maybe you're right. Perhaps ready is not a luxury we have right now.' He sipped thoughtfully on his drink, staring into the red-hot embers of the fire. 'Somebody's killing the Brokers, Herr Voss. This is about the Seven Families; you know that, don't you?'

'It would appear that way.'

'It will be your first ever mission.'

'There's a first time for everything.'

Herr Hesse fixed him with a grave look that said any kind of levity was undesired right now. 'If you take this on, the fate of the Seven Families will be in your hands.'

If Luca doubted himself, he didn't show it. All his life he had wondered how he would feel if offered the role of the Broker. This wasn't quite that offer, but it was certainly a first step on the road, and the feeling—more wariness than excitement—was unexpected. 'I'll do whatever is necessary.'

Herr Hesse wagged a cautionary finger at him. 'This is a simple expedition. Nobody is expecting you to kill anybody.'

'What if my life depends on it?'

'Then you will have messed up and overstepped your remit. This is North Korea we're talking about, Voss. A firecracker going off in Kim Il Sung Square could start the third world war right now.'

The younger man's mind began to work over the logistics of the trip, the equipment to pack.

'Voss, you know that if three Brokers die in quick succession we have to call a meeting of the Families? That's a

terrible risk, to have them all in one place. For their sake—
and yours—you must stay alive.'

'For how long?'

'Perhaps for longer than you have any right to expect.'

Luca nodded dispassionately. 'I'll need an assistant.'

'One will be provided.'

'I'd like to use my own.'

'You mean your lady friend?'

Luca shifted in his chair, trying not to look defensive and
ending up doing just that. 'I mean somebody I trust, and
someone able to take care of themselves.'

'So you do mean your lady friend?'

The old man stared hard at Luca until he conceded the
point with a shrug.

'Well, Voss, since this is not meant to be an eventful mission you can use her, this once. Let us review it afterwards.'

'Once it's done, I want to complete my training. I want to
be the next Broker.'

'We will see.'

'Herr Hesse—'

'We will *see*.'

The General Counsel had reminded Luca in tone if not
in deed that his word was final. The young man sat back in
his leather seat nursing his drink, putting the politics of his
situation out of his head as he watched the fire and saw a log
split in two, sending small red sparks up the chimney.

'Are you coming to Davos?'

Luca made little attempt to conceal his surprise. 'Is that
still necessary?'

'We need to show certain parties that it's business as usual.
Just stay for the first evening, and stay out of trouble.'

Hesse had attempted to lighten the tone with a reference
to Luca's midnight skiing antics of the year before, but Luca
was too engrossed in thinking about investigating Franz's

death to notice. Wondering why he had immediately wanted to take JJ and whether or not he could stay out of trouble, he finished his drink with an air of finality.

Outside, Luca slipped behind the wheel of the Bentley and took a moment to think about the meeting. Then he remembered his conversation with JJ on the boat, how he had surprised himself by telling her something he had never even told himself: that everything he had was borrowed. He looked about him at the car with its luxury interior, a car that could accelerate from zero to sixty in under four seconds, and keep going above 180 miles per hour. A car to die for, maybe. He had taken pleasure in driving JJ around the winding mountain roads of his native country and speeding along its highways, but right now it seemed alien to him. When he thought about it, he owned nothing, not even the shirt on his back. JJ was right, there was something unusual about that, very unusual. He remained for a while sitting behind the wheel of the car wondering whose life it actually was, feeling for all the world like a drifter.

After a minute or two, he slowly reached forward and pushed the ignition button. The Jurassic growl that met him woke him from his pensive reverie and he slowly eased the car out of the castle grounds and around the lake.

★   ★   ★

Two hundred metres up, on a mountain slope opposite, hidden among sparse Alpine foliage, a tanned, bald man knelt behind a camera, taking pictures. Its telescopic lens captured Luca travelling from the castle door to the car, just as it had captured his arrival two hours earlier.

The bald man pulled his head back from his camera. Any observer would have noticed that alopecia had taken his eyebrows and eyelashes too, his face like a strange, unfinished waxwork. He tapped a button on his headset and spoke with a thick French-Algerian accent into the microphone curling round one side of his face.

'He's leaving. I'll pick up his trail as he passes by.'

He clicked off the call and began to dismantle his equipment, placing it all in a leather satchel, before picking up a motorcycle helmet and heading for the nearby ridge.

5
Davos, Switzerland

JJ turned to her partner with a smile that was perhaps more rictus grin than delight. 'Luca, I will not lie. These past six months have been some of the most exciting of my life. The holidays, the meals, the fancy cars, apartments, the sex—I'd like to emphasise the sex—all of them have earned you one big, fat tick. When we were driving here tonight, again, I was kind of excited. You know, the town covered in snow, mountains rising up behind it, that lovely tall, narrow, church spire standing high above it all. The view would have done the cover of any chocolate box proud. But now we're here—actually in this ballroom—I'm really worried you're going to spend all that good will you've built up.'

Luca looked out at the hundreds of delegates, the men in tuxedoes, the women in evening dresses, and gave a small groan. 'The World Economic Forum is not quite the Grammys is it?'

JJ shot a look at a passing politician. 'Was that a war criminal? Was that a war criminal who just walked past us?'

Luca looked after the European statesmen disappearing into a flock of happy-to-see-him handshakes. 'Alleged war criminal, I think he just picked up a peace prize in New York, so, you know, it probably all balances out.'

JJ considered his mischievous smile but her suspicions were only partly allayed. 'Tell me again, why are we here?'

Luca scooped up a couple of flutes of champagne from a passing waiter and handed one to JJ. 'The same reason everybody is here.'

'Because this is where all the global wheeling and dealing is decided?'

'Oh, God, no. All the big deals are done at the Burning Man Festival in Nevada these days.'

JJ stared wide-eyed. 'Then what are we doing here?'

'We're doing the same as everybody else. We're showing our face.'

JJ drained her glass in the vain hope it would liven up her evening. 'Would you mind terribly if I got *off* my face?'

Luca had to take a moment to place the English idiom his partner had just used, but the speed with which she swapped her empty glass for a full one made it clear what she was saying.

'You know if you're good I'll take you to the Bilderberg Group one day.'

JJ's eyes sparkled. 'Well, you told me last night I was "very bad" so there's not much chance of that. How's the back, by the way?'

Luca gave her a careful smile; he could still feel the smarting across his shoulders from the belt she had chosen to use on him. 'Hmm… Think of tonight as payback.'

'Bit out of proportion, don't you think? Hey, there's Bill Clinton. So is it true about Bilderberg? Is that where all the governments get together to decide global policy?'

'Global policy? Governments don't decide global policy, corporations do. Governments, JJ, are merely the restraining hand.'

His partner scrutinised his face for any signs of humour but found none. Luca's attentions, however, were elsewhere. For the third time that evening a short man of Kazakhstani, Mongolian or maybe North Chinese appearance had snuck a glance at him. The man had a scar the length of his face and on his arm was an undeniably beautiful blonde Caucasian woman who was noticeable not just by her height but by having, by the modest standards of the night, the most revealing dress on display. Its tight fabric was as bright red as the lipstick she wore. Probably an escort like a few of the women—and some of the men—present, he thought, but an oddly ostentatious one at that.

'Herr Voss.'

Luca turned to be met by Stefan Hesse, sporting an evening jacket and tie, a rare departure from his signature Bavarian-influenced attire.

'Herr Hesse. This is my companion, JJ.'

The General Counsel nodded his head, a gesture that the Chinese woman half-expected to be accompanied by heel clicking. 'Ma'am,' he said, before looking at Luca to signal that he was all business. 'Can we talk?'

JJ raised her glass accommodatingly. 'Don't mind me. If I was having more fun they'd have to arrest me.'

Luca rolled his eyes at her and left.

Hesse had taken them to a bar at the side of the makeshift ballroom where he ordered a glass of wine for himself. 'Did you notice the Mongolian fellow?'

That placed it for Luca. 'The one with the arm candy?'

Hesse turned, talking into his wine glass due to his constant fear of lip-readers when in public. 'His name is Mr Butakhan but more often he goes by "Butakhan".'

Luca looked to an angled mirror that ran along the length of the bar to see that the man in question and his female friend had somehow reached JJ and all three were now enjoying a seemingly pleasant conversation.

'What else do we know about him?'

'There's the problem, Voss, that's all we know about him.'

That was significant in itself. Through their relationships with the world's security agencies, even those on opposing sides, the Families had access to information on everybody

41

and anybody. A 'ghost' was a rarity and always a cause for concern. A ghost at Davos meant only one thing: trouble.

'This must be the friend you were talking about.'

To Luca's ear, Butakhan spoke with a crisp Etonian accent, an almost ostentatious, upper-class English with a dose of entitlement for good measure.

'Oh, she'll talk about anyone given the chance.' Luca accompanied his words with a warm smile aimed at Butakhan and his companion. JJ smirked mischievously.

'The name is Luca, Luca Voss.'

Butakhan shook his hand, but felt no discomfort in failing to offer up his own name. 'This is my friend Scarlett.'

Scarlett extended her hand to Luca in a slightly theatrical manner. 'A pleasure to meet you, Mr Voss.'

'West Coast?'

Scarlett raised her eyebrows at JJ. 'Gorgeous *and* clever. South San Diego, for my sins. Mexican drug gangs on one side, the US Navy on the other. A real joy.'

Butakhan smiled with a hint of criticism. 'She likes to talk.'

Scarlett gave him an admonishing tap on his shoulder. 'Somebody's got to. He can go hours without saying a word. I mean, what is it with men? Me? I could talk all day. My mother always said there should be a job where all you had to do was talk, because that would be like getting paid to do my hobby.'

JJ allowed herself a private smile. 'Luca, these nice people were telling me about the skijoring event tonight. You didn't tell me about that!'

Scarlett put a hand on Luca's sleeve. 'Skiers being pulled by horses. These Swiss are crazy, you could kill yourself. I'm beginning to wonder if it's just the cheese that's got holes in it,' she added, swirling her hand near her head to make her point.

Butakhan smiled indulgently at his partner, but in such a way as to communicate that she should take it down a notch or two. 'And what brings you to Davos, Mr Voss?'

'Hedge funds. You?'

'The winter sports. Do you skijor?'

'Not for about ten years. Last time I did so I broke my leg, so, you know, happy memories.'

'You've lost your nerve, have you?'

Luca was intrigued by the implicit taunt behind the smile. 'The appetite, perhaps.'

'It's a pity. Your friend here was asking me if I knew of a casino nearby and I was thinking that if you were the gambling type we could race each other and have a little wager, make the skijoring all the more interesting.'

'I think you'll find skiing behind a horse around Davos interesting enough.'

'Ah. Scared of skijoring *and* of losing a bet. I'm beginning to wonder what JJ here finds so attractive about you.'

It was said with a warm smile but nobody missed the undercurrent of belligerence. It was strange and swift. Luca was suddenly curious to know where it would lead.

'What sort of wager were you thinking of?'

'Nothing major. Ten thousand euros, perhaps? Unless that's a little steep for you?'

Scarlett's eyes widened and Luca didn't doubt that the little man's self-image was propped up by grandstanding of this nature. But before he could reply an aide leaned into Butakhan's ear and whispered a message.

'You must forgive me, I must say hello to the Japanese prime minister. I will be back presently.'

He turned away with Scarlett to a group of Japanese dignitaries nearby.

JJ laughed. 'Well that was a fun dick-swinging competition. He must find these bashes as boring as I do.'

Luca pondered the colourful couple for a moment. 'Actually, I think he's targeting me for some reason.'

'What do you mean?'

'I mean…' Now Luca could have kicked himself for putting off a conversation he should have had before. 'Look, you know I said I've got to jump on a plane tomorrow?'

'Yeah.' JJ felt a small surge of sadness, the last twenty-four hours having been an exercise in not thinking about Luca disappearing on one of his travels again.

'I was in two minds about whether to ask you to come along.'

JJ felt a rush of excitement but did her best to cover it with a poker face. She smiled at him curiously. 'Well, when you've made up both your minds the answer's yes.'

'You don't know where I'm going.'

'As long as it's warmer than here it's a yes.'

'It's minus twenty where I'm going.'

JJ gave a charmingly ingratiating smile. 'Then you'll just have to buy me some furs. Where are we going?'

The brief encounter with Butakhan, a person of unknown intentions or threat, caused Luca to pause. It wasn't a casual thing to bring JJ along to Davos, let alone the Korean–Russian border. He was realising he didn't want to put her in harm's way: danger wasn't something for which she had been prepared and it wasn't necessary; besides, deep down, he knew that she was untested. The plan to take her along was a romantic notion, not a practical one. He nodded in the direction of Butakhan.

'The thing is we don't know anything about that man.'

JJ paused, perplexed, wondering if he perhaps had more to say. 'Who are *we*?'

'The people I work for.'

'The people you don't want to tell me about?'

'JJ, you're not—you're not ready for this. I need to get closer to this guy, and that is something in which you don't need to involve yourself. Go home. I'll arrange for you to fly to wherever you want tomorrow, but I need to get on with this. I'm sorry, really I am, but something's come up.'

Everything slowed to a halt.

JJ didn't speak because she never spoke when her heart was breaking.

'OK,' she said, after a while.

'You're angry at me.'

'No. You're busy.'

'Well I am busy.'

'Fine.' Her monosyllabic reply was underlined by the draining of yet another glass of champagne. 'I'd be in your way, I'm just a helpless woman, and this is a man's job.'

'JJ, I don't think I'm a very good bet—'

'What? Now you're breaking up with me as well?'

'That's not what I meant.'

'What do you mean?'

'Do you really want to know what I mean? I mean that two of my associates have been murdered and somebody tried to kill me, and I hate the fact that you were anywhere near me when that happened. And now, from nowhere, a man I know nothing about wants to stake ten thousand euros on a bet that he can beat me in a race. A race that in all likelihood will get one or both of us seriously injured; and I'm probably going to have to take on the bet, because right now I can't think of any better way of finding out what his angle is, OK?'

For reasons that baffled Luca, far from his words having a sobering effect, they seemed to have left JJ smitten. 'You were really upset that I almost got killed in Mexico?'

Luca paused to take in her remark. 'That's what you took from what I just said?'

JJ shrugged. 'Well, that, and that you need help.'

'I didn't ask for help. How was that asking for help? When did I use the word help?'

'So, have you changed your mind about the wager?' Butakhan had returned unnoticed, wearing his Californian trophy on his arm and a goading smile on his face. Luca had been about to say 'no' with a few expletives added for good measure, but he was beaten to it.

'Luca would love to accept your challenge. Only we'd like to change the terms of the bet.'

Butakhan smirked condescendingly at JJ. 'The stakes are too high?'

'Actually, the stakes are a little low. We were thinking that instead of money the winner wins the other's partner for the night.'

A stunned silence met JJ's suggestion, Luca quickly wiping the disbelief from his face. Scarlett did not react for her own political reasons, but Butakhan had been wrong-footed, until a grin crept into his face. 'Scarlett, what do you say to an evening with JJ and me?'

When Scarlett had first noticed JJ in her black evening dress, a slit tantalisingly rising all the way up her thigh, she had to admit to herself that some guy in the room was very lucky. The prospect of exploring her body, even with the inconvenience of Butakhan between them, was a delight she felt travelling south from her stomach. She went to answer her benefactor, but JJ interrupted her.

'You're assuming you're going to win. The only thing certain is that Scarlett and I will be spending the night together. The rest is yet to be decided.'

JJ moved over to Scarlett and slipped an arm around her and the pair of them—far and away the two most beautiful women in the entire room—took no small pleasure in lording over the two men the delights that awaited one of them.

Luca looked from Butakhan to Scarlett to JJ and despaired at JJ's idea of helping.

On the roof of the Davos Congress Centre snipers in winter camouflage were questioning the orders they were being given. More than one of them had asked for their orders to be repeated. One demanded to know the exact name of the person at Davos who had allowed it, so that he could personally tear a strip off them the next day. From their perch, they witnessed four hundred of the world's most high-profile—and therefore high-risk—politicians and business people and their partners, pouring out of the building below. Not to their bulletproof cars at the front, but out onto the completely exposed snow-covered lawn at the back. A bomb outside the building right now would destabilise half the world's governments and leave the fifty largest companies leaderless. It was everything security forbade the organisers to allow and it was exactly what was happening.

Word of the skijoring race had spread like wildfire among the presidents, prime ministers, crown princes and CEOs in attendance. As eager as they were to talk to their peers, the prospect of something of a diversion happening saw every last VIP exiting the Davos Congress Centre. The starkly geometric wood-clad rear of the building flowed onto a wide slope that led down to Kurpark, the town's main open space. The large parkland with a ring of trees around it was the perfect venue for skijoring, with a tiered viewing area for the delegates.

'Shall we say three laps?'

As Luca, dressed in a red winter jacket and trousers, stepped into his skis he looked down the length of the park. The route, a large loop marked by flaming torches, hooked round four trunks on the inner edge of a thick border of trees, just under half a kilometre at Luca's estimation. Around this, two horses would race, pulling the skiers behind them. Skijoring was typically performed at a racecourse or in an unobstructed space like a town square, but this route, with trees to navigate, was dangerous for the horses and suicidal for the men.

Luca gave a small nod towards Butakhan. 'Sure, why not. Which horse would you like?'

There were two horses: one a white Arabian stallion that its young female rider was chiding with little tugs of the reins to keep it calm; the other, slightly smaller to Luca's eye, had a black coat that appeared to ripple in the moonlight.

Butakhan, dressed head-to-toe in a burgundy snowsuit, slapped the black gelding proprietorially on the side of its neck. 'Forgive me, Herr Voss, but Saikhan is my own horse from my native land. I don't think she would take kindly to pulling somebody else.'

The smile that accompanied his opponent's statement could not hide the man's pride in the magnificent beast. It was, Luca knew, too large for a pure Mongol-bred horse; evidently it was a cross with a Western breed to bring the best of other breeds to bear. And it seemed significant to Luca that this man had flown his own horse all the way to Davos. *He's nothing if not competitive*, Luca noted to himself.

The two horses were guided by their young female riders to the makeshift starting line where ropes were tied to the backs of their saddles for the skiers. Luca exchanged a tight smile with the attractive twenty-something freckled redhead racing his.

She greeted him in German but with enough of an Italian accent to suggest she came from the southern region of the canton of Graubünden.

He addressed her in Italian. 'Win this and I'll give you a thousand euro bonus.'

The Swiss girl rewarded him with an excited grin, replying in her native Swiss-Italian dialect, 'Well, I promise to deliver on my part if you deliver on yours.'

Luca indicated with a serious smile that he liked her even more for her fair response. He looked about him and could see the Davos security team running to secure the outside of the park. He understood the security nightmare this had created, that any plans would have had to be torn up and revised. For a terrible moment he wondered if he had played directly into Butakhan's hands. Was this his plan, to lure the delegates out from the protection of the Congress Centre and its ring of steel? Had Luca taken the bait that had never been about the race, never about the man's apparent rampant ego, but a ruse to blow wide open the security of Davos? If it was, it was brilliant. Luca felt stupid and impressed all at once until he thought of one thing, one flaw: Butakhan would necessarily be implicated in whatever happened and even a helicopter-led escape would never succeed with the aerial protection at hand. If that was his thinking, it was incredibly high stakes, but then everything about the Mongolian man so far was consistent with a taste for risk.

'You don't have to do this if you don't want to, Luca.'

As Luca strapped a red racing helmet into place, he turned to see JJ, a winter coat wrapped round her black evening dress, beside him.

'Thanks, but I came here to show my face, not lose it.'

JJ gave him an encouraging and perhaps apologetic smile and then looked admiringly at Butakhan's female friend. 'Think of the fun we could have with a filly like that. Win this race and we'll give you a night you'll remember for the rest of your life, Mr Voss.'

'You're assuming I'll win then?'

'Oh, you can beat a fool like that, surely?'

'JJ, he brought his own horse from Mongolia.'

She was speechless for a moment. 'His own? So, he's done this before then?'

'I think it's safe to assume that.'

JJ blanched at the implications. 'Jesus, I'm screwed.'

'Well, I'm glad you've got your evening planned out.'

A marshal in brown lederhosen, a white shirt and an appropriately Alpine hat complete with jauntily positioned feather held a Swiss flag above his head.

'Herren...'

Both horses walked forward to the improvised starting line and Luca, tightening the skiers' ropes, pulled away from a worried JJ, both of them realising at the same time that Butakhan had received the inside line of the race.

'*Eins...*'

Butakhan gave a small nod to his opponent.

'*Zwei...*'

Luca returned the gesture, lowering his goggles over his eyes.

'*Drei...*'

The two men crouched slightly, adopting starting positions.

'*Gehen!*'

As the flag was brought down, the two female riders urged their horses on with everything they had. A cheer went up from the onlooking dignitaries as the two horses made furiously swift headway, the fresh, foot-deep snow flying up in clouds behind them, the skiers neck and neck as they raced away to the delegates' right.

Surrounding the parkland were tall fir trees, not so tightly packed as to prohibit a careful course between them. It was towards one of these they raced. As they reached the first tree-cum-marker, the reason behind why Butakhan had brought his own horse became clear. It had edged ahead by a neck, which was enough for his rider to use the inside line to force Luca's mount to go wide around the black gelding and the tree, gifting the Mongolian man a full length's lead once they hit the next straight.

The parkland was not natural skiing territory and the uneven ground was less forgiving than the usual flat skijoring course. Looking ahead at his rival, Luca could see the Mongolian man absorbing the unexpected dips and rises, and wondered if an advantage was to be had, his own experience having been in cross-country events where flats were a luxury. But, as they approached the second corner, Butakhan expertly swung wide of his horse like a waterskier describing a wide arc, a spray of snow showering nearby foliage before the skier got in tight behind his horse.

Butakhan kept his horse-length lead around the third tree, but the fourth and final tree of the lap looked trickier and the riders could not take it at full pelt; a clump of nearby trees was ready to receive reckless competitors with their thick, unyielding trunks.

Luca had hoped his rider might mount an attack—insane though it might prove—but caution prevailed, the narrow gap forcing her to allow her competitor's horse to pull ahead the entire length of the beast plus the trailing Butakhan. However, once out of the corner, the Swiss-Italian rider seemed to summon up a hidden reserve as their horse burst into a sprint and found the inside line. Angry to be surrendering the lead, Butakhan's rider could do no more than track Luca's mount round the corner, earning a threatening order from Butakhan.

The momentum had shifted and Luca's rider was steering the horse like the wind towards the next corner a length ahead of the black gelding. Luca soon found himself alongside Butakhan's rider as they raced to the fourth corner. The Mongolian man barked another order in his native tongue. Luca couldn't translate it but the meaning was swiftly understood: as they dropped out of sight of the spectators, behind the trees of the fourth corner, Butakhan's rider slashed at Luca's arms with her crop. Once, twice, three times, before Luca took a hand from his rope-handle to grab it the fourth time, catching her in the act, and yanking the short whip out of her hand as they went round the trees. The undulating ground betrayed him as he lost control and a cry erupted from the four hundred or so delegates watching as he had to abandon his rope and fight to keep his balance. Luca's rider pulled up to watch as he corrected himself and skied with painful loss of speed towards her, while Butakhan's mount raced past them in a cloud of white powdery snow.

Luca scooped up the ski-rope handle and looked up to see his rider mortified that she might be to blame.

'Win this race and I'll make the bonus five thousand euros.'

Luca's young female rider, who was from a family of limited means, felt a thrill at the jackpot that instantly transformed into energy. She turned and smacked her heels against the horse, urging it on with a defiant command that saw them explode after Butakhan. They chased him towards the first tree, closing on him into the second and third, though the outside line betrayed them each time. Just then the Mongolian horse stumbled, losing precious time out of the third corner, and the two horses drew neck and neck as they raced back up the hill with only the narrow gap of the last corner between both teams and victory. Luca batted away the thought of JJ's insane wager, anticipating the raw anger he would experience not just at the thought of her going with another man, but *this* man. His rider exhorted her horse to give everything it had, both horses exhausted and driven on; the corner racing towards them, only one team able to squeeze through the unforgiving space, a crash a certainty unless somebody backed off. Luca's rider waited for the instruction to quit, but nothing was forthcoming. The money he'd offered saw her throw everything she had at the calamitous event about to happen. Broken bones were a small price to pay for the promised reward. Feeling a lump in her throat at the thought of what her parents could do with the prize money, she committed everything she had to getting through the gap.

Luca looked across at Butakhan, letting him know he would not quit—the reply on the Mongolian man's face an undeniable look of hatred before he turned from Luca and yelled at his rider: '*Zogsoogooroi.*'

His rider pulled up and Luca's horse cut past, the gap suddenly opened to him. His rider's nerves were shredded but not surrendered and she slowed her horse as little as she dared, while Luca pulled away from Butakhan.

It was then that Butakhan's rider kicked Luca in the face.

Her boot came out of nowhere and slammed into the side of his head. The Swiss man, caught unaware, was unable to stop it or to hold onto his rope as he veered into the tree that marked the fourth corner, its lowest branches grasping at him as Butakhan accelerated past.

A collective gasp met Luca's headlong crash into the snow where he rolled to a stop, while a muted cheer greeted Butakhan's crossing of the finish line, the lederhosen-dressed marshal finalising it with an emphatic lowering of the flag that signalled Butakhan's victory.

From the front of the crowd, JJ ran to Luca's inert body in the snow, sick to her stomach at what she had brought about.

Before JJ reached him, Luca was rising up on one elbow and undoing the strap of his helmet, fighting the myriad emotions running through him. The idea of breaking Butakhan's neck seemed particularly satisfying, though with all the expert security present about them, this wasn't the best time. He realised that the entire incident would have been blocked from view so that only he, Butakhan and the riders would understand the real reason for his rage.

'Oh Luca, I'm so sorry,' JJ said.

He pulled off his helmet. 'I did my best.'

Any further words were smothered by JJ's kiss.

'I'll tell him I'm not going through with it.'

'You gave your word.'

'I'll run away from here before he speaks to us.'

'JJ, really? I've watched you lose six-figure sums on the turn of a wheel.'

She put on a face that was braver than she felt. 'But I always won them back for you.'

'Who knows, maybe this is for…' Luca trailed off.

'For what? The best?' JJ felt like Luca had punched her in the stomach with those words.

'An excellent race, Mr Voss.' A shameless Butakhan dropped his gloves into the helmet he was carrying. 'I couldn't see what happened at the end there, you seemed to lose control. I've heard that about you.'

Luca got to his feet, using the time it took him to get up to decide what to do. He knew that if he gave Butakhan the treatment he deserved the world's elite would take him for nothing more than a bad loser.

'I see you're lost for words. Well, I promise not to do much talking myself tonight.' With a gloating and unabashedly greedy look in his eye, Butakhan proffered his arm to JJ, who, still reeling from what she saw as Luca's cruel words, put her hand distractedly onto it.

The Mongolian man walked her away, Luca wracking his brains for something to say to put a halt to it.

'Is that your idea of being a discreet Broker, Herr Voss?' Luca turned, unprepared for Hesse's angry glare. 'An embarrassing display in front of the entire delegation of Davos? Well, is it?'

Before Luca could find the words to reply, Hesse made his position known by stalking off. Luca watched as his former mentor disappeared up the slope along with the last of the delegates and wondered just how drunk he would get on his return to his chalet that night.

'I'm sorry.' It was the redheaded rider, standing meekly beside him, disappointed for him and personally devastated. Luca looked around them, the park almost abandoned now.

'You did well.'

He gave the girl the best smile he could muster and received a sad one in return, but the smile wavered when she saw what he did next.

'Five thousand wasn't it?' Luca pulled out a clip of notes from inside his snow jacket and, unclipping them, handed them to the girl. 'It's all there more or less.'

'But—'

'You didn't lose the race. I did.'

He gave her an encouraging smile.

The girl stared at the money; it was more than she had ever held in her hands. Then she stared at Luca, athletic without being muscle-bound, handsome without seeming to know it. She recalled how she'd felt when she had seen JJ going off with the other skier, relief that she wasn't Luca's girl as she'd thought. Buoyed by this and the adrenaline of the race she did something she had never done before.

'If you're not doing anything for the rest of the night, neither am I.'

Luca looked at her as if for the first time and saw a very attractive, freckled young redhead. In that moment he knew two things: the first was that when it had come to the crunch Butakhan had lost his nerve; the second was that this evening wasn't going to prove as devastating as he first thought.

★ ★ ★

Luca stood on the balcony of his chalet, looking down on the sleepy town of Davos as the sun began to rise over the slopes, the snow renewed by a heavy, silent downfall in the night. He rested his cup of black coffee on the thick wooden balcony rail, its warmth melting the snow where it sat, the rest of the rail covered by three inches of perfect powdery white. He looked at the few wood-clad chalets about him, not the largest to be had, but undoubtedly the best in the resort. It was all 'the best' he found himself thinking: the Thai coffee he was drinking, the English Grand Tourer sitting in the porch, the Swiss watch on his wrist, but none of it was his. JJ had made him aware of his dependency of late. Smiling darkly, he found himself wondering if it was all an elaborate metaphor for life: *You can't take it with you—especially if you didn't own it in the first place.*

He sipped his drink, enjoying the warmth it provided against the chill that wrapped around him as he wore nothing more than a white bathrobe. Down a nearby narrow street, he heard the soft, effortless purr of a powerful engine and the crunch of tyres on fresh snow. Round a corner at a sedate pace appeared a black Mercedes limousine with heavily tinted windows. With chauffeur-driven care, it gently glided to a halt outside his residence two floors below. A small Asian man—maybe Mongolian—exited the driver's door and made his way to the back, which he opened. Out stepped JJ. She was dressed as she had been when he last saw her. *Still in her evening dress*, he found himself thinking. Luca decided he needed to finish packing for his flight.

JJ had removed her shoes before padding up the stairs to their bedroom. She eased the door open quietly with infinite care and then stopped. Luca was stooped over the end of the bed, fitting clothes into a small suitcase.

JJ closed the door behind her and rested her back against it. She considered her lover, remembering how she had walked away from him the night before, having offered the wager, how everything that had come about had come about because of her. Luca looked up and paused to regard her. She tried to read him and could see the thing he would never admit to her, that he had pulled down the shutters, locked her out, to protect himself. He would deny it, but she had seen it before, and not just in him.

She took him in, his tall frame so poised, the body with its hint of primal animalism. She almost smiled, recalling their first ever workout in the gym together, both of them silently egging each other on by training harder and harder to see who would call quits first. He was the first well-toned man she had known who didn't stop to admire his physique in floor-to-ceiling mirrors. This man, with something of a V-shape to his upper body, trained as a duty, not for vanity's sake. It had made him doubly attractive then, and it made him doubly attractive now. However, his ability to shut down, to lock her out, hurt her.

Realising Luca had nothing to say to her, JJ made her way to the en suite bathroom. The bedroom, overlooking the town, was enormous and the silence between them became more oppressive with every step. Both of them felt a rising sense of foolishness. Luca reminded himself that Brokers did not let their personal life get in the way of business.

JJ was almost by the bathroom door when he spoke.

'So… was it a good night?'

She stopped and turned, watching each muscle movement of his reaction.

'Educational.'

Luca nodded slowly. 'What did you learn?'

She raised an eyebrow for ironic effect. 'That Mongolians can't take their drink…'

Now she had to applaud him. Not a hint of relief, not a whisper of gratitude that Butakhan hadn't had his way with her. Luca nodded again to acknowledge the information and resumed packing his suitcase.

'… and that West Coast blondes can go for hours.'

Luca raised his head slowly, looking at her blankly for a moment before he allowed a mischievous amusement to appear in his face. 'Is that so?'

JJ gave him an admonishing stare as she turned to the bathroom then turned back again. 'Why does it not bother a man if his woman has sex with another woman?'

Luca acted nonplussed before shrugging. 'Kinky I guess.' This was accompanied by a wide, wolfish grin.

The Chinese woman rolled her eyes before announcing her real news with a wry self-satisfied air that told him she knew how clever she had been. 'Anyhow, he's got six passports and eight of his last ten phone calls were to places in Myanmar.'

The Swiss man was impressed. Very impressed. He knew in that instant that he had underestimated this woman he had chosen, then dropped, and now re-chosen, to accompany him on his investigation of Franz's death.

But now, the ice broken, JJ was in the mood to enjoy her coup. She wandered slowly and victoriously towards the head of the bed and sat down. 'Anything you want to say to Miss Super Spy?'

'Pack your bags for Siberia?'

She winced theatrically in a way that said he would have to work harder than that. 'I was thinking more along the lines of, "Well done JJ", "That's important information JJ", "I'm helpless without you JJ."'

Then the levity evaporated in an instant as her eyes fell on the pillows.

'Rough night?'

Luca knew what was coming. 'Why do you ask?'

'These pillows have both been slept on.'

Luca stood in a manner that suggested curiosity more than concern. He watched with a detached interest as JJ lifted something off the nearest pillow.

'A *red* hair.' She shot a look at him that warned of a rising temper. 'You brought that jockey back here, didn't you?'

Now Luca was intrigued, not just at how the tables had turned, but at how she would react to the events of the night before.

'Was she good?'

Luca didn't quite see the wisdom in answering that, and began to wonder where JJ would take this as she rose and began to approach him.

'Was she as good as me?'

Luca answered this with a look that told her it was a stupid question. She had reached him and put her hand on the belt of his white bathrobe.

'Do it to me.'

A quizzical look overtook him. 'Do what?'

She looked up into his eyes as she loosened the belt, causing his robe to fall open, her fingernails gently clawing down his torso to his manhood. She wrapped her hand around it.

'Do everything you did to her to me. Now.'

'Why?'

'Because then I'll own the memory. And then I'll own you.'

Pleased at his response to her touch, JJ moved her hand to his chest and pushed, directing him back to the bed, her lover holding her by the waist, bringing her with him. JJ lifted up her dress and straddled him as he lay back, putting her hand between his legs and easing herself onto him with a sigh. Then she leant forward and scrutinised his face as if it were the last time she would ever see him.

Speaking in a whisper that would brook no opposition, she said: 'You're mine.'

★   ★   ★

Every futurist's prediction that technology would make face-to-face meetings redundant was rebutted by events such as Davos. They were proof, if proof were needed, that face time—as the suits referred to it—was the undisputed preference for top-level meetings. Video conferencing was convenient, but being in the same room was how all the best deals were done. Besides, there was another crucial factor not lost on any of the world's movers and shakers: video and phone calls could be recorded whereas face-to-face conversations could be denied.

All of the meeting rooms in the Davos Congress Centre were the same: white, well-lit and minimally furnished with a table and chairs. There was one room with a difference though, one room where every adjacent room and space was occupied by American Secret Service personnel. Their role was to keep unauthorised, eavesdroppers out using hi-tech RF-jamming devices—or by force if necessary. For all intents and purposes, the conversation taking place in this room was not happening.

Butakhan took a seat on one side of the long, bland conference table opposite eight senior members of the American Council on Foreign Relations. It felt like someone was trying to drill his brain in two and were it not for the rarity of having access to these people he would have called off the meeting and stayed at home. The night before, he had returned to his chalet, the largest in Davos, and slipped into a whirlpool with Scarlett and JJ, all of them naked and all enjoying a whisky. Then, nothing. When he had woken that morning, Scarlett had told him what a tiger he had been the night before, but he couldn't remember any of it. Still, any feelings of regret or frustration at not being able to recall events would have to wait until he had stumbled through this meeting.

The eight men from the Council on Foreign Relations were composed of two Republican senators, a former Republican vice president, two Wall Street bankers, the head of the biggest arms manufacturer in America, the head of a petrochemical conglomerate, and Washington's leading political lobbyist. Even in the Mongolian man's weakened state, he managed a grudging admiration for their organisation. Formed in 1921, it was essentially Davos before Davos, Bilderberg before Bilderberg had even been invented.

With the shift of global power to the American empire, the Council on Foreign Relations became America's imperial brain. Although every member would deny it, the Council on Foreign Relations was the think tank that powered the long-term strategy behind America's economics, its wars, and foreign policy. Everything from the Cold War to trickle-down economics, from the CIA's pan-global regime-destabilising agenda to drone attacks, emanated from the organisation. If corporations listened to any formal body, it was the Council on Foreign Relations. That was because it was made up of these corporations, along with the highest ranks of the CIA, the NSA, the military, the government, and every strategic industry that boasted a global reach. Davos was merely the shadow it cast.

At the centre of the eight was seated Senator Ralph Huxley. His clothes matched his expressions: tight and uncomfortable.

'Mr Butakhan, I will not pretend to fully understand why we have been asked to allocate time for this meeting, so if we could get straight to the meat of it, we would all be very grateful.' His accent had that southern states quality, both homely and menacing.

Butakhan sipped some water then rallied himself, mastering his hangover the same way he mastered all obstacles in his life. His clipped, English accent came as something of a surprise to the others present.

'Thank you for being here, gentlemen. Incidentally, it is just Butakhan, no 'Mr'. I do understand how precious your time is so I will be brief. My organisation understands that the Council on Foreign Relations is agitating for regime change in North Korea and we would like to offer our assistance.'

Butakhan's announcement both stunned and bemused the men who saw every non-Council on Foreign Relations player in the world as nothing more than a pawn on the board, to be moved about at their will. The senator spoke for them all when he leaned in to brush Butakhan aside.

'Sir, I don't wish to be rude, but all we know of your organisation… The Six, is it?'

Butakhan nodded. 'You could call it The Six.'

'All we know is that it was the first to start the run on the Wall Street banks back in 2007, and that this is an action for which we have never received a satisfactory explanation.'

'The explanation is simple, gentlemen. We wanted to see who ran America.'

'I don't follow you.'

'Well, when the government wrote the banks a blank cheque we knew who called the shots, as you Americans say. It was Wall Street. We were very pleased.'

'Pleased?'

'Oh yes. We find it very difficult to do business with governments—but corporations, on the other hand…' Butakhan made a gesture to indicate this was another story altogether.

The overweight senator was as fascinated as he was irritated. The Council on Foreign Relations' intelligence on the so-called Six came to almost nothing, though there were rumours, unsubstantiated, of the organisation funding terrorism across the world, talk of secret holdings in major corporations, of even being the outright owners of one of the world's major tax havens. None of their sources had been able to generate concrete information on anything, though, and for that reason alone the meeting was worth having, intelligence being the Council on Foreign Relations' primary currency.

'What is your organisation's interest in North Korea, Mr... sorry, Butakhan?'

Butakhan smiled to let them know he was not here to seek their blessing, but to tell them, unapologetically, how it was.

'My organisation is funding The Alt-NK, a North Korean government in exile.'

A ripple of consternation ran through the eight men present, the hawk-nosed former vice president being the first to speak. 'You're behind that? Do you understand how destabilising that has been for the region?'

Butakhan felt a calm descending on him. Their fear was his strength, their confusion his certainty. 'Yes we do, almost as destabilising as the last sixty years of US foreign policy.'

A Wall Street CEO, with brilliant white teeth, pointed a finger at the table. 'You're a player, is that it? You feel you are equal to the Council on Foreign Relations? Do you understand the knife-edge to which your Alt-NK has pushed that country? Do you understand the game you're playing?'

Butakhan smiled serenely at his outburst. 'Well, if we don't, I assure you that China does. They are courting us as a potential partner in this, but I will make no secret of the fact that you are our preferred ally.' More than one of the men went to respond, but the Mongolian man pressed on in such a way as to hold their attention. 'Allow me to explain. As you know, developing the next generation of technology is impossible without the requisite supply of rare earth metals and China has a monopoly on over ninety-five per cent of these resources. Or so it was thought.'

The room was silent; there was only one thing the men present understood more than power and that was money. If Butakhan was the real deal, he was about to point the way to more of it. The Mongolian man was relishing what he was about to say, knowing these men would guess exactly what he was getting at but that they wouldn't be able to say anything due to the risk of exposing themselves.

'We have recently received the results of some extensive geological exploration we performed across various parts of North Korea.'

The American general shifted in his chair, the senator beside him discreetly applying a calming hand on his arm that said: *Do nothing*.

'I am pleased to report that North Korea is to rare earth metals what Saudi Arabia is to oil. Managed correctly, it will be the wealthiest country per capita in the world within a generation of the regime change. Perhaps even Korean unification could become a reality, creating a new front against Chinese expansionism.'

Now the general spoke, his voice a subterranean growl. 'What exactly are you offering, Butakhan?'

'North Korea is the loose cannon itching to use its nuclear arsenal. We are offering to facilitate this regime change in a way that leaves America with clean hands and makes it acceptable to the wider world for her to secure exclusive rights over all and any resources in the country, at rates to be agreed by ourselves.'

The general was torn between outrage at Butakhan's presumption and the appeal of his offer. He chose the latter. 'You think you can do this, how?'

'Forgive me if I don't reveal our methods.'

The overweight senator could contain himself no longer. 'Then forgive me if I speak for all of us when I say, we choose not to do business with you and your organisation.'

Butakhan smiled in a way that wrong-footed the others. 'Gentlemen, the geopolitical map has changed, the world is in constant flux, and China has overtaken the US economy. It is time for new and imaginative alliances. It is a poorly kept secret that if China chose to dump its treasury bonds on the open market it could achieve with capitalism what it failed to do with communism: it could break the US economy forever. The dollar would be abandoned as the petrocurrency and US debt would be worth ten cents in the dollar. We think our proposition, to work with you and not China, is advantageous to your organisation.'

'Don't you mean our country?'

'Exactly.'

'Who are you?'

'We're your new allies.'

'We have allies.'

'You don't have allies who can bring China to its knees. You don't have insurance.'

The eight men swapped looks that, far from any kind of firm agreement, were close to a collective interest in what was being proposed.

Senator Huxley spoke with the loftiness worthy of any patriarch. 'And what exactly does your organisation want from us?'

Butakhan felt the small thrill of reeling in the big fish after the struggle; standing before these men was the moment that he had worked so long and hard to organise. He had to fight an urge to smile.

'The Seven Families.'

Nobody on the other side of the table said anything but every one of them was shocked. No one had raised their name at a meeting in living memory. No one outside the tightest circles should have even known their name.

The vice president spoke. 'What of them?'

'They owe us a debt. Reparations, if you will, for damages done.'

A silence met his remark. Everybody and nobody on the other side wanted to say something until the senator spoke.

'We're not going to move against the Seven Families without very good reason.'

'Would the fact that they have aligned with China and are plotting to support North Korea in a war against Japan be a good reason?'

This potential bombshell elicited caution across the table and more than one look of disbelief. This time, nobody found a voice. The game had been taken to a different level.

Butakhan shrugged calmly, sipped his water, and then stood to indicate he needed no more of their time.

'You can afford to be sceptical, gentlemen. You cannot afford to be wrong.'

6

Tumen River, Russian Far East

Who knew hell would be so white? Who knew it would blind you with snowflakes? Who knew that instead of lakes of fire there would be ice in every direction, ice that can break the spirit as surely as it can freeze you? Poor bastards. These and a hundred other despairing thoughts swirled around JJ's mind, like the blizzard in which she and Luca were caught. She had the consolation of knowing they were only paying a visit, but that was cold comfort at best.

They were being watched over by a nearby group of Russian border guards, one of whom pointed to the frozen river and spoke in his native tongue above the sound of the wind.

'What did he say?' JJ asked.

Luca leaned into her, his voice muffled by the storm. 'He said they found the body on the edge of the river. It had frozen to the bank.'

JJ nodded her acknowledgement and tried to look beyond the river, the bank opposite virtually consumed by the near-whiteout in which they found themselves.

'What's over there?'

Luca asked the Russian the same, the reply sounding more like a complaint than any useful information. He shouted to JJ what he had gleaned.

'He says that's North Korea. There's an armed outpost across the river, but you can't see it in this weather. He says the body could have come from the Chinese side or the North Korean side, but it didn't come from the Russian side.'

JJ looked about them. They really were in the back-end of beyond. This place that meant nothing and everything to their respective countries; this point at which three such volatile countries met might be a source of repeated international incidences, but here, on the southern tip of Russia, it was one big white nothing. Besides, if Luca was to be believed, it was the first incident even to be entered into a logbook here in fifty years. The only sign of civilisation—if you could call it that—was the low, cinder-block guardhouse close by.

'What's over there?'

'Over where?'

JJ pointed to their right. 'Over there.'

Luca asked the question of their armed babysitter and got a curt response.

'The Chinese border crossing.'

'Do they know anything?'

Luca asked the question and got a curter answer still.

'They don't talk to each other.'

JJ looked at the Russian through the deep recess of the ruff of her arctic jacket. He looked back at her and attempted a smile that somehow looked threatening. Even in the wall of snow, JJ could see he had breakfasted on potato vodka. She stomped off to their right.

'Where you going?' Luca asked.

He watched her, realising her plan as she began to recede into the whiteout. Within twenty seconds she had disappeared. The Russian said, or slurred, that Luca's companion was very beautiful. The Swiss man gave him a non-committal look, interested that he had reached that conclusion from the few square inches of her face the parka revealed. After ten minutes, Luca resolved to go after JJ until he saw her figure emerging from the wall of white.

'They said the body was there at first light five days ago. He said it was a clear night but nobody from their side saw anything.'

Luca nodded.

'Nice guys. Offered me a bed for the night.'

Luca couldn't see the irony in her eyes but could hear it in her raised voice.

'I just don't understand why they would leave the body here—why not lose it, or destroy it?'

Luca peered at what they could still see of the river. 'Because somebody wanted it found.'

'Who?'

'That, JJ, is the sixty-four million rouble question.'

They stood in silence for a moment, the noise of the wind abating, but the swirling snow showing no signs of following suit. Luca felt slightly stupid. It was a long way to come to find out close to nothing about Franz's death. If the Russians wouldn't give him the information he needed then he would just have to take it.

'JJ, I need a distraction so I can get into the building.'

'Why?'

Luca nodded to their left. 'There are closed-circuit television cameras on the walls and there's a chance we might learn something from them. These guys, they're just grunts. Do you think you can go back to the Chinese guards and start an argument? I'll get these guys to investigate, then slip inside and see if I can get a copy of the recording.'

JJ looked at him concerned. 'What if they don't follow me?'

'Then I'll neutralise those who don't.'

'What if nobody follows me?'

'Then I'll neutralise all of them.'

'What if the Chinese guards shoot me?'

'I said start an argument, not a war.'

JJ gave him a look that said she was not impressed and marched off in an altogether different direction towards the frozen river. After watching JJ disappear into the haze of snow, the sound of silence was broken by her screaming seemingly for her life, which suddenly caused everyone to move at electrifying speed in one direction.

'Genius,' Luca said, shaking his head and smiling.

★　　★　　★

Everybody had moved indoors. After JJ had 'slipped', throwing herself onto the frozen river and breaking the ice, the guards had almost fought each other to win the honour of escorting her to the guardhouse, no less than four of them donating winter jackets.

Many words might have described the guardhouse, but 'miserable' summed it up best. The station on the axis of the North Korean–Chinese borders was clearly one of those necessary evils, an afterthought almost, bare of amenities. It struck Luca as a micro-army base, all of it condensed into one long, soulless building. JJ and Luca were led down the corridor past sparsely furnished rooms: a small kitchen and canteen, barracks, what Luca thought was a locked store room and a communications room. It was a gloomy place, almost designed to make its occupants feel isolated.

Only the last room they reached showed signs of life. It was the rest and recreation room, or R&R. A surprisingly large television was pinned to one wall, an Xbox and PlayStation wired up to it. There were enough Soviet-era chairs for everybody to sit down, but not in comfort. The tables, too, were serviceable without adding any life. Luca did notice, though, that the place was clean. *Somebody runs a tight ship*, he observed.

JJ was freezing. The moment she had hit the ice, she berated herself for not thinking of fifty different ways to draw the attention of the guards away from Luca. Her clothes were wet and frozen and she knew with certainty that were it not for the speed with which the Russians had rushed to her and wrestled each other, hypothermia would be a certainty. The jeep that had brought them here had said minus twenty-two on its dashboard and she was feeling every one of those minus-degrees as she staggered to a chair in the living quarters.

A young Russian arrived with blankets, but he was rebuked for reasons JJ was unable to grasp. As a tussle began, she glared briefly at Luca, partly as a reminder for him to execute his plan and partly to express a certain indignation that he had not moved sooner to end her ordeal.

The most senior Russian soldier present shouted down his comrades then spoke to JJ, another soldier repeating his words to Luca.

'He says she needs to get out of those clothes.' Luca nodded firmly to signal that this was true, as well as being helpful to his cause.

JJ, her lips turning blue, knew the wisdom of changing out of wet clothes if not that of doing so in front of six sex-starved Russian conscripts. She began to pull at her parka zipper, every Russian leaping to her aid, until the senior officer barked again and stepped in before their openly resentful eyes.

It was a scene of controlled chaos, rebellion brewing among the jealous and hungry men: a good time for Luca to make his exit. Asking the youngest soldier the way to the bathroom, Luca was pointed dismissively out of the room.

Luca made his way back towards the small comms room, which, predictably, was unmanned. Without hesitating, he began flicking off any controls that might give access to the outside world, interfering with some wiring for good measure. Any attempt to make outside communication now would take a good half hour, time that might prove invaluable if they had to make a dash for it.

Checking that the coast was clear, Luca made his way back past the R&R room. The raised voices of the Russian conscripts reassured and alarmed him in equal measure. Inside he saw the senior officer holding up a blanket to screen JJ while she undressed—the idea of offering her privacy in another room evidently not an option.

With all eyes on the beautiful Chinese woman, Luca slipped past to the last door in the corridor. It had a white sign with red writing in Cyrillic script that read 'Restricted Access'. He took this as a positive and slipped inside, pleased to find he was at the top of a concrete stairwell lit by a row of wall lights. Their glare was hard on the eyes and it took him a moment to get used to the light.

Satisfied he was alone Luca cautiously made his way down, reminding himself of the Russian for 'I'm sorry I was looking for the bathroom' as he did so. Reaching the bottom, he saw only three doors along the right-hand side of the corridor and another at the end. The far one he guessed correctly would be a holding cell; its prisoners would be wayward soldiers awaiting collection by the Russian military police. The other three would be an engine room, an armoury, and, by his estimation, a rudimentary IT room. This last room was where the hardware that formed part of Russia's creaking global-weapons defence system would be stored, he hoped, along with the CCTV footage.

With infinite care, Luca opened the first door, the power room—a space in almost total darkness, lit by no more than the small lights of the equipment. The air was thick with the stench of years of burnt oil from the generator. The door ajar, he stepped inside and pulled a small cigarette-box-sized device from his pocket. He punched in a number on its screen then slid it underneath the generator.

Back in the corridor, he made his way silently to the next door. It was closed and when he attempted to turn the handle, he discovered it was firmly locked. He listened at it, trying to hear any IT equipment within. Nothing; he concluded it must be the armoury. He moved to the next door, listened, and could hear the hum of servers and workstations. After looking back down the corridor and reassuring himself he was alone, Luca slowly turned the handle.

No resistance.

The handle down, he calmly and silently swung the door open.

'Is this what you're looking for?'

Luca pulled up sharp. A middle-aged and scruffy Russian officer was sitting before a bank of monitors. The officer, sporting a curiously dated Lenin beard, tossed a USB stick in the hand that wasn't holding the gun. He had a confidence that told Luca he had more than just a memory stick up his sleeve.

'I suppose it depends what's on it.'

'In Russia nothing is more valuable than secrets, no?'

Luca glanced at the monitors behind the officer. Many of them appeared blanked out, white, reflecting the snow outside. One showed JJ curled up in a chair wrapped in a blanket, half a dozen frustrated soldiers jostling with ill-concealed impatience before her.

The officer's demeanour was relaxed and somewhat self-satisfied. He noted Luca's concern at the CCTV footage showing the woman and was impressed that he had replied to him in Russian, taking that almost as a sign of respect.

'Here we are left to freeze our arses off for years on end without so much as a visitor, then three sets of visitors in almost as many days.'

'Three?'

'First the police to take the body to town; then some nice FSB gentlemen threatening us with all kinds of prison sentences if we didn't tell them everything, very old school, and then you.'

'Did you give them a copy of whatever's on the USB stick?'

The officer grinned slyly. 'It slipped my mind.'

'Any particular reason?'

'Why give it to some jackbooted, faded-KGB types for free when I can sell it to a nice gentleman like you?'

'And what's the price?'

'Well, it just went up. You see, I added some bonus footage, you know, for the DVD extras.'

'What would that be?'

'You, breaking into this restricted area.'

'Oh, this area's restricted?'

'Didn't you see the sign?'

'Well, the truth is, I speak Russian better than I read it. So what is your price?'

'Price? You think I am merely motivated by money?'

Luca paused, perplexed. 'What else is there?'

The officer smirked unpleasantly and moved out of the way to show a freezing JJ standing behind a blanket screening her as she changed; the men jostling to grab discreet glimpses of her. In this view, the camera looked down from the corner of the room at her bare breasts, which were exposed as she buttoned up the shirt she had been donated.

'I'm motivated by that as well. Very clever of her to engineer that fall and use her change of clothes to distract my men. In truth, I don't see how I can keep her all to myself. Probably best to merely say that I will get first use of her.'

'I'm not sure you'll find her very co-operative.'

The officer pulled a face. 'In World War II the advancing Red Army raped over two million women. What is one more?'

Luca did not react except to unhurriedly check his watch causing the officer to notice it for the first time.

'Perhaps if you throw in the timepiece I can agree to go easy on her after you've gone.'

A change came over Luca that the Russian couldn't place, almost disinterest, as if he had somewhere else to be. 'My timing's off. I thought I'd be out of the building by now.'

'Oh dear, has your plan not gone to plan?'

Luca gave him a cold smile.

Then an explosion erupted in the adjacent generator room, rocking the building and plunging it into darkness in the same instant. Before the boom had subsided, Luca had stepped to one side as one, two, three bullets burst from the gun, the flare helping him locate it in the dark. Closing his hand round the officer's, Luca twisted the weapon out of his grasp with a wrench that left the Russian with two broken fingers, followed by an elbow that knocked him to the floor.

A moment later an emergency generator in another part of the building geared into action, its inferior power doing no more than booting up the CCTV monitors and emergency lighting. It was enough to show the Russian huddled in a corner, looking up to see Luca with a gun pointed at him.

'Get up.' The Swiss emphasised the instruction by gesturing with the gun. The Russian complied, keeping his hands on his head.

'The things I said about the woman, I didn't mean them. I was joking.'

Luca had to keep the hate from his eyes as he considered the officer's now wretched form. 'In World War II, twenty-four million Soviet people died. What's one more?'

An ugly look spread across the officer's face as he weighed up the situation. Years of bitterness at being stuck in the Russian quasi-prison welled up inside him, urging him to make a charge at his assailant. Perhaps death would be his only release from the soulless existence of this outpost. Then he saw Luca's face and knew it would prove fruitless; the intruder seemed to be alert to every movement, alive even to the thoughts in his head. The Russian offered the USB stick slowly to Luca.

'There's something else on the stick, a bonus, in exchange for my life.'

Luca held out his hand to receive the memory device, asking for an explanation with a look.

'There was a fourth visit. The footage is on there.'

'Do you have a name?'

'No, but he was escorted by high-ranking Russian officers and he sent a message from this computer, which tracks all of the key strokes inputted.'

The Russian gave what he hoped was a winning look, but his fear turned it into a snarl. Somehow, his physical ugliness prompted a sharp reminder in Luca of what the Russian had promised to do to JJ, of the kind of animal he really was. Then another darker thought haunted him, goaded him: *I haven't killed anybody yet.* This man trembling before him had proved himself perhaps unworthy of living.

'Turn around.'

'Please no. I have a wife, a daughter—'

'You were just about to rape somebody's daughter. Turn around.'

The Russian turned white, then did as he was told, his knees beginning to buckle. His death seemed a sudden and inescapable reality.

'I have money. I can get more secrets. I could be of use to you...'

Luca gripped the gun tighter, thinking this man would be a good start, that perhaps killing him was all that stood between him and being the Broker.

'Please—'

The man's shoulder-shaking sobs had no effect on Luca but something was staying his hand. There was no denying it, the *presence* of the man's life somehow made the idea of ending it diabolical. To blow him up with a bomb or shoot from a distance was one thing, but this, so close, so cold…

The gun smashed down on the officer's crown rendering him unconscious.

Luca stood over him, a feeling of nausea rising up inside, not at what he had done, but at what he had failed to do.

Then JJ screamed.

A snatched look at the CCTV monitors showed the six Russian conscripts aggressively circling JJ as she held them off with a chair. Whether they had linked her to the explosion or feared an attack, or had somehow decided that in the dimness of the emergency lighting all bets were off, was impossible to read. All Luca knew was that JJ was in danger.

He raced from the room, remorse mingling with anger as he sprinted along the concrete corridor, past the generator room with its door blown off, acrid black smoke pouring out, before reaching the stairs. He took them three at a time and kicked through the door at the top.

Red emergency lighting lit his way as he raced into the R&R room to see one Russian moaning on the floor and the other five furiously circling JJ with knives in their hands. Without pausing, Luca had his knee in the side of one soldier before finding another with his whipped-round elbow; both went down like sacks of potatoes. At the same moment, JJ span round on the spot delivering a roundhouse kick to one conscript, finding the windpipe of another with three relentless punches that slammed him back into the wall-mounted television. The last conscript couldn't begin to comprehend the speed of events and twisted left and right between his two opponents in desperation, slashing the air with his knife. This meant he was facing Luca when JJ slammed her foot into the back of his head causing him to bend over at a violent speed into Luca's rising knee which sent him flying backwards, unconscious before he hit the ground.

Silence.

JJ, dressed only in a man's shirt, looked from the six bodies to Luca and dared to hope that the danger was over, while trying to comprehend the combination of fear and exhilaration she was feeling. She pointed an uncertain finger at the prone bodies.

'What just happened?'

'I think you just happened.'

'Are we in trouble?'

'Not as much as they are.'

JJ tried to take it in; the few who were conscious groaned pitifully.

'Oh God, what have we done to them?'

'The plan was to kill me and rape you.'

It took a moment to register, but when it did, a volcanic look flared in JJ's eyes. A soldier prostrate on the floor near her murmured painfully as he reached for a knife near his hand. She dropped to her knees, landing on the man's face and neck, the blow rendering him unconscious.

'*Sons* of bitches,' she said.

Luca looked on, impressed, before he remembered himself. 'We should go.'

'OK. OK.'

Luca could see something was bugging her. 'What is it?'

'Did you see if they have any spare winter clothing? I'm not sure I'm dressed for minus twenty.'

7

Chinese Airspace

'You OK?' Luca asked.

'Are we out of Russian airspace?'

'We're about halfway across China.'

'Then I'm OK.'

JJ, now dressed in casual wear, did her best to give Luca a reassuring smile. He could see she needed time to think things over and returned to working on his tablet.

JJ looked around, trying to take in not just what had happened at the Russian border but what was happening *now*. Where had she found herself? The last question brought on a small ironic smile, because even this aspect of where she found herself was surreal to her: a private jet, with twelve luxury leather chairs, and the two of them the only passengers. An attractive Somali air stewardess attended to their every need, serving them gin and tonics before preparing salmon en croute for dinner. The gin was the best JJ had ever tasted.

The billionaire lifestyle was just another surreal aspect to the life she'd arrived at. In her schooldays, the head teacher had told JJ she would end up on drugs, in jail, or worse, if she carried on in the direction she was going. After her expulsion from school, every penny JJ earned from her work at casinos in London went to pay the debts accrued at other casinos round town. Eventually gambling debts had forced her to skip town and when she made a substantial sum in Monte Carlo JJ was obliged to send back every penny to pay off the debts. Her winning streak saw her turned away from enough casinos across the south of France for her to seek out other venues, other games. This was how she'd stumbled across poker and the myriad dens and dwellers attached to it. While poker was more colourful than other games on the casino floor, it was more nefarious, with more than one game abandoned due to a police raid. One memorable game had been brought to an abrupt halt by an armed robbery. That was before she had known Luca.

They met in a palatial villa on the outskirts of Rome belonging to a major Mafia *caporegime*, though JJ didn't know it at the time. She had seen Luca before that, though, at a casino in Cannes. She remembered him because he was handsome and sober and quiet, three traits missing from the rest of the players at the table. She also remembered him because she happened to be the blackjack croupier when he won the biggest pot of the year, only to walk over to the roulette wheel and lose it all. It was the smile at that moment of their encounter that was seared into her mind. It was a smile not so much of acceptance as relief, as if Luca might have been dreading doubling his money. He had tipped her and the woman running the roulette wheel in a big way and then disappeared into the crowd of people still agog at what they had just witnessed. That was the other reason she had remembered him. Her shift ended at that exact moment, and she had raced to grab her coat and find him on the street only to see a sporty looking Bentley pulling away from the kerb.

The encounter at the *caporegime*'s villa was an altogether different story. She had gone with her friend Chantal whom she loved and hated in equal measure: loved, because she was her oldest and best friend and hated, because she was the more beautiful of the two and, unlike JJ, wasn't a drifter. She was a marine biologist who had forged a successful career

80

studying dolphins. 'How am I supposed to compete with somebody who talks to dolphins?' JJ had once complained, to which Chantal had reassured her, 'Anybody can talk to a dolphin, getting them to understand you is the hard part.'

The villa was so garishly full of bling that Chantal had said it looked like somebody had consumed the Harrods sweet counter and vomited it over the walls. JJ had to agree. Since they were invited to the party and not the poker game in play downstairs, she resolved to leave; that was, until curiosity made her drop in on the poker game to see who was playing. And there was Luca again.

But it was a different Luca to the man she had first set eyes on a few months before. This Luca was unshaven and she didn't recognise him at first. He was dishevelled, the opposite of the crisp, sharp look he had sported in Cannes. Then there was the drink, which he was gulping down as if his throat was on fire. Intrigued, if privately disappointed, JJ had stayed and forced Chantal to stand and watch the game, though Chantal failed to see what JJ saw in Luca now. JJ was mesmerised, however, finding this other side to the man undeniably riveting. He was a mess and she wanted to watch all of it.

As the night wore on Luca became increasingly drunk, knocking his cash off the table and spilling his drink. Still, he had managed to stay in the game until one pot grew and grew. One by one, every long-distance player folded either for lack of funds or fear of being wiped out. This left Luca— who seemed more concerned that a bottle of Jack Daniel's was put on the table—and the host himself. The *caporegime* was a small wiry man with a flat boxer's nose and silver hair tied back in a long tail. They called him *Il Macellaio* (The Butcher) and it was his party. It was clear that The Butcher believed this should be his hand, a story to tell the morning after the night before.

Word of the head-to-head had spread upstairs and any dancing and cavorting stopped as everyone squeezed into the cellar to watch the game. JJ was told later that if the *polizia* had raided the villa that night, they could have closed down the Mafia's operations in northern Rome for good. However, the police didn't show that night, perhaps because at least four people watching the game were from police headquarters and good friends of the host.

It was clear that both Luca and the *caporegime* were all in, and soon the middle of the table was littered with piles of money. A charged silence descended as everybody waited to see who had the winning hand: the lethal host or the drunken stranger. The result produced a collective gasp.

The host turned over his hand. A flush: five hearts. His hand was matched by a smile of wistful sympathy for the man about to be beaten. Then Luca slowly tipped his over. A full house: a pair of kings and three twos.

That was not the remarkable moment for JJ, though. It was the change that came over Luca that surprised her most. Incredibly, he turned from drunk to sober in a second. It was nothing he did, just the look in his eye, a look that was not missed by the *caporegime* who felt the sting of having been played for a sucker by a superior opponent.

The collective gasp was not just at the drama of the result either, it was fear at the response it might ignite from the *caporegime*, infamous for his bloody regime in the Mafia. At first, he did nothing. His considered reaction was to smile and then speak in his native Italian.

'Well played, my friend. Would you do me the favour of playing again so that I might win it back?'

The mood in the room became quietly nervous. He had chosen his words carefully; no one present was under the illusion that it was in any way a request. His honour, and money, were at stake.

'JJ, let's go.' Chantal whispered.

This was another reason JJ loved Chantal, she had the survival instinct. But JJ was determined to see how this played out; she had to learn more about this man.

'You go if you want to, but I'm staying for a bit.'

'A bit of what?'

JJ looked at her friend and smiled admiringly; as ever, Chantal understood her to the quick.

Then Luca spoke: 'If you don't mind, I've won enough money for one night.' He spoke not out of fatigue or boredom but as a challenge.

'Perhaps we gamble for something else? A car? One of the girls? Something more exotic?' The *caporegime* was two rungs down from the head of the family, but he spoke as the person he wanted to be, a king, dealing out largesse like it was his birthright.

Luca, who even the dullest person in the room could now see was sober, turned the Jack of Diamonds over in his hand while he considered the offer.

'Do you know how much money is lying there?' He nodded at the pile of euros on the table.

'Sixty, sixty-five thousand?'

Luca nodded very slowly. 'Seventy-one thousand, one hundred and eighty euros.' He reached over and picked up five thousand euros, which he folded and put inside his jacket. 'That's my original stake, but that still leaves over sixty-six thousand.'

The calmness with which he had acted, the loaded intent, made the *caporegime*'s henchmen calculate how quickly they could pull out their guns, and the police officers calculate how quickly they could get away from the place.

Everyone felt the buzz of fear, the nervousness before a violent eruption. But to JJ it was like a light in a dark abyss, something so fascinating, so immediate, so alive, and all orchestrated by the man she'd chased in Cannes. She was determined not to let go.

'A month ago a friend of mine, Sir Stephen Devereux, approached you to ask that you forgive a debt against the Siriaco family, who own a factory in the town of—'

'I know what they own. But they owe me money.'

'How much?'

The *caporegime* evidently didn't like where this was going, but his ego and reputation were at stake. He clicked his hand. 'Antonio, how much?'

A henchman, more ape than *homo sapien*, spoke up with caution, knowing the consequences of making a mistake. 'Sixty-five thousand euros, *capo*.'

The *caporegime* stared at Luca, his humiliation deepening with the realisation that the money—a pile of cash that included his money—was to pay off the debt. A stack of cash, not a penny of which was Luca's. This fact was not wasted on any of the guests gripped by the scene playing out before them.

Later that night, after dropping off Chantal, Luca told JJ that the manner in which the *caporegime* reacted to the repayment of the debt could have defined both their futures.

Everyone around the table had begun to plan an exit route at the first sign of the *caporegime*'s famous temper; all of them recalled that *Il Macellaio* had once shot seven innocent people at a wedding party while seeking to settle a perceived slight. Then he showed his hand.

The *caporegime* stood up. Without realising it, everybody in the room took in a breath and held it. Then he started clapping, slowly at first, then faster, until he matched it with laughter.

'Now this—*this*—is how to do business.'

As his laughter grew, people joined in. The relief and happiness it created meant that the group's laughter became hysterical.

First, they called for more drinks and then very quickly the party moved upstairs.

Luca thanked the host for the evening and made to leave, but the *caporegime* insisted on escorting him to the door. Once there, he took Luca's hand in a double handshake: 'Signor tonight was entertaining,' he said. Luca waited for the rejoinder. 'But like all jokes, not so funny when you've heard it more than once.'

They remained in the handshake for a few moments, Luca not deaf to the meaning, the *caporegime* satisfied he had made his supremacy clear.

Luca left and found JJ and her friend waiting for him by his car. The *caporegime*, meanwhile, went to find out which of his underlings had allowed Luca to attend the party. The man was found swinging by his neck under the Ponte Sant'Angelo in Rome a week later.

★   ★   ★

The smell of salmon wafting up to JJ's nose snapped her out of her daydream.

'Your dinner, madam.'

JJ smiled at the polite air stewardess, who smiled back at her radiantly as she walked towards the cockpit.

The Chinese woman looked over at her partner and once again tried to understand how in hell she had gone from being expelled from a string of schools to flying away from the scene of a crime—an international incident—in a private jet. Her attention was then caught by something else. Luca leaning in close to his tablet staring at the screen.

'What is it, Luca?'

'I know who killed Franz.'

JJ got up from her seat and stood next to Luca. The tablet on the table showed grainy footage that JJ immediately recognised as the view from the Russian border guardhouse across the river towards North Korea. The night-time scene was relatively well lit, the sky clear, a strong half-moon illuminating the ground.

JJ watched as nothing happened, squinting to see every detail, until the tiniest movement caught her eye.

'Do you see it?'

'By the river?'

'That's it. Keep watching.'

The movement became a dark mass as it approached the bank on the other side of the frozen river. Luca put his fingers on the small point of interest on the screen and pulled them apart, zooming in on the pixelated detail that suddenly became visible as three people approaching the river, two of them carrying a long bundle under their arms.

When they reached the river they kept going, their dark bodies silhouetted against the shining ice, crossing to the bank on the near side. Here, the two men carrying the load stopped while the third continued, moving in the direction of the guardhouse.

'Watch what happens,' Luca said.

JJ did just that and understood immediately. As the two men dumped their burden on the near river bank it was immediately obvious from the size and shape of it what they'd been carrying: a body.

'Is that—?' JJ asked.

'Franz. Yes.'

The two men positioned the body on the bank and then recrossed the frozen river before retreating into the darkness, out of view of the camera. Meanwhile, the other man was walking almost directly towards the camera, staring at the ground. JJ noticed he had not looked back once.

'So they did come from North Korea?'

'Probably, but they might have turned north and headed to China. It's too dark to know for sure, but it's an acceptable working assumption. Watch this…'

The walking man had disappeared from view and Luca reapplied his fingers to the tablet screen to zoom out. The man was close and clearly in focus, but still looking at the ground. He must have thought he heard something, because he looked up, alert, straight into the camera.

Luca paused the scene to allow JJ to take it in.

'Butakhan…'

His face was caught, pin-sharp, close to the camera. It was unmistakably him and to the Swiss man it was deeply unsettling.

'What's wrong, Luca?'

'It's too—'

'Too what?'

'Too perfect.'

'What do you mean?'

'I mean, a man crosses from North Korea to Russia in the dead of night, has a body dumped, then walks straight up and deliberately gets his picture taken?'

'But he was rattled by a noise, wasn't he? Isn't he just looking up at something?'

'Maybe.' Luca was bothered by something, bothered by a detail he was missing.

'What is it?'

'The Russian officer, the one that gave me the USB. I think he was expecting me.'

'You said somebody had arranged for us to be shown around.'

'No, no, more than that. He knew I would come looking for this film. And he was meant to kill me.'

'Why didn't he?'

'Because he was greedy. He wanted to get paid by Peter *and* Paul.'

'Is Butakhan that sloppy?'

Luca was bothered by JJ's question, not because he felt it was wide of the mark but because it was a bull's-eye. He looked at her, annoyed that he hadn't realised sooner. He had to review his thoughts; he was unsure which side of insane or accurate his theory was.

'I don't think he cared.'

'What do you mean?'

Luca almost smiled, almost impressed. 'I mean, I think it's a game to him. Either I died today or I brought back a message for the Families. It was win-win for him.'

'The Families? Is that the organisation you work for, the Families?'

Luca felt an idiot for letting it slip. It was a reminder that either he had to get the General Counsel to agree to co-opt JJ for more than just this investigation or he had to cut her loose before she learnt too much, or said too much.

JJ put an affectionate hand on the back of her partner's neck and rubbed it. 'I wouldn't read too much into what the Russian officer said. I was always taught that when in doubt assume cock-up over conspiracy.'

Luca looked at her, telling himself that he might want to start appreciating her at some time in the future. 'The officer gave me one other thing, access to an email account.'

'Whose?'

'Butakhan's and whoever he's been talking to. The officer had set up the computer to record Butakhan's keystrokes.' As he spoke, he switched from the frozen film scene to an email app on the tablet.

JJ watched as he clicked on 'Inbox'. It was empty. Next Luca clicked on the 'Sent' folder. This was empty too.

'Hasn't it been used?'

He nodded and clicked on the 'Drafts' folder. One email with no subject line was present. He double tapped it and it popped open. It was a list of three names. Franz Wetzell. Raoul Escobedo. Luca Voss.

JJ recognised the first as the name of the man found at the Russian border, but didn't understand the significance of the others.

'Why are there three names sitting in a draft email?'

'It's a trick used by terrorists. Once you send an email you create a digital signature that can be tracked, but not even the NSA can read your draft emails. You save the file in 'Drafts', your partner in crime reads it, deletes it, and replies with another email from their own account. Two people have the password to the same account and communicate via draft emails in complete privacy.'

'OK, I get that. But what do those three names mean?'

'Well, the first two were murdered in the past week. So, if I had to take a guess...'

Luca pulled a face to finish the sentence and looked up.

He was met with JJ's look of dawning horror.

'You're next.'

The silence was broken by an incoming videocall on Luca's tablet. He tapped to accept and Herr Hesse's stern face filled the screen.

'I have received your account of the trip and I wish for you to return to Ticino.'

Luca nodded. 'I'd still like to find out how Butakhan learned about Franz; I'd like to know how he tracked him down, and why.'

JJ, out of view of the tablet's camera, studied the General Counsel's face. Close up, it seemed more severe than she remembered it being when they had met in Davos. It was stony, seemingly devoid of emotion. Somehow, this lack of humanity made her more concerned that he had influence to direct Luca's life in any way.

'Herr Voss, please return. We will discuss the matter further here.'

Luca was matter of fact in pushing aside the instruction. 'But we can turn this plane around and be in Shanghai in an hour. I'd like to understand what Franz was working on to get him killed.'

'Herr Voss, you have already encountered more danger than you are trained for. In fact, I am surprised you have survived it unscathed. Let us not tempt fate another time.'

'This is different, I would be visiting unannounced.'

'We will discuss this on your return.'

JJ was struck by the subtle emphasis he put on the last word. It was more than emphatic, something akin to holy writ.

Luca paused, wondering whether to persist. 'We should inspect the apartment to see if we can learn anything.'

'You must come back. Need I say it in stronger terms?'

Luca paused again, this time his mind made up. 'No, Herr Hesse. I apologise.'

To JJ, the General Counsel's face seemed to relax, an underlying stress abating. 'Then we're agreed. That's all for now.'

Luca tapped off the app before sitting back in the wide, cream-leather passenger seat. While he pondered the conversation, the Learjet's engine hummed hypnotically. JJ shifted in her seat, alarmed by what she had heard.

'What did he mean about this being more than you are trained for?'

'There's a programme. I haven't finished the programme yet, that's all.'

'Is that where you were heading after Mexico, to finish your training?'

Luca remembered her reaction to that news. She had fought with disappointment and he had felt uncomfortable upsetting her; their closeness had become a hindrance to his cause.

'Yes. Yes it was.'

'Where was the training taking place?'

'Japan.'

She nodded, piecing together a puzzle they had never spoken about. 'And then you could be the Broker or whatever it is they call it?'

'One can be considered for the role.'

'Why do they call it that? The "Broker"?'

'Well, whoever is chosen to be the Broker has three roles. They act as financial broker across the world's markets, as power broker between the world's movers and shakers and as arbitrator between...' Luca's voice trailed off.

'Between who?' JJ said, leaning forward in her seat.

'The Families.'

JJ watched him. The prospect of such a position seemed to weigh on Luca. The realisation began to dawn on her that it was not her companion's ambition to fulfil the role, but an obligation, almost. 'Do you want to become the Broker?'

'I want to find out why Butakhan killed Franz and, presumably, Raoul.'

JJ noted the sidestep, choosing not to pursue it directly. 'And you want to know why he wants to kill you?'

'One follows the other, doesn't it?'

The plane was jostled by mild turbulence briefly before settling down to its smooth course again. JJ tried to grasp where Luca was coming from, not wanting to come right out and ask just yet. Then the sense that Luca was in danger swept over her. The threat had stalked him in a remote outpost in Russia and, therefore, could stalk him anywhere.

'Well, maybe it's for the best that Herr Hesse has ordered you back to Switzerland.'

'Why?'

'Well, look at the reach of these people.'

'You think I should run and hide?'

'I think you should be careful.'

The door to the cockpit opened and the elegant Somali stewardess approached them.

'Can I get you any more drinks?'

Luca lifted his empty glass. 'The same again, please.'

'Yes Herr Voss.' She bent down to retrieve the glasses.

'Oh, and tell the captain to change course.'

'Certainly. Where to?'

'Shanghai.'

'No,' JJ said.

'No what?' Luca replied.

'No—we're not going to Shanghai.'

Luca met JJ's defiant stare with a crooked smile. 'Who said *we* were going?'

Now JJ was wide-eyed. 'You're not going without me.'

'Well, which is it?'

JJ didn't know whether to scowl or to laugh at herself, and so she made do with turning her own seat to face Luca's across the aisle of the Learjet until, understanding her point, he turned his to face hers.

Luca was confronted with a look that demanded some kind of an explanation but no words were forthcoming. 'What?'

JJ met him with mock surprise. 'You're asking me "What?" What the hell do *you* think you're doing?'

'I'm going to inspect Franz's apartment, see if I can find out why Butakhan acted against him. If Herr Hesse is angry, so be it.'

'Not that. What do you think you're doing not taking *me*?'

'JJ, this is no place for a—'

Now JJ was more than surprised, she was outraged. 'A woman? Is that what you were about to say? Some whimpering female, am I? Just a helpless "little girl" back in Russia, was I? Curled up in a ball crying, was I?'

'This is no place for an outsider.'

This gave JJ pause for thought. Half-embarrassed, half-amused to have risen to imagined bait. 'I'm Chinese and we're over Chinese airspace. So who exactly is the outsider here?'

Luca smirked mischievously. 'You're only three-quarters Chinese.'

'I get the stubbornness from my Ukrainian grandmother.'

The Swiss man went to smile at the beautiful woman opposite him, went to say that she got more than mere stubbornness from her ancestor—the exotic Asian form with its dash of Eastern European beauty a testament to that. He found himself grimacing instead. 'JJ, I shouldn't—'

'Shouldn't what?'

'I can't involve you. You're not a member of—' Luca felt Herr Hesse's presence sweep over him, felt the chains of his education, centuries of tradition hemming him in. He sensed a rebellion within himself, but it was unfocused, ill-formed. He also knew from long experience that whenever he was in doubt, it was best to wait for an answer to present itself. Annoyed at himself, he sighed. 'You don't come from—'

'One of the Families?'

'Yes. One of the Families.' He looked at her with as much of an apologetic expression as he could muster in his increasingly foul mood.

'Luca, who are these families that keep coming up? Are they all related or something?'

'No, it's not that.'

'Then what? Tell me. I keep hearing them mentioned but you don't explain who they are.'

'Because I'm not meant to.'

'You don't want to.'

He saw the truculence in her face and it didn't help the mood. 'I'm not *meant* to. I would if I could.'

'Why? Who's here stopping you?'

Luca smiled again, only this time at himself. Her words, as ever, went to the heart of it for him and he wondered just what was stopping him, except for the centuries of history perhaps. He considered her words in a new light, a light that included her. As the Broker, he would be appointed an assistant, a facilitator to coordinate logistics, equipment and supplies. This individual would act as wing person on certain missions. They would require physical prowess, intelligence, and grit, qualities JJ had in spades. Only this person had to come from within the Families.

Or did they? Luca felt more than the shift of time, he felt another bigger truth: he wasn't sure he wanted to be the Broker if it meant having anyone other than JJ by his side. Not just because she was more than able, or because of the sex, or the fun they had together. It was something else. She was the first thing, the first person, to have ever taken him off his preordained course. His life, mapped out almost to the day, had only ever become his own when he had spent time with her. She made the call to duty bearable when the billionaire's playthings had long lost their lustre.

'Your drinks, Sir, Madam.' It was the stewardess, who placed a tumbler beside each of them. 'The captain says we should land in Shanghai in approximately eighty minutes.'

'Thank you.'

Luca watched her walk away absent-mindedly before his eyes drifted back to JJ who was waiting with a mock-threatening glare.

'Get a good look at her derrière?'

He smiled despite himself, her tongue-in-cheek possessiveness shaking him from his meditation. He'd come

94

to the decision to tell her. This being JJ, he would let the cards fall where they may.

'The Families, JJ…'

Luca's companion dropped her jokey expression, sensitive to the mood change, but didn't speak lest she disturb his delicate and apparently confessional demeanour.

'There are seven of them today, though at one time there were thirteen. Many, many centuries ago for better or worse, they effectively ruled the world.'

He watched JJ for a reaction, but she was waiting, waiting for all of it. Luca considered the ice floating in his drink, bobbing gently, hypnotically almost. He was flipping a coin in his head, wondering whether to push on. He decided that the coin was double-headed.

'They were, I guess, the powers behind and above the thrones that ruled over each land. To be honest, it's not that hard to dig up the names, but forgive me if I don't speak of them now. For over five centuries, they were a self-styled council of Philosopher Kings that were meant to steer the world along the most peaceful path possible. While nation states were driven by self-interest, the Thirteen Families believed they were driven by a collective interest.'

'The collective good?'

He wore a look that conceded her point. 'They weren't saints, they profited, enormously at times, but their interests were—they believed—aligned with the wider world interests.'

'And these families ran the world the whole time?'

'No, no, they were never all-powerful. Genghis Khan pushed them back, as did the Church in the Dark Ages, but otherwise they dominated behind the scenes. Except that over time, increasingly, they failed in their own mission. Over time the very atrocities they were meant to ensure would never gain a foothold in the world—total war, religious persecution, slavery—emerged, and nation states broke the silent concord and the Families' power was reduced to influence.'

'When did it change?'

'The end of the Napoleonic era was the end of the Thirteen Families.'

'What happened?'

'It transpired that six of the Families had been pursuing personal gain and that these pursuits were behind many of the recent global problems.'

'Then what?'

'A council was held and they were banished. The six rogue families went their own self-serving ways and, pretty soon, tore each other apart to the point of oblivion. We're not even sure if their descendants know of their illustrious past.' Luca gave a small shrug to indicate it really was ancient history.

'And the rest?'

'Well, the Seven Families somehow became known as the Seven Pyramids of Power. I think Napoleon coined the phrase. They resolved to continue their relationship with the world powers. I think, somehow, over time, it had just become what they did—like a set of religious beliefs—almost true, by virtue of having existed for so long.'

'And do these families kind of still run things?'

'Not in the way they did. The world has changed beyond recognition, perhaps for the better. In fact, the Seven Families have moved so far into the background that most people think their existence is just rumour. The Families have no sovereignty, no home, no standing army, just influence.'

'I don't understand, how do they influence things? Do they own banks and things?'

'Yes, they have interests in financial institutions, as well as in various global industries. They always have done, really. They started a lot of them. Never underestimate the sway this sort of connection has with governments.' He pulled a face that said that such things were the way of the world. 'But they prefer diplomacy. Almost every nation state has had a relationship with them since as long as they care to remember. The Seven Families have done everything, from funding wars to funding building programmes. But whereas nations and empires have fallen and risen, risen and fallen, the Families—the Seven Families, at least—have remained constant.'

JJ nodded taking in the story methodically, not wanting to overlook how the pieces fitted together. 'And that's it, they don't do anything else?'

Luca sighed, reluctant to touch on his next point, but he was committed to telling her now. 'Direct intervention is sometimes undertaken, but only very reluctantly.'

'But it is undertaken?'

'When necessary. You see, the Seven Families know how easy—how tempting—it would be to become sucked back into orchestrating world affairs. If they do that, however, they can't claim to be impartial, which is vital to their mission. So, to stop themselves doing it by degrees, since the eighteenth century, they have limited themselves to one and only one agent of change: to prevent the accidental creation of any kind of militia.'

JJ looked at him as if seeing him for the first time. 'What can this agent do?'

'Pretty much whatever he or she deems necessary.'

'With limits?'

'Without limits. This one individual is—'

'The Broker.'

Luca nodded.

JJ sat back in her chair, the story washing over her, the details and the implications drifting in and out of view.

'Weren't Franz and Raoul Brokers at the same time?'

'No, Raoul stepped in when Franz went missing. They like continuity.'

'And you might step in next, once you have completed your—?'

'Training, yes.'

JJ nodded contemplatively, addressing in her mind an angle Luca could not guess.

'Franz dead, Raoul dead, you wanted dead. What's the average life expectancy of a Broker?'

'Short.'

'Because of all the fun and games, like we had in Russia?'

'To be honest that was an easy assignment.'

If this bothered JJ, she did not let on. Instead, she turned over the facts in her head once again while looking round at the cabin.

'And that's why you get the toys and the lifestyle, isn't it?' Luca said nothing, knowing she was about to spell it out for herself and him. 'All this is the price you have to pay for doing your job. All this is the price they put on your life?'

Luca waited to see what JJ's reaction to this ultimate truth would be. She was considering the cut-glass tumbler, knowing even this would be hugely expensive glassware. Somehow, its luxurious nature was tainted in her eyes now, now she knew the real price.

'Why are you telling me all of this?'

Luca made a helpless gesture with his hands. 'I wanted you to understand. And I wanted you to know that when we get to Shanghai I'm going to ask the pilot to fly you home.'

'But I want to come with you.'

'It's too dangerous.'

'For me or for you?'

'For anyone. The difference is, you don't have to do it. I do.'

'You don't have to do it, in fact, you were just told *not* to do it.'

'I think Herr Hesse is wrong, JJ. The Families are under threat, and I can't walk away from that. But it's not your problem, it's nothing to do with you.'

'Don't talk to me like that.'

'Like what?'

'Like I'm excluded.'

Luca could see the heat rising in JJ's face and felt foolish. She was adopted, a Chinese child of white, English parents, and therein must lie its own tale.

'I'm sorry.'

'You should be. We were a good team in Russia. And you need an assistant, you said so yourself in Davos.'

'I know, I know. They'll give me one. So go home.'

'I don't want to.'

'I'm not asking you.'

'I don't care, I'm staying.'

'JJ, you're going home.'

'I'm not, Luca.'

'I'm sorry, but I've made my mind up, you're going—'

'I don't have a home. I have you.'

The restrained vehemence with which she spoke brought Luca up short. He tried to read her but she looked into her drink instead. In the silence, Luca looked out of the window at the constellation of science fiction lights that was Shanghai, and thought about what JJ had just said; he could say the same thing to her. They were both alone he realised, only they didn't have to be. He didn't know whether he was thinking with his heart or his head. Maybe she had a point, or maybe she was the point. He looked back at her and let himself smile until she half-smiled back at him.

'You mean I'm stuck with you?' he asked.

JJ had to play the words through her mind once more and then struggled to read Luca before detecting a glint in his eye, which she matched with an even more mischievous one of her own, sliding off her chair and onto his lap.

'Stuck with me like a bad penny.'

She looked into his eyes, scared and excited about liking somebody this much. Then she planted her lips on his and gave him a long, slow kiss before resting her head on his shoulder.

'Talking of bad pennies JJ, since we're a mile up, I wondered if I could interest you in membership of my club.'

The beautiful Chinese woman sat up on his lap and looked at him with intrigue, biting her lower lip as she did so. 'A mile-high club? Does it come with one of those initiation ceremonies?'

'Well, it's funny you should say that…'

The Somali stewardess stepped out of the cockpit to ask the passengers for any last requests before landing, but what she saw made her turn around immediately and step back inside. Once she had closed the door abruptly behind her, it took a moment for her to register what JJ had just done from her position underneath Luca.

'She winked at me,' the stewardess muttered.

8

Yangon, Myanmar

It was not the exclusivity of the Rolls Royce Phantom that Butakhan liked most, although there was no denying the pleasures of its cocoon of leather and walnut and the air-sprung ride that wafted him from location to location. It wasn't the communications system built into the back of the driver's seat in front of him, which allowed him to direct the affairs of his global organisation from this car, nor the cool-box beside his elbow that always held a bottle of his preferred drink, Krug 1928. Nor, even, was it the pneumatic platinum blonde, bubblier than his champagne of choice, luxuriating next to him on the sumptuous rear bench-seat in a pleasingly short dress. It was not even that the car, like the woman, was shipped wherever he went. It was the shell.

The specifications for the car's shell had been personally overseen by him: constructed from bullet and bombproof materials it was able to withstand bullets fired at the windows or bombs set off under the chassis. In such an event not only would the integrity of the shell remain intact, the car's bullet-proof wheels would also ensure the car was able to continue on its journey until the fuel ran out. Admittedly, the weight of all that armoury was significant: the Phantom had started out as a three-tonne vehicle with a retuned engine that enabled his bodyguard to accelerate to a hundred kilometres per hour from a standing-start in just over five seconds. The added armour took the weight of the vehicle to over seven tonnes and reaching sixty took a positively sluggish ten seconds. It was a price worth paying though; it was his home away from home; his one-man war room, and it made life on the move almost acceptable. What was unacceptable was the traffic.

He hit a button on the armrest.

'Ivaanjav, why did we take this route?'

Up front, his heavyset Mongolian driver winced at his boss's irritation. 'Sorry Sir, there are roadworks on the way into town so I thought this route would be easier and quicker.'

Butakhan wanted to say more, but to do so would have achieved nothing.

'Buty, I like it. We've never come in this way before. Look at all the houses, they're so quaint.'

His Californian co-passenger was alive to the volcanic nature of his temper and was always keen to placate it, though she was vividly aware that she was not always on the money.

'Scarlett, don't call me Buty, and the houses are not quaint, they are shanties. I wouldn't house my pigs in them.'

Yeah, well, these people don't have the odd billion to pay for penthouses for their porcine friends. The American thought it, but wasn't dumb enough to say it. Instead, she looked out at the shacks and thought how her sponsor could change it all with a wave of his chequebook.

'Maybe we could pay them to get out of the way, Buty. Toss some money in the air and start a riot. Oh, I've always wanted to do that, can we?'

Butakhan looked at her with sleepy, unimpressed eyes. 'I do not throw money away, Scarlett, I invest it.'

She gave his words some consideration and then a smile spread across her face. 'Oh, Buty, you are always splashing the cash with me so you mustn't think you're throwing it away where I'm concerned. You're such a romantic.'

She was squeezing his elbow as he tried to fathom the logic of her statement—and the notion of being romantic—when the car phone rang. Butakhan was grateful for the interruption.

'Yes?' he said.

'He has read the email.' The voice was male but robotic, the result of a voice-modifier. This was unnecessary on a secure line, but its owner was more cautious than most.

'How are we able to ascertain that?' The Mongolian man's brow creased at the possibility of knowing whether a person had read draft emails.

'We were able to pick up a digital footprint, which we traced to his location. Also, the last name on the list has been changed.'

Curiosity had already caused Butakhan to lean forward and type in the email details on the laptop of his mini-comms station. He clicked on the 'Draft' folder and saw the three names as they were now: Franz Wetzell. Raoul Escobedo. Butakhan.

The Mongolian man sniffed, not amused. 'Yes, I see the evidence. Good, so he knows he's being hunted. Do we know where he's being hunted to?'

'Shanghai. He is heading to Wetzell's former safe house, an apartment in the Shanghai Tower.'

'Just as you predicted, bravo. If we finish him there, it will send a very powerful message to the Families. They will know there is a fox loose in the hen house and we can expect them to act like headless chickens.'

Butakhan grinned, pleased at his wordplay. He turned to Scarlett but she was staring out of the window at the local peasants.

'Do you wish me to expedite the matter?'

The Mongolian man nodded slowly to himself. 'Yes, well put. Expedite the matter.' He remembered the skijoring, how he'd nearly been beaten by the better team, how he would have enjoyed another chance to prove his superiority. It was not to be. 'How quickly can we get our people there?'

'We have a team on standby in Taiwan. They can be on site within two hours.'

'Good. Call me in two hours to tell me Luca Voss is dead, then.' He killed the call and replaced the phone. 'Champagne, dear?'

Scarlett was still gazing out of the window, her eyes squeezed tight at what she had just heard. She began calculating when she could next slip away to send a message. She put on a game face and turned to Butakhan, all smiles.

'Champagne? Of course. What are we celebrating?'

★　　★　　★

A team of twelve men were sitting in a hangar by the side of an airstrip between a freeway and the sea in Hsinchu City, Taiwan. Most were Chinese, employees of Butakhan's organisation. They were highly trained in guerrilla warfare as well as close-combat martial arts, edged weapons, guns, and explosives. They lived to fight and took enormous pleasure in their well-paid jobs but the sitting around irritated them. As they so often complained to each other, they were trained to kill, not to sit around on their backsides.

Also present were the three most senior members of the group. One was a heavily bearded Japanese man who was sitting on a crate flicking a knife with exotic blades at each end, backwards and forwards and around his hand.

And then there was the African-American, who, like the Japanese man, was a gun for hire. He had a pure-white handlebar moustache and white dreadlocks bound tight to his head. He was a large bear of a man and from the ammunition belts criss-crossing him it was evident his weapon of choice was big, loud, and aggressive.

The last man, Jean Picardie, was the most senior. He knew the most and said the least. The alopecia-bald French-Algerian was antsy and frustrated that he may miss out on the action as a result of being stationed in Taiwan. He had last seen Luca Voss when photographing him from the mountainside in Ticino. Marooned in the aircraft hangar in Taiwan, he had developed the habit of checking his phone almost every other minute, a scowl meeting every confirmation that no call or text had been missed.

The American watched him do it for the umpteenth time that hour and had to bite. 'I don't know who she is, but I'm telling you, she ain't worth it.'

Those that understood English smiled at his wisecrack while some chuckled belatedly after having it translated by colleagues. Jean looked up from his phone with a neutral expression that told everybody he did not care for their small talk.

Finally his phone rang. He put it to his ear before the first ring had even finished.

'Yes?'

The robotic voice was matter of fact. 'Shanghai Tower, now.'

The call dropped off and the Frenchman looked up at everybody. He didn't need to get their attention, he already had it.

'Let's go.'

9
Ticino, Switzerland

Once it had been a dungeon, when the Families had ruled as the Thirteen, before the schism from which they never recovered. Back then the chateau had been more than a global meeting point, it had been a base from where soldiers would ride out to impose the will of their masters. Back then the world was different, power more brutal and tangible; the borders of countries shifted with the deaths of kings, alliances moved wealth and strength from region to region, overnight. The world had not settled.

In those times, the dungeon had been used to imprison those who opposed or rose up against the power, those who threatened the bonds the Families had worked so hard to forge. The dungeon had once had a darker purpose as well: it held, like so many of the castles of Europe and beyond, the instruments of torture and death. During times of brutality, the rulers had themselves been brutal.

But the dungeon had long been stripped of its barbarism. It was a cavernous space, inexplicable when dormant yet startling when in use. Since World War II, it had been known as the control room.

In the centre of the room was a state-of-the-art armchair, its wide arms fitted with computer touch-pads from which the user could control everything surrounding them. It was a meeting room where rarely more than one person was present in person.

Herr Hesse was sitting in the control seat and surrounding him were the seven people to whom he answered, each sitting above a podium in simple seats. Though they appeared to be present, each was in fact a hologram, a near-perfect projection, exactly to scale, realised in light. Within each pillar of light was the patriarch or matriarch of their respective family. There were four men and three women, no one younger than sixty, and more than one in their eighties. The location of their personal control rooms was kept secret even from each other, such were the security concerns of the two Americans, two Asians, and three Europeans.

Herr Hesse was comfortable in these encounters. As he had informed Luca, his family had served the Seven in one capacity or another since medieval times. They were his masters and he was their trusted General Counsel, their 'brain', as he often told himself. What he was not comfortable with, however, was the rare presence in the control room of another person: Sir Stephen Devereux. Hesse understood that he did not have a free hand to govern the Families' affairs, of course. Still, it was the fact that Devereux, a cardinal, was his counterweight in these matters that antagonised him, even if he was one of the Vatican's most senior clerics and the Grand Master of the Order of St Ambrose, the grandest of all the old orders of the knights.

'Herr Voss disobeyed a direct order.'

Stephen Devereux, resplendent in his vivid red cassock, stood before Herr Hesse's seat. 'Herr Hesse, is it possible that the wrong order was given?'

The General Counsel smarted at this slight. '*If* I was in error, his course of action was not to resort to disobedience, but to return and discuss it. He assured me he was flying directly here, only to divert his plane to Shanghai. He is not fit to be the next Broker.'

'I think it is premature to judge Herr Voss on this one assignment—'

'Brokers follow orders.'

'It's called spirit, Herr Hesse.'

'It is called ill-discipline, Sir Stephen. It is called being unfit for the role. Did you not hear about his skijoring stunt at Davos? Perhaps, as his godfather, you are not detached enough on this subject.'

'If you are suggesting—'

'Gentlemen...'

Hesse and Devereux immediately ceased their dispute and looked attentively at the speaker, both simmering from their mutual contempt.

The speaker was a Nordic woman, her hologram seeming to shine brighter with her intervention. She was strikingly handsome, apparently in her fifties, but in fact twenty years older. Her white hair was pulled tight behind her head and her sober black dress gave her the overall appearance of a widow in mourning. She was secretly pleased at the spat between the two men believing that it kept complacency at bay.

'Forgetting Herr Voss's suitability to be the Broker, what is your reading of the situation, Herr Hesse?'

The German straightened his back against his chair. 'We believe a Mongolian known only to us as Butakhan is behind the death of both Franz Wetzell and Raoul Escobedo for reasons as yet unknown.'

'Were we acting against him?'

'Certainly not intentionally, he was unknown to us. He appears to head a shadowy organisation that has singled out the Seven Families.'

'In what way?'

'He met with representatives of the Council of Foreign Relations in Davos and offered assistance in executing regime change in North Korea in exchange for cutting all ties with ourselves.'

The Nordic woman's eyebrows rose, concerned that such a conversation was even possible. 'Did they accept?'

'We are told that they did not. But they are worried that North Korea will be toppled and that they will have little or no influence in the region.'

An aged Japanese man, more donnish than patriarch in his owl glasses and tweed jacket, spoke from his hologram. 'Do not underestimate the importance of this play. There will be a race for the rare earth minerals of that region. This could define the next century and these territories could overtake the Middle East as the world's primary flashpoint. The Americans will be tempted by his offer.'

'I do not believe America will waiver.' It was a septuagenarian from Texas who spoke now.

'On the contrary, I believe history has shown that the American empire does not trade in loyalty, but in money.' The Japanese man was inscrutable as he spoke. 'The Families' own relationship with it was built on money, therefore it could be broken by the same.'

'Well, I disagree—'

The Japanese man smiled indulgently. 'What was it Henry Kissinger said? "America has no permanent friends or enemies, only interests."'

The Texan eyed him unhappily.

'Gentlemen, before we disagree, can we agree on what it is we agree on?' It was the Nordic matriarch, her white hair shimmering in the hologram's lights. 'Two of our Brokers have been killed; an attempt was made on Luca Voss's life. In some shape or form, we are all under attack. Herr Hesse, how quickly could we get the next Broker online?'

'I'm sorry to say that nobody is field-ready.'

'What about Luca Voss?'

'As I have said, I do not believe he is right for the role.'

'Then what is our strategy moving forward?'

The General Counsel went to speak, but Devereux was quicker off the mark, keen to guide the discussion. 'Luca Voss is hoping a comprehensive search of Franz Wetzell's apartment in Shanghai might bring to light vital information. I think we should await his findings and reconvene first thing in the morning.'

'Can we trust Luca Voss's motives?' asked the Texan.

'What do you mean?'

'Well, how do we know he's not working to his own agenda? He has disregarded orders, and I understand he took a woman with him from outside the Families.'

'I should take some of the blame for that, Mr Furst.' The General Counsel was contrition itself. 'I allowed him to take her on what should have been the low-key trip to Russia. He is not yet a Broker and not bound by those rules, but in hindsight I made an error of judgement.'

The Nordic woman looked at each of the heads of the Families in turn. 'Right for the role or not, Luca Voss is in the field. I agree with Sir Stephen. We should allow him his investigation. But if Luca Voss is terminated I believe we should consider a period of limbo.'

'Limbo?' The Texan was almost out of his chair. 'We agreed never to return to that unless in the most extreme circumstances.'

'What could be more extreme than the assassination of two of our agents? It is the prelude to the play. We must be their ultimate targets and limbo has served us well in the past. It will not be the first time we have all withdrawn from global affairs. I suggest we give consideration to fifty years.'

The General Counsel rose at the suggestion. 'Fifty years? That's almost a lifetime.'

'Since when did the Families measure history in lifetimes, Herr Hesse?'

A cold silence descended over everyone present, eventually broken by Devereux. 'We are agreed. We wait to see what is discovered in Shanghai. Luca Voss, although untried and untested, is our last hope.'

10
Shanghai Pudong International Airport, China

Outside the airport, Luca and JJ ducked into a waiting cab.

'What, no limousine?' JJ asked, giving Luca a wry smile.

'The occasional understatement never hurt anybody.'

JJ squinted with concern. 'Why, are you expecting someone to be waiting for us?'

'Hope for the best, plan for the worst. Anyway, you're meant to be the facilitator. If you want a limo, go book one next time, isn't that what you were doing on the phone back there?' He gave her a half-admonishing, half-ironic stare, to which she nodded in acknowledgement.

A noisy off-road motorbike pulled up beside JJ's window, its rider immediately tapping her window. She turned to Luca and put her hand out.

'Money.'

'What for?'

Her eyes widened at his recalcitrance. 'Money…'

Luca rolled his eyes as he pulled out a money clip. 'How much?'

'Two thousand dollars should cover it.'

Luca warily peeled off twenty notes. JJ lowered her window and handed over the money. The motorcyclist stuffed it inside her jacket, then handed JJ a heavy paper bag and drove off.

Luca and JJ sat in silence, JJ apparently not intending to explain herself.

'OK, you win. What's in the bag?'

JJ pulled out its contents: two automatic pistols.

'What the hell are those?'

'You told me to facilitate, so I facilitated.'

At the rear of the taxi rank, another motorcyclist was waiting on his Ducati. Inside his mirrored visor, he spoke into a mic.

'They are in a taxi outside the airport.'

Butakhan's voice came through crystal clear on the rider's earpiece. 'Watch them for now. Do nothing until the others arrive.'

'Understood.'

Five cars ahead of Luca and JJ's taxi, a Volkswagen Santana pulled out and motored to the exit. The Ducati rider turned the ignition and his bike roared to life. He pulled into the slow-moving traffic behind them.

★   ★   ★

Standing 632 metres high, the Shanghai Tower would dominate even the tallest skyscrapers in New York. As Luca stood at its base, its summit out of sight, he remembered his last trip to the city. The tower had still been incomplete but Franz had just overseen the purchase of an apartment at the top, one floor shy of the penthouses. Franz, who had trained as an architect in case he failed to be chosen as the Broker, had become mildly obsessed with the construction of what was then the world's second tallest tower. They had enjoyed a beer in a sky bar across the river in the Bund, Shanghai's former financial district. Even then, there was no mistaking the scale of the city's ambition.

'You see how it's made out of nine sections, Luca? Each one will have its own atrium with shops, cafes, gardens,' Franz had said.

'Gardens?'

Franz had grinned at Luca and stroked his blonde beard, a tic the Swiss man had noticed the German had since the first time they had met over a decade earlier.

'Of course, the Chinese dragon has awoken. *Now* we will learn the types of structures humankind is capable of erecting. I told you about the elevators?'

Luca had smiled to see Franz so energised. 'No, but I have a feeling—'

'OK, OK, now remember the structure. The sub-levels are car parks for up to 1,800 cars. That's *1,800*. Then you have the shops and businesses from the ground floor up. Above that residential, then, get this, the *tallest* hotel in the *world*. Floors 84-110 are all *one* hotel. Above all that business and residential space, the twenty-six floor hotel. And think of the views—*look* at the views.'

From their high point in the Bund they could see across the water: Lujiazui resplendently lit, worthy of the futuristic city it was fast becoming; neon lights casting electric hues of red, purple, and yellow across the night-time water. This was more than just a collection of buildings; it was a statement of intent.

'Do you ever think you're in the wrong job, Franz?'

Luca's friend had looked at him thoughtfully before pulling a rueful face. 'What can I say, Luca? When I was at school, I wished to be at college, when I was at college I wished to work. Before I was the Broker all I dreamed about was being the Broker and now I am the Broker all I dream about is being an architect.'

'Why not quit and become one?'

Luca remembered vividly the look the tall German had tried to cover up by draining the remains of his beer: it was pain. Luca knew that the pain was caused by the job to which he had finally risen. This trip to China fitted into Franz's schedule only because of a mandatory recuperation from an unspecified assignment. However, given that a leading terrorist and his entourage had been killed the week before in a shootout with an unidentified assailant in a bank in Sana'a, Yemen, Luca felt he could hazard a guess as to what the assignment was. Franz's face revealed to Luca the virtually physical effort required to push down whatever it was he actually wanted to say. Instead, a hardy smile fixed to his face.

'Why don't we talk about that after Christmas? There's a little job to do in North Korea first, but don't worry, we're not assassinating any dictators. Who knows, maybe I'll hang up my gun then?'

Luca's whole life had been a long journey to possibly becoming the Broker one day, and he could not deny the slight thrill he felt at the prospect of the job looming a step closer. This, however, was matched by the growing awareness that his friend had paid a heavy price for taking on the role, and the growing knowledge that he should expect the same. 'Will you really retire after North Korea?'

Franz had met the question with a shrug, before staring out across the water. 'I don't know if I told you, but that building will have the world's highest travelling elevator: almost 580 metres, in *one ride*.'

So he had gone on, rambling in his own inimitable way. That had been their last meeting together, the Broker and the Broker-in-waiting.

'I wonder what he would have built?'

Two cars in the street behind Luca had an angry exchange of horns.

'What?'

Luca looked round to see JJ standing beside him, a perplexed expression on her face.

'You wonder who would have built what?'

Luca saw that their taxi had driven away without him realising. They were standing outside the entrance area to the Shanghai Tower, an enormous bus-shaped edifice that seemed somewhat aesthetically at odds with the cylindrical skyscraper above.

'You OK?'

Her friend nodded, refocusing on the task in hand.

JJ chose not to pursue it—Luca was often alone in his thoughts.

'Which floor did he live on?'

'119.'

'This thing has 119 floors?'

'More,' Luca said, looking from the building up above to JJ beside him. 'Have you ever used a gun before?'

The seriousness with which he had asked the question made her pause before answering. 'Well, I've pointed one at someone before; a poker game gone wrong. But, no, I've never actually used one.'

Luca looked her in the eye in a manner that told her that the time for levity was over. 'A word of advice about using a gun up there, JJ?'

'Sure.'

'Don't.'

JJ looked back at the elevator that had deposited them on floor 119.

'How fast is that thing?' she asked.

Luca looked both ways along the corridor.

'Eighteen metres per second.'

JJ looked at him askance. 'You making that up?'

Luca pulled a face to himself. 'Trust me, I know.'

He set out along the corridor.

They arrived outside a door with the number '8' in the centre. Beside it was a sensor pad, cutting-edge technology, like everything else in the building. JJ nodded at it and spoke in a whisper.

'There's no lock.'

'No, it's fingerprint recognition.' As he said this, Luca remembered how Franz had been found without any digits on his hands.

'What's the plan? Can we bypass the security, or shall we bust it down?'

Luca's brow creased as he looked at her before knocking on the door. JJ had to fight the urge to slap her forehead, annoyed at both of them.

After a short minute, the door was opened cautiously by a young woman. She appeared to be Japanese.

'Yes?'

Luca spoke kindly but firmly. 'I'm a friend of Franz's.'

'He's not here right now. You'll have to come back.'

Luca heard the fearful lie in her voice. 'We both know he's not coming back.'

The apartment was expansive, with staggering views over the river towards the Bund and the west of Shanghai. Somehow, Franz's girlfriend seemed to fit in with the city if not with Franz. Her name was Kitty and she was Japanese with baby doll looks to match her blue hair. In her torn jeans and slashed white t-shirt, she could have been in a pop band or had a career as a TV presenter. Despite her unusual appearance, JJ was not surprised that Franz, or anyone for that matter, had fallen for her. She had fallen for her, admittedly on a primal level, but even in her current nervy state the young woman exuded sexuality. JJ couldn't guess at the emotional level of Franz's relationship with her, but she could guess at their sex life.

'I heard about it on the news a week ago but I don't know what happened to him.'

Kitty was following Luca as he methodically opened every cupboard in the living room in which they now stood. JJ noted that like all the apartments and villas she had visited with Luca this one was sparsely furnished. This time the theme was slightly modernist: Eames chairs, Le Corbusier recliners. The difference, here, were the signs of another life: models. Scale models of various skyscrapers made meticulously out of card. Some she recognised: the Burj Khalifa in Dubai, Makkah Royal Clock Tower Hotel in Mecca, and Taipei 101 in Taiwan. Others she wasn't so sure about, maybe they were just fantasies, but the detail was fascinating; they were perfectly realised models, complete with balconies and antennas, and more.

What Luca was looking for, searching the myriad concealed cupboards, was anybody's guess. In his silence, JJ decided to speak for them.

'We don't know what happened to Franz. We're here to find out.'

'What is it you're looking for? I might know where it is.'

Luca looked at her with what JJ perceived as a hard expression. 'What were the security arrangements here?'

The Japanese woman pointed at the enormous television on one of the walls. 'CCTV, everywhere.'

'Show me.'

Nervously she picked up a remote lying on the side of a leather and wood armchair and turned the television to another channel. A large screen appeared, divided into eight sections, each showing different views around the building: street scenes outside the main entrance, the lobby, underground car park, the atriums, and the corridor from the elevator to the apartment door. Luca nodded, it made sense, Franz would never have lived in a building with less.

Kitty and JJ trailed Luca into the white kitchen, where he proceeded to go through each cupboard and drawer in the same exhaustive fashion, running his fingers around the insides, the back, the top, and even underneath. Kitty looked on nervously, unsure how to handle these strangers, unsure what they meant to her. She cast a poorly disguised look of anxiety at JJ, who gave her arm a reassuring rub.

'Don't worry. We're here to help.'

'Sorry, it's just that I've been so scared since I saw the news about Franz. I haven't known what to do. Are you looking for something in particular, I might have seen it?'

When it was clear that Luca was not interested in answering her, JJ decided to be the good cop. 'How long had you known Franz?'

'Not long. I only moved in six weeks ago, and he left the next day.' She watched Luca inspecting the inside of the microwave. 'Can I get you guys a drink?'

JJ replied with a shrug. 'Thanks, I'll have a glass of wine.'

Luca opened a slim cupboard next to the oven and pulled out a small fire extinguisher. Without hesitating, he proceeded to unscrew the bottom from the rest of the device. It resisted at first, but then started to turn, the seal seamlessly disguised. After a few twists, the base was in his hand and he put the main section on the work surface.

'Where did Franz keep his car?'

'I'm not sure, there are five floors of car parking and I don't know which one he parked it on.'

Luca nodded thoughtfully. 'Don't worry I think I'll know it when I see it.'

He tipped the base over. A set of car keys dropped into his hand.

★　　★　　★

The Gulfstream G650 jet deposited Butakhan's twelve men onto the private airstrip, delivering them in comfort and at speed. The drive across town to the Shanghai Tower

119

would have been unacceptably slow, so to overcome this two Sikorsky S-76 helicopters were waiting for them on the runway tarmac.

As six of the Chinese militia jogged to one of the helicopters, both aircraft began to accelerate their rotor blades in preparation for take-off. The remaining three Chinese soldiers, the Japanese, African-American, and French-Algerian mercenaries ran to the other.

Barely had the last man boarded when the helicopters began their ascent.

Sitting in one of the jump seats beside the wide open door, Jean Picardie checked his phone for messages. There was one waiting.

'He's gone to the underground car park, U4, bay 121.'

★   ★   ★

As the elevator descended to the basement car park, Luca pulled out the gun JJ had obtained: a Type 54 pistol. It was a Chinese knock-off of a Russian knock-off with, if memory served, an effective range of around fifty metres. The fact that she even knew people in the city who were able to rustle up weapons at such short notice was itself an insight into her character, he realised now. After this, if he could possibly smooth it over with Herr Hesse, he hoped to plug JJ into the Families' own arms suppliers. Knocked-off black-market weapons would be no good on their travels. It was military standard or nothing. As far as Luca was concerned, the gun in his hand was only fit to scare people off. Even if it worked, the results would be unpredictable at best.

Luca had left JJ babysitting Kitty in Franz's apartment. He had yet to decide if she was friend, foe, or freeloader. As the elevator arrived on floor U1, Luca hoped JJ would heed his advice not to let anyone in and to call him if anything happened. The CCTV channel would give her a heads up if trouble was brewing, but if people were coming for them, they were likely to be fast-paced and well trained. He knew he had to check Franz's car and get back upstairs as soon as possible.

He took a single step out into the car park, keeping one hand on one of the elevator doors to stop it from ascending. Wandering up and down every parking bay was not in his game plan for now, especially given that the vehicle was doubly difficult to make out since every other car parked up here was either a high-end luxury executive car or supercar. Squeezing the car's key-fob, he was met with silence. The odds were against success so he stepped back into elevator and hit U2.

It wasn't until Luca arrived on level U4 that he came up trumps. A squeeze of the key-fob earned a deep electronic chirrup. Luca turned his head in the direction of the sound, catching a small wink of lights as he did so. Alive to the space and shadows about him, he made his way to the far corner, away from the ramps leading up and down to the other basement levels.

The Swiss man walked past rows of cars until he got to the one he was looking for. He shook his head when he saw it, a Bugatti Veyron Super Sport, in yellow and red. *Insane*, he thought when he saw it. Still, he understood the mega-rich circles the German had infiltrated. As his late friend had said to him over their last beer together, 'Sometimes, Luca, you have to stand out to blend in.'

Luca opened the driver's door and slid behind the wheel. Instinctively he assessed the best escape route if he needed to leave, his training kicking in. He noted the four rows of bumper-to-bumper parked cars, three aisles between them, a ringway around all of them, the arrows painted on the floor that pointed him the long way, left, when the exit ramp was to his right. He never felt over-zealous or paranoid for taking a moment to plan for the worst. Franz's fate proved just how important this was.

Luca attended to the task and looked about him, studying the interior, remembering how Franz had joked that they used real unicorn hides for the seats. He smiled at the memory. Luca had sat in the passenger seat when Franz had taken him for a spin, but he'd never driven the car himself—nor did he plan to. Even on the city's freeways, surrounded by traffic, the presence of the car's titanic engine could be felt. Franz, as ever, had rattled off the stats. The fact that it had ten radiators had impressed Luca the most.

Typically, Luca would have looked for a concealed compartment at this point, but this being a Veyron he knew there would not be any space for such luxuries. He opened the glove compartment. Empty. He fruitlessly explored the limited storage compartments before scouring the dashboard. Nothing. He peered inside the air vents, felt the back of the door handles, touching anything that might have a reverse side. His mood sank at the prospect of feeling under wheel arches, as at that point it would be needles and haystacks. But, no, it would be somewhere clever, somewhere practical. *Right under my nose*, he mused. Then he smiled. *Or my foot.*

He reached down and felt the underside of the accelerator pedal, his fingertips touching a small, flat square. Luca unpeeled if from the pedal. Sitting back upright, he looked at the tiny case he had found and popped it open with a thumbnail to reveal a micro SD memory card.

Then, from the far side of the car park, the elevator opened. Luca, in his poorly lit corner of the car park stopped stock-still and watched as a young Chinese man in a black suit walked out to a nearby Jaguar XK. His relaxed demeanour was almost enough reassurance for Luca, but to be on the safe side he waited as the man switched on the engine and drove the car away and up the exit ramp. Silence returned and Luca pulled out his smartphone, accessed it with a fingerprint scanner, and then swapped its memory card for the one on the end of his finger. His phone's screen, though not the largest, was pin-sharp and as he accessed the contents of the memory card, he quickly became fascinated.

Luca discovered a cache of photographs, first of a decrepit-looking colonial building, a hotel perhaps or an embassy, whose stone façade was weathered and worn. From the architecture Luca guessed the building was in Asia somewhere and this was confirmed by some wide-angle shots where a number of south-east Asians, Cambodians, Vietnamese, or Burmese possibly, were seen passing by on bicycles, in ramshackle cars and on motorbikes. Exactly where the picture was taken was something he could easily check. Another photograph caught his eye for the street name it showed: Yadanar Bon Street. Luca had no idea as to its significance, but if it was important enough to Franz that he saved and hid it under a foot-pedal in the car, that was good enough for him. The second group of photos were more interesting still.

These were of a mega-yacht, the class above the previously unrivalled super-yachts, a craft worthy of a Russian oligarch. It had a discreet aquatic design which hid most of its external details from the outside world. Still, it was clear there were three stories to it and a helipad jutting out of the rear. More importantly, its name could be seen: *Charon*. The reference to the ferryman of the underworld wasn't lost on Luca. Again, it was not obvious where the pictures had been taken, but this dockside had a militaristic look. Alongside the boat were various vehicles, jeeps, and transport trucks, and the pictures had obviously been taken in a hurry because they failed to frame the detail needed to pinpoint locations easily.

Luca paused; there, at the rear of one of the trucks, was a yellow triangle, a 'Hazardous Load' sign. Luca mentally apologised to Franz for doubting he had caught the most important information. He placed his fingers either side of the triangle and began to expand the image. It was then that he heard the screech of tyres. They were coming for him.

In an instant, Luca's mind sprinted through the avenues still open to him. With the rows of cars between him and the elevator, he would never be able to reach it in less than six seconds. Even if he did, he would still have to wait for the elevator to arrive. If he got out of the Bugatti and hid between the cars he would still be too exposed. This left Luca with only one option.

The sound of screeching car tyres changed to a roar as the vehicles thumped down the ramp to where the Bugatti was parked. Luca strapped on the seatbelt and fired up the engine. Normally the sound of the engine stopped traffic and wildlife, but now the Jurassic bellowing was matched by the arrival of four black GL-Class Mercedes SUVs. Luca didn't doubt they were prepared, noting that two had stopped at the bottom of the down ramp and two at the up ramp. The message was clear: he wasn't going to be driving out of there.

He looked down the passage ahead of him and saw that two SUVs had stopped approximately eighty metres away. Their heavily tinted windows gave no clues as to the identities of their occupants. To his left, the other vehicles had also stopped, their occupants also a mystery. Each aisle had room for two cars to pass each other, but if he allowed the SUVs to block him in, Luca knew there was only one outcome. He needed to get out of the corner he was in as quickly as possible. He put his pistol on the passenger seat to his right, cursing that he hadn't asked Herr Hesse for something better. Then, remembering that he was out in the cold the moment he had disobeyed Hesse's orders and come to Shanghai, Luca realised he only had himself to blame for what was about to happen.

At that moment, in a coordinated move, each of the four passenger doors of both SUVs opened, blocking the ramps. Four Chinese males then climbed out of each SUV; they were clearly military, Luca could tell from their black combat outfits. They were also kitted out with hardware, knives, grenades and sub-machine guns. Initially they stayed close to the doors of their vehicles, the harder to target. Then they hoisted their gun-straps over their shoulders and began to march in his direction, all eight barrels of their sub-machine guns pointing at him. Herr Hesse's words came back to him like a taunt: *You haven't learned how to assassinate someone.* This was followed by the memory of Russia, how Luca had held the officer at gunpoint but chosen not to kill him. Now it was a question of kill or be killed.

Four gunmen were in his path, four were coming from his left. Shooting his way to the exit was not an option. They were sixty metres away. Driving his way to an exit was not an option. They were fifty metres away. Sitting and doing nothing was the worst option of all. They were forty metres away. Then it occurred to him there was still something he could do in a car that hit sixty in 2.2 seconds. The gunmen were thirty metres away. They stopped and raised their guns at him. He could hit them.

The car leapt at the four assailants, smacking the men in front of it before they even knew what had hit them, crashing through them like a set of bowling pins. They flew into the air and over the car.

Even as the yellow and red Bugatti had catapulted forward, it was being chased by bullets from the other four Chinese militia; they had been slow off the mark, but still quick enough to destroy the nearside rear headlight. The four men stopped firing to avoid their four comrades as they flew through the air and landed on nearby cars, setting off alarms as each of them did so. Luca heard the impact of the men as they landed, but he didn't register the emotional impact of most likely having killed four men.

Now was about his escape, now was about getting back to JJ before these men made their way up to her—if others hadn't already.

The Bugatti's brakes had stopped it from slamming into the jeep parked on the up ramp, it slid left, around the outside of the cars, left again, until it was racing towards the second jeep parked on the down ramp. But now both doors were opening, the nearest revealing a large, black mercenary who had the wisdom to leap as far away behind the car as he could. Unfortunately the Chinese passenger didn't have the same foresight; the last thing he saw was the Bugatti sliding left, then using its rear to slam into the jeep to pin him between it and the wall. The man was trapped; his shattered legs, causing him to scream as he clawed uselessly at the bonnet across which he was lying.

Luca was away before the African-American could bring his weapon of choice—an M16 assault rifle—to bear on the disappearing car. The gunman fired after it angrily all the same, catching the rear as Luca fishtailed left into an aisle, turning on a dime right into a one car gap. He bolted into the slot, barging into a gold Lamborghini Aventador as he did so, scraping his car alongside it as he emerged from between two more rows of cars. Beyond these, the Chinese soldiers still standing were weaving between cars and firing furiously at him, puncturing the windows and bodywork of the high-end cars around them, setting off alarms with every bullet.

Luca knew time and luck would run out quickly like this. He reached for his gun but saw it was no longer there on the passenger seat. Looking down, he saw it wedged between the seat and the passenger door.

'Christ. No.'

With mixed feelings, Jean Picardie had watched the beginning of the execution of the Swiss national from the cab of the last Mercedes GL to arrive. On the one hand, it was undeniably botched, though easily remedied. On the other hand, the hairless French-Algerian had been agitating to handpick his own team since arriving at Butakhan's organisation, and the sacrifice of a few Chinese mercenaries to make his point for him suited his purpose perfectly. However, enough damage had already been done, and now it was time to put the matter—and Luca Voss—to rest.

Jean turned to Kawabe, the bearded Japanese soldier who was sitting beside him in the jeep. 'Bring out the big guns.'

Luca raced the Bugatti to the end of an aisle, four Chinese soldiers jumping out from between cars to spray his car from behind with bullets. He slammed the brakes on, hit reverse, and tore backwards towards them, all of them ready to leap back between cars if the Bugatti veered into them. Luca leaned over and pulled the door lever on the passenger side; pushing open the door, he reached for the pistol, but it fell out of the car and cartwheeled across the car park floor. The Chinese soldiers in his path had not anticipated the car door opening wide and the impact scooped them into heap with such violence that their skulls cracked into each other as the door's outer edge hit a concrete pillar, tearing it and the men clean off the car.

Now the Chinese men on the opposite side of the aisle were tracking Luca, taking advantage of a clear view of him as he passed by to spray his car with bullets, the driver's window splintering before shattering over him. He slammed on the brakes, skidding the car round 180 degrees. The side and rear of the car were drilled with bullets, meaning it would come to a standstill any moment. He knew he had to get the hell out and fast.

Luca tore the car round the outer ring of the car park as the African-American mercenary, crouched between two red Ferraris, pummelled the space where the windscreen had been with gunfire. Luca, dropping down out of view, drove blind, knowing he had to keep moving. Spinning the car round on the spot, acutely aware they were closing in on him, Luca accelerated towards the elevators and leaned through the shattered window on the driver's side to hit the 'call' button. Then he stamped on the accelerator once more and the car tore off to the right. The Swiss man's peripheral vision told him that the African-American mercenary and the two Chinese were running between cars to cut him off. But then, just as he turned right, he saw something unbelievable: it was game over.

Jean Picardie had never been worried about terminating Voss but he had been concerned about getting out of the city afterwards. Butakhan had given strict instructions that *nobody* was to be caught. If the risk was there, they were to be killed if necessary. However, since the French-Algerian did not intend to fall foul of that edict, he had decided to bring enough firepower to blast his way out of Shanghai if necessary: an M2 tripod-mounted machine gun. If it was good enough to open up a street blockaded by the Shanghai Municipal Police, it was certainly good enough to bring a halt to Luca Voss's vehicle. Fifty-calibre bullets that could stop a charging rhino in its tracks wouldn't just stop a Bugatti Veyron, they would shred it to pieces.

Luca saw this weapon just as he slid round the corner in the car; he saw the sandbags across the base of the tripod to keep the M2 in place against recoil. He knew in an instant from his time in the Swiss Army that sandbags meant a serious weapon. He knew it was a 50-calibre before the first volley was launched and did not dare to charge towards it, continuing his slide round into the next aisle; but not before Picardie and Kawabe started to bombard him with gunfire. The bullets punctured not only his rear tyre, but the wheel itself, pounding it to a mess. As sparks flew up off the nearside rear of the car, Luca knew he was running out of road. The soldiers manning the cannon tracked him behind a line of cars, punching holes through Mercedes, Jaguars, Audis, Ferraris, Aston Martins, Bentleys and others, as they continued their assault on him.

Through the thunderstorm of glass, metal, and carbon fibre, the wounded Veyron continued round in a long slide that came to an abrupt uncontrolled sideways slam into the jeep blocking the down ramp. *Get to the elevator, just get to the elevator*, Luca screamed in his mind. Yet before he knew what had happened, the American mercenary jumped into the passenger seat beside him. Luca hit the accelerator. The American raised the butt of his M16 rifle and, as the crippled car catapulted down the roadway, slammed it against the side of Luca's head just as the car crashed headlong into a concrete pillar.

While the American launched from his seat and shot through the windscreen, Luca's seatbelt held him, slamming him instead into an airbag. At the far end of the aisle, the M2 machine gun began to spew another torrent of bullets at the car. Knowing he did not have a moment to spare, Luca rolled out and away from the Bugatti on the gunman's far side, while pieces of the American's lifeless body spat against the wall as machine gun rounds hit it.

As the car disintegrated into debris, shards, and dust all about him, Luca ran at a crouch to the elevator just as the doors opened.

Behind him the gunfire had stopped.

He jumped inside the elevator, chose the highest floor available, and stood out of sight.

Picardie and Kawabe did not wait for the dust to settle around the Bugatti, but sprinted towards it with their sub-machine guns ahead of them. Approaching it, they saw no one was inside the wreck. Running round the back, realising quickly that Luca had escaped, they both looked at the series of near-by elevator doors.

Picardie jammed the closing elevator doors open with a foot and then jumped back out of view as the doors slid apart again. To avoid setting himself up as an easy target he rolled into view of the elevator car—his back on the floor with his gun facing inside, machine-gunning bullets into the elevator's far corner.

Nobody was there.

Luca had been standing on top of the elevator when he heard the footsteps running towards him. Above him, the elevator shaft soared so high that it disappeared out of his sight. Beside him were two other elevators. He looked down and saw that the ceiling panel he'd just climbed through had not dropped cleanly back into place and then he heard the sound of footsteps approaching. Just as he was considering whether to lean down and try to make it less obvious, bullets started tearing through the side of the elevator below him. Luca hopped to the roof of the adjacent elevator as bullets began to eviscerate the roof panel that had concerned him a moment ago. As he sought to regain his balance on the roof of this elevator as silently as possible, he heard muffled voices talking excitedly in the car park below. He willed the elevator he was standing on to start ascending, realising the poison chalice this would prove—travelling at eighteen metres per second would not make for the safest ride up into China's tallest skyscraper.

As Luca stood there, another car descended with frightening speed, braking with surprising subtlety as it stopped beside him. He was weighing up whether to step atop this elevator when the frenetic conversation he could hear nearby stopped abruptly. Now he feared they were listening to him, and if he stepped across the noise would be like an elephant tap-dancing on a timpani drum. He stood absolutely still. Then, to his relief, both the elevator car on which he was standing and the one that had just arrived began to ascend.

Gripping the cable that pulled the car up at almost seventy kilometres per hour, Luca braced his body against the harsh rush of air buffeting him as if on some unholy fairground ride. Behind and before him other elevators whipped down, the air cracking as they passed. Then, in the sheer violence of the ride, he questioned his own eyes as he watched the roof panel of the neighbouring car open and a bearded Japanese man pull himself up athletically onto the roof. He sat there, grinning malevolently.

Though he knew it was lunacy, Luca saw no option other than to jump across to the next car if the man pulled out a gun. Instead, the man approached him and then—seemingly from nowhere—an ornate, curved knife appeared in his hand. With practised speed, he squeezed the handle of it causing four further blades to separate out, so that he was holding a star-shaped weapon at the centre. Luca knew one thing: if the Japanese man had chosen a knife over a gun he was probably very good at using it.

Kawabe stepped to the edge of his elevator, describing slow swirls in the air with his blades, a ritualistic act before the slaughter.

The Japanese man swiped the air between them, forcing Luca to step back behind the steel wires of the elevator. His opponent's game was clear: he wanted to push Luca back to the edge and either slice him, or force him off the edge into the abyss. Neither seemed advantageous to Luca, who allowed another swipe to pass before him, and another, but on the last, stepped in and blocked the armed hand. He went to deliver a blow to Kawabe only to see him immediately hop backwards. The Japanese man found his foot on the seal of the elevator's missing ceiling panel and needed a moment to move to firmer ground.

Luca grabbed the cables of his own car and swung round in the air, delivering a kick to Kawabe's chest and knocking him backwards off the elevator. The Japanese man snagged his star-shaped blades on the cables of his own car, leaning backwards over the edge, over the abyss, and grinned at Luca, gloating that his luck—and knife—had held. But seeing Luca swiftly looking up and away, Kawabe followed, his gaze shifting to see an elevator plummeting down the shaft he was overhanging.

The base of the elevator smashed into Kawabe's face and dragged his body out of sight, before it braked, having sensed a mechanical aberration. A cloud of blood hung mid-air in the shaft, just for a moment, before following the assassin down.

When the apartment door was buzzed open, Luca entered and closed it swiftly behind him. He paused to listen for signs of activity. If nothing else, his unorthodox ride back up the skyscraper had given him a head start on the remaining mercenaries in the car park, though he knew there might still be others elsewhere in the building. Luca's mind ran over recent events; by his estimation, at least two Chinese mercenaries and one of the M2 machine-gun operators were still at large; the latter dark skinned and bald, but that's all he'd managed to see in the confusion. It was then he realised the mercenaries would have no trouble finding the apartment now that they knew exactly which parking bay the car had been in.

Ahead of him, the apartment's wide lobby was dominated by a limestone human-sized angel with two massive wings that spread up towards the ceiling; at this height, Luca wondered if the angel was meant to symbolise touching Heaven. It was beautiful, in a gothic, kitsch kind of a way, though Luca was more interested in whether or not he'd be able to hide behind it in a shootout than its aesthetic qualities.

'JJ?'

His heart sank. Even if she was in trouble, he had nothing with which to arm himself against any intruders, and if the intruders were racing up behind him, he needed to move as quickly as possible. He decided to make his way to the kitchen, edging silently round the statue, ready to react to the slightest movement, slightest sound, slightest... giggling...

He stepped up to an oak door and listened again. The sound was undeniable—giggling of not one, but two women. Now his heart sank for another reason.

The door swung open just as JJ and Kitty—naked—rolled off the end of the bed together, tangled in a sheet that had contrived to wrap itself around them. More giggling followed, interrupted only when JJ looked up to see Luca standing in the open doorway. The terms of their relationship being what they were, she felt no self-consciousness or shame and her giggling increased at having been caught in the fumbled act.

'Ooh, Luca, just the man—we could do with another set of hands,' JJ said.

Under the sheet, JJ squeezed Kitty's breasts, which elicited a shriek of laughter, setting JJ off again.

'The thing is, JJ, we're on a bit of a schedule. Get dressed.'

She went to complain playfully, before the humour was sucker-punched out of her. 'Your hand, it's bleeding.'

If Luca heard the remark, he ignored it, as JJ, now angry with herself, untangled herself from Kitty.

'Weren't you watching the security cameras?' He looked up at the large television on the wall of the room they were in, on which a muted lesbian porn flick from the 1970s was showing. He knew immediately what had happened: Kitty had lured JJ into the bedroom, switched on the TV and with little or no resistance seduced her.

JJ was already pulling down a white dress over her naked body as she spoke remorsefully: 'Luca, I'm so sorry, what do you need me to do?'

The blue-haired Japanese sex kitten was standing up using the sheet as a dressing gown, jumping with playful petulance, her exposed breasts bouncing up and down as she did so. 'No, no, you said we could include him.'

Luca scooped up the remote from beside the king-size bed and aimed it at the television. The CCTV channel came on, pandemonium filling its various rotating windows: police cars pulling up outside the building, police officers crawling over the lobby, dozens of cars ablaze on U4 of the underground car park.

'Oh my God, Luca, I'm so sorry.'

Luca's anger was reserved for Kitty. 'No. I should have known how dangerous it could be. I should have known how dangerous *she* could be.'

Kitty looked shocked, but more than that, she looked scared. 'No, no, I don't know anything.'

Luca looked with disgust at a length of silk rope that was lying coiled on a dressing chair. 'Planning a spot of bondage, were you? Perhaps tying up the pair of us?'

He was stepping towards Kitty as she backed up against a dressing table. 'No, no, I'm innocent.'

'Who said you were guilty?'

She smiled in an attempt to placate him, but her fear and distracted mind turned it into a grimace. 'Here, let me show you my papers—'

She half-turned, pulled open a drawer, and fumbled for what was in it with one hand, only to have Luca's foot slam the drawer against her wrist. She screamed at the violence of the kick, the Swiss man stepping back as she pulled out her useless hand, a small 38-calibre pistol falling helplessly from it to the floor.

Luca scooped up the weapon and levelled a hard stare at her. 'Who paid you?'

'Nobody.'

The gunshot seemed to come out of nowhere, quicker than even Kitty could register.

'My leg, my *beautiful leg*,' she whined, the shock at the sight of the ripped skin somehow appearing to be greater than the pain.

Luca repeated his question. 'Who paid you?'

She looked at him, terror rising in her eyes, yet terrorised not just by him, but something else as well, something she was thinking of. 'I can't—'

'You could assist in the death of Franz. Who paid you?'

'I don't know, really.'

Another bullet, this time her left leg, a flesh wound to match the other. Kitty fell to the floor, wailing in pain. 'I only met a middleman. I would tell you if I could, please, please let me go.'

Luca grabbed her, scooping her up, and began to frog-march her to the door; Kitty barely able to walk, half-moaning, half-howling in pain and fear.

Luca shot JJ an admonishing look. 'Bring the rope.'

'Don't do this,' Kitty said.

JJ was tormented by the effort not to look at Kitty as she wrapped the rope around her where she stood, bound to the stone angel.

'Please, I've got money. I'll tell them you left, anything—' Then her weeping was replaced by thrashing as she tried to escape the bonds, but it was useless, and the weeping returned. '*Please*—'

JJ had offered to tie Kitty up as her penance for not realising the gravity of their situation, not grasping the world into which she had stepped. Once she was sure Kitty was fastened tightly, JJ stopped resisting the urge to be sick and emptied her stomach to one side of the statue.

'*Please*—'

Annoyed and horrified, regretting their position at the centre of the situation, the Chinese woman ran back into the bedroom. Luca was emerging from the en suite bathroom and saw the queasiness in JJ's face before she spoke.

'What will happen to her?' JJ asked.

'Whatever she had planned for us.'

'*PLEASE*—'

Luca was deaf to Kitty's cries as he crossed to the floor-to-ceiling window, squeezed a toothpaste-like tube into a large 'X' across the glass and planted the tube's lid near the centre. The plastic explosives ready, he hit a discreet switch inside the lid and walked swiftly to the bathroom.

'I'd get down behind the bed if I was you.'

JJ looked from the window to Luca confused and alarmed. 'What? Why?'

A rising beeping was coming from the window.

'*Now.*'

She dropped to the floor beside the bed and Luca stepped out of sight into the en suite bathroom as an explosion shattered the window into thousands of pieces which then blew out into the night sky, a strong wind immediately gusting through the room.

JJ rose cautiously and approached the gaping hole, six hundred metres above the city. Across from them, the Jin Mao Tower and the tall, thin wedge of the Shanghai World Financial Centre were all that could be seen; fog hid anything beneath the penthouses, the world below an unfathomable cloud. Clinging to the wall with undisguised nervousness, JJ turned to her partner. 'Are you expecting us to jump?'

Luca spoke as he jogged across the room and grabbed the heavy dressing chair, crossed to the door kicking it shut, and then wedged the chair under the handle.

'Not without some help.' He returned to the bed where he pushed at imagined panels, seeking a hidden compartment. 'Brokers always have escape equipment. I just have to find where Franz hid it.'

JJ looked out at the towers rising from the fog below, a sudden blast of noisy wind blowing her and the curtains back almost horizontally. 'Luca, I can't do it.'

Gunfire broke out at the front door to the apartment. Kitty screamed. JJ looked from the windowless space to Luca. 'OK, I can do it.'

In the apartment's lobby, Kitty saw the front door lock shot to pieces by a burst of gunfire. The shock of it caused her to scream and slap her head back in terror against the statue; in doing so she nearly knocked herself unconscious. She could see the smoke drifting slowly off the splinters of wood at the door and tried to form the words in her mind, knowing she had to shout something stark and clear, or she would be the first thing shot when they raged through the door. She tried to shout the words, but they seemed to get stuck in her throat as she watched semi-conscious, in slow motion, the door being kicked open, a bald man in black combat gear appearing, crouching, looking down the barrel of a sub-machine gun, fire blazing from it, fire piercing her body ten, twenty, countless times—

Picardie watched as the blue-haired Japanese woman, tied up and wrapped in a sheet, the angel's wings spreading out behind and above her, wriggled spasmodically while his bullets drilled into her. He knew almost instantly that she was a decoy, that she was their girl on the inside, but his survival instinct—his instructions—left him no choice.

He stopped firing and paused as the two Chinese mercenaries stepped carefully past him, their own sub-machine guns at the ready for Luca, intent that he too should join the fallen angel before them.

'They're here.'

JJ's whisper was hoarse. She was scared; these weren't unarmed Russian conscripts, but brutal mercenaries who had proved themselves deadly. Luca kept pressing his fingers against the panels around the head of the bed. There was another burst of gunfire as the killers entered another room off the lobby.

JJ jumped in her skin; she found Luca's near serenity surreal. Then the Swiss man felt a portion of the cladding to the left of the bed compress with a click. He gave her a reassuring smile as a panel fell forward on hinges, the smile falling away as he reached into a recess, pulling out a piece of paper. He read it aloud: 'Were you hoping to find two parachutes?'

JJ's eyes snapped open at the words, and then another burst of gunfire, closer now, underlined the seriousness of their predicament.

'Are we screwed?' she asked.

'If Franz didn't have a plan B, then maybe.'

He leaned into the recess and pressed at the rear wall. Kitty may have discovered the first hidden compartment when she was combing the apartments but she may not have thought to look for another; a panel fell forward, and Luca pulled out some heavy equipment and a huge coil of thin metal cabling.

'What the hell is that?'

'Plan B—our ticket out of here.'

He dropped the loop of cabling by the open window, lifted what looked like a stunted harpoon gun, loaded with a large titanium bolt, and aimed it down to the Shanghai World Financial Centre.

'Stand back.'

JJ did so and he pulled the trigger. There was a small explosion as the bolt rocketed from the harpoon gun through the air in a slightly descending arc, the cable whipping along behind it, the wire feeding furiously over Luca's shoulder until a distant *clink* was heard. The cable slowed, only gravity gently tugging the wire further out.

Luca immediately looped the wire over a heavy light fitting in the wall, pulling it tauter, before repeatedly wrapping it round and tying it off.

JJ watched aghast. 'I... I can't go down that, Luca. What if it doesn't hold, what if we both fall to our death?'

Luca surprised her with a genuine look of amusement. 'You say that as if you have a choice.'

Machine-gun fire riddled the door of the room, the handle reduced to nothing as it popped off with the force of the onslaught. JJ leaned into Luca, more frightened than she had ever known. When he spoke, in a voice calmer and warmer than made any sense in the situation, it gave her the strength she was lacking.

'Time to leave.'

One of the Chinese mercenaries kicked the bedroom door but was knocked backwards by the weight keeping it closed. Immediately Picardie knew the reason: it was barricaded—they were in there.

The French-Algerian nodded fiercely to the two Chinese men and they immediately formed one unit to pour bullets into the door, the gunfire hailstorm reducing the target and anything behind it to splinters, leaving only tiny chunks of wood hanging from the hinges and dust where the door had stood a moment before.

As Picardie threw a flash grenade into the room, all three mercenaries stepped away from the doorway and braced themselves for the concussive bang that followed. The grenade briefly filled the room full of smoke, which was swiftly blown away by the strong winds buffeting the tower.

Switching to automatic pistols the two Chinese men followed Picardie, who swept the room cautiously, before noticing the makeshift zip wire and stabbing his pistol back into the holster.

'*Merde.*'

He moved over to the wire and his eye followed it down as it disappeared into the depths towards a huge skyscraper that was dwarfed by the one he stood in. He slammed his hand against the wall.

'*Putain.*'

He looked angrily at the two junior members of his team.

'Go after him.'

They looked uneasily at him and didn't move so he took his pistol from the holster and pointed it at them.

'I said, go after him.'

One of the men reluctantly started patting himself down, searching for something. Eventually he pulled out a carabiner clip which he attached to the strap of his sub-machine gun. This done, he stood on the precipice of the window ledge and hooked it onto the wire.

'What are you waiting for?'

With no idea how to slow down at the other end, the Chinese mercenary stepped off the ledge and out into the night. His cohort didn't wait to be told, doing the same and following the first man down the zip wire.

Picardie watched them go, furious that his prey had escaped, and then cast an angry glance round the room. His eyes were caught by the television where he saw that each CCTV view showed police officers and SWAT teams running through every part of the building.

'*Salaud. Salope. Putain de merde.*'

The mercenary hurried from the room before his options ran out.

As the first Chinese man slid down the wire, a sag developed towards the very end and slowed him, his ride stopping two metres short of a high window through which the bolt and wire had travelled. He began to edge ahead by grabbing the wire with his hands and clambering along the cable, but then he sensed the heavy, bouncing vibrations of the other mercenary and feared that the violence of his arrival might dislodge whatever the wire was attached to in the room ahead. His fears were instantly realised; as the second Chinese soldier arrived, there was a crunching sound. As the bolt flew backwards out of the room, the wire dropped and the men screamed, but the barbs of the harpoon bolt caught on the sill of the window.

The cable steadied.

The two Chinese men, now at least four metres from the window, were clinging to the wire five hundred metres above the financial district, holding their breath lest it dislodge the fragile grasp that held them. A wind rose up and the two men swayed, powerless, the harpoon head shifting an inch or so, both men yelping in fright. Then they steadied.

That was when the bolt slipped off the sill, men and wire falling together, accelerating down to the Shanghai Tower, helpless as its exterior approached them faster and faster.

Luca looked down at JJ where they lay hidden in the bath of Franz's bathroom. They were covered in plaster and tiling after the bedroom door had been reduced to nothing.

'You OK?' Luca asked.

'Am I alive?'

'I think so.'

'Then I'm OK.'

Luca and JJ emerged from the en suite into a room torn to pieces, almost everything ripped to shreds. The zip wire was swinging gently in the wind, clearly not attached to anything. JJ put an arm round Luca, which earned her his arm round her shoulder.

'Somebody doesn't like you, Luca.'

'I'm starting to dislike them, too.'

Luca and JJ stepped out into the hallway, JJ giving Kitty's corpse the widest possible berth. They paused to look back at her as they left; the rope holding her was completely soaked from her blood. Luca contemplated her impassively, JJ felt sick again.

'Look what we did, Luca.'

'What *she* did, JJ. She made the call. They came here to kill us. Remember that.'

11
Ticino, Switzerland

Nobody spoke for more than a minute after the General Counsel delivered his report; they were not so much shocked at Luca's unknown fate but concerned for their own.

A hologram presence shined slightly brighter on its pedestal. 'You can't turn on the television without seeing pictures of the Shanghai Tower. Even if he is alive, his first mission has become a global event. Questions will be asked, we will have to deny things that were done, we will have to lie. This is not how it should be done.' It was Alexander Oakwood, scion of the Oakwood family, a refined Englishman, speaking as much self-critically as to apportion blame. Despite his understated appearance, he was head of the world's largest private bank.

The diminutive figure of Sir Stephen Devereux rose from his chair in the darkness and approached the centre, ignoring the disdain on Herr Hesse's face. 'We have yet to hear from Herr Voss, we have yet to establish the facts.'

Furst, the Texan, bridled in his holographic seat. 'Sir Stephen, the Chinese are furious about what happened yesterday, telling anyone who will listen in Intelligence circles that these men were enemies of the state—their state. Coming at a time when there is talk of overthrowing the government of North Korea, the Chinese are linking the two. And let me tell you something, the finger is being pointed at the Seven Families.'

Devereux turned sharply, his crimson cassock swirling slightly about him. 'Mr Furst, they are making political capital out of this. Perhaps it is a timely reminder that our ties with China are not as strong as they should be.'

The Texan eyed him with ill-hidden irritation. 'China is the future, is that it? America is the past?'

'What if I told you that everybody could be the future, and that not only can we afford to, but we should look to, make alliances with everyone and anybody?'

The owlish Japanese octogenarian spoke with his usual dryness. 'The Council of Foreign Relations is also concerned that we are stirring up trouble for our own reasons.'

As he stared from one family head to another, Ulla Thord-Gray, the Nordic matriarch, spoke up. 'Whatever else we can ascribe to the events of last night it has certainly sown discord among ourselves. Could that be the intention?'

A certain collective foolishness was felt by everyone having understood her point.

'Do we know who instigated the attack on Voss? Is it linked to the individual you mentioned at our last meeting, this Butakhan character?'

The General Counsel went to speak, but instead sighed. 'He is, to all intents and purposes, invisible. We are still digging but he appears to have come out of nowhere.'

'What of the other intelligence agencies, the CIA, FSB? Nothing?'

'A blank. But trust me everybody is working to find out.'

Thord-Gray considered this for a moment before turning from Hesse. 'What do you suggest, Sir Stephen?'

Voss's godfather almost sighed with relief to be allowed the floor. 'I believe our priority should be to find Voss. I believe, if he has survived, that he should not be left out in the cold. And once we know what he knows, we then secure the situation and paralyse it, before it spreads.'

She nodded, evaluating his views, before turning to the General Counsel. 'And Herr Hesse?'

The German sat forward in his seat and rested his chin on his prayer-like hands in thought. What he said next he said with great hesitation. 'I'm concerned about Herr Voss. His disobedience, his wilfully high-profile behaviour that puts us at risk, his silence… I feel terrible saying it but what if he has been turned?'

Devereux's face turned a shade of red that matched his robes. 'Turned? Luca? Are you insane?'

'No, I am cautious and caution serves us well.'

'But to suggest such a thing—'

'Is my job. I am fully aware that if he has been turned by the Chinese, North Koreans, the Americans even, that *I* and *I alone* am to blame. His training is my responsibility and any failing is my failing.'

Sir Stephen appealed to the room with his next remarks. 'This is beyond the realm of reason, speculation of a most wild nature. We might as well ask if any of us are working for the other side. Am *I* in league with the enemy? Am *I* the enemy within?' He looked from figure to figure but was met with a stony silence, which somehow made a speech that was meant to shame, a shameful one itself.

Ulla Thord-Gray turned to face the General Counsel. 'What would be a reasonable and measured course of action, Herr Hesse?'

'Pull his credit lines and all support until he returns and explains himself. Should he try to use them, or his passport, he will be made visible to us immediately. If he keeps on running then our fears may be justified.'

The seven patriarchs and matriarchs swapped looks that concurred, and then Thord-Gray nodded. 'It is decided.'

12

Shanghai Pudong International Airport, China

'Two first-class one-way tickets to Yangon International Airport, please.'

JJ looked from the smartly dressed Chinese woman at the check-in desk to Luca. 'Are we in trouble with the Families?'

'No, we're not in trouble.'

'So, explain again why we're not going to Switzerland?'

'We are going to Switzerland. We're just going via Myanmar, that's all.'

'That will be 4,700 Yuan, please, sir.'

Luca handed over his credit card.

'And why are we slumming it rather than using the family jet?'

Luca met her irony with a tight smile. 'They took the jet away.'

'I'm terribly sorry, sir, but your card hasn't been accepted.'

Luca's brow creased, this was a first for him. JJ put a hand on his arm.

'Is that normal?'

Luca closed his eyes for a moment, pained by the implications. 'No, no it isn't.'

JJ reached into her bag for her purse. 'So it's not just the jet they've taken away?' She handed over her own credit card and regarded him with gentle criticism. 'But we're not in trouble?'

★　　★　　★

JJ set her champagne on the table and eased back into her seat, rubbing the wide arms of her chair, appreciating the comfort. 'I mean, really, why would a person choose a private jet over this?'

Luca, working at his tablet in the seat beside her, spoke absent-mindedly. 'Some people hate the queues.'

'We were treated like royalty.'

'Some people like the flexibility.'

'We live in a mobile world where you can work anywhere. So what, if you can't snap your fingers and fly somewhere right *now*?'

'Some people like to have sex on planes.'

'This place is a dump.' She took a swig of champagne, then remembered herself. 'You still haven't told me why we're going to Rangoon?'

Luca shifted his tablet to give JJ a better view of the photo of *Charon*, the mega-yacht included in the set of photos Luca had found concealed in the Bugatti.

JJ peered closely to read the name of the craft. '*Charon*? Isn't he the guy who ferries the dead across the river Styx?'

That earned a wry smile from Luca. 'I thought I was the only one to have Greek mythology forced on me?'

JJ was sincere in her response. 'All those tormented women and strapping heroes, what's not to like? Anyhow, *Charon*, sounds a bit ominous, doesn't it?'

'Trust me that is not the ominous part.' Luca set his fingers over the rear of an army lorry in the picture and expanded the image, a yellow triangular sign growing with it, but the words on it pixelating, becoming illegible.

'Can we decipher that?' JJ asked.

Luca shook his head. 'It's clearly hazardous waste, but no, Franz was using a very poor camera, a phone most likely. But we can do the next best thing.'

He tapped 'Start' on one of the tiles on the screen and the tablet began immediately to purr furiously as it processed all the photographs, half a dozen per second flashing in and out of view. With some difficulty, JJ began to discern that they were all pictures of ports. Some flashed red.

'What am I looking at?'

'Herr Hesse has cut off all my support, but hasn't locked me out of the computer network, yet. This is an algorithm to identify locations in photographs. Once it has enough matches it—'

At that moment, the screen switched to an atlas, North Korea at its centre. Then a circle appeared around the west coast port of Nampo and the map zoomed in.

'Is that where the boat was photographed?'

Luca nodded. 'Seems like a curious destination for a mega-yacht.'

'Why would it be there?'

'Well, UN trade sanctions would make selling it to the Glorious Leader an international crime. And about the only thing North Korea has that's worth exporting is—'

'Hazardous materials? But...'

'But what?'

JJ didn't like it. 'But isn't it a long shot, one photograph?'

'One photograph that Franz went to a lot of trouble to get. Look, I traced the ownership of the boat through a series of shell companies and I've followed the trail.' He paused, switching apps to the picture of the once-grand blue colonial-era building. 'To here.'

'Where's that?' JJ asked.

Luca double-tapped one corner of the picture and the previous atlas came into view, panning west until it arrived at Myanmar and zeroed in on the major port city of Yangon, the old Rangoon.

'Myanmar? As in where this plane is heading, as in to where Butakhan made those calls?'

'Exactly.'

'And do you think Butakhan is behind all of this?'

'Seems like a fairly sensible working assumption. But what I am certain of is that whoever it is was behind the party thrown for us in Shanghai last night.'

JJ glared at her companion. 'We're going *to* them? We're going to find those people? Are you mad?'

'JJ, we have three choices: go into hiding; spend our lives on the run; or take the fight to them.'

'But why not let someone else do it?'

'Because they weren't trying to kill someone else.'

'But we can hide until it blows over.'

'I don't want to hide from it, I want to stop it.'

'Why?'

'What do you mean, why?'

'Why not let someone else do it, why not let some other Broker or government agency do it?'

'What sort of question is that?'

'It's a gambler's question. We've had an incredible run of luck, Luca, but there's one thing I've learned about luck at the poker tables: it runs out. Why do this?'

Luca went to answer, but paused, unhappy with what he was about to say. He reframed it, then went to answer again, but was unhappy with that reply too. Instead he laughed.

'What?'

'If I told you I was determined to see this through to the end, would you walk away and leave me to it?'

JJ knew that there was something darkly amusing about what he'd just said, but didn't feel like laughing. 'I don't think it's taking the fight to them, Luca.'

He gave her a quizzical look. 'What is it then?' He felt a pang inside, his gut falling slightly at his awareness that even in the pyrotechnics of yesterday he had not once taken another person's life close up. Every kill had been at a distance, the killer blow never quite taken with his own hand. He wondered for the briefest of moments whether Hesse had been right and if indeed he was not yet ready.

'Well, if you must know, I think—'

An air steward stopped by their seats with what looked like a large mobile phone. 'Mr Voss, there's a telephone call for you.'

JJ gave Luca the look the moment deserved. He raised an eyebrow and took the phone from the air steward.

'Hello?'

Herr Hesse's voice was like an Alpine stream: crystal clear and ice cold. 'Do you mind explaining what happened in Shanghai?'

'We had to deal with an unexpected turn of events.'

'A Broker plans for the unexpected, Herr Voss. Maybe this is a sound reminder as to your true calling.'

'I thought we dealt with it fairly well, all things considered.'

'All things considered, Herr Voss, you're meant to be an agent of stealth, but instead you prove yourself a wrecking ball.'

'One could argue that the other party played their part.'

'A party you should not have encountered, Voss, because you should have been here.'

'Look, we've picked up a lead—'

'Have you, Herr Voss? Then why not share it with us?'

Luca paused. It was a fair question, going to the heart of his actions. 'We've got some new information and I'd like to check it out.'

There was a silence from the other end that was impossible to read; when Hesse did speak, it was distinctly unfriendly. 'The Families need convincing you're one of us, Voss.'

'What? Of course I am, I'm doing this to *protect* the Families.'

'Are you really? Or are you working to your own agenda, Voss?'

'No, no, not at all.'

'Then I will send a plane to collect you from Rangoon.'

Luca took a deep breath at Hesse's smart move. 'Herr Hesse, you don't understand –'

'The problem, Voss, is that I do. Make the plane.'

'A few hours, that's all I need. Herr Hesse?'

Luca pulled the phone from his ear and looked at its screen. The call had been terminated at the other end. He was annoyed at Hesse but furious at himself.

'They're sending a plane.'

JJ looked at him sceptically until he felt provoked into responding.

'What?'

'I presume that call wasn't to tell you that you'd been nominated employee of the month?'

Luca knew JJ's remark deserved a smile but he pursed his lips instead. 'They're closing us down.'

'So why didn't you mention *Charon*?'

'Hmm?'

'You almost died retrieving those photographs, wouldn't that have persuaded him?'

'I don't know, JJ, I don't know.'

She sensed something was wrong; he was avoiding answering her question directly. 'What's up? What is it you're not telling me?'

'We walked into a trap in Russia and in Shanghai. That's more than bad luck.'

'You think somebody's tipping them off, Hesse maybe?'

'No, not that, but it could be that our channels of communication have been compromised, or...' He said no more, just shrugged.

'Or somebody's tipping them off?'

Luca drained the whisky in front of him, needing the kick to speak the words: 'Seven families, JJ, that's a lot of people and sources, a lot of tongues. I have no idea about the level of secrecy they work at, so why risk letting them in on what we're up to?'

'Because otherwise they might conclude we're the enemy?' JJ shook her head in despair as she looked away and down at the vast expanse of China below. 'Maybe it's a good thing they're sending a plane.'

★   ★   ★

As Luca and JJ walked past the double-storey windows that ran the length of the passport control building at Yangon International Airport, they had a good view of the runways. Three passenger jets were plugged into the gangways and then Luca spotted the Learjet coming into land. It touched down just as the immigration officer returned their documents to them.

JJ looked from the plane to her partner with a sense of resignation. 'There's our ride.'

Luca gave the aircraft a cursory glance then walked to the exit with their carry-on bags.

Leaning against the driver's door of his yellow taxi was a young man holding a newspaper. Luca indicated that he wanted a ride and found his bags swiftly taken from him.

As Luca climbed into the back, JJ muttered to herself as she followed: 'OK, so fine, the plan is not to get on the plane they sent.'

'Where to sir?'

'Nat Sim Road, please.'

JJ was less than impressed by Luca's decision. 'OK. So what's the plan?'

13
Yangon, Myanmar

JJ had used binoculars before, even night-vision ones once, but she had never used anything like this. The telescopic lens belonged to a rifle, which brought subjects eerily close and rendered them pin-sharp, albeit overlaid by the scope markings.

She scanned the building opposite across a four-lane road, from floor to floor, window to window. The facade, like all the buildings around it, was decrepit. A colonial gem in its day, its century-old name, The Ambassador Hotel, was still chiselled in stone above the entrance. Each floor was double height with arching windows and ornate railings, but its grandeur ended there. Other than some vestiges of its former status, the building matched all the buildings in this run-down district. The peeling blue paint had been applied decades before and electrical and telephone wires criss-crossed their way up to numerous floors.

Only two details revealed its true condition: every room had windows in a neighbourhood where windows were a rarity; and the roof was host to three twenty-first century satellite dishes that would not have looked amiss atop a major TV station. As JJ noted, however, they were set back from the front of the building so that most people would never even notice them.

A view through the windows of the building revealed more information. There were beefed up, serious looking men in sharp-looking suits and, in an office on the third floor of the building, she instantly recognised the figure of Butakhan behind a desk.

JJ felt her mouth go dry. She looked down one side of the imposing, detached building and saw beyond it, moored on the river next to the building itself, a mega-yacht. The name was impossible to make out, but having seen the photos, it was unmistakably *Charon*. Somehow seeing the vessel moored so close, knowing it had sailed from North Korea, seemed to pull her towards some imperceptible sense of danger. At the sound of approaching feet, she lowered the lens.

Luca walked into the room, a large open-plan clothing factory floor dominated by long tables, which were cluttered with industrial-size sewing machines, endless rolls of cloth standing against every wall.

'The factory owner has given everybody paid leave for the rest of the day courtesy of yours truly, and you are the proud owner of a motorbike,' Luca said.

He dangled the keys from his finger and dropped them into her extended palm. JJ glanced at the battered key without excitement. 'When you say motorbike—'

Luca winced slightly. 'A vehicle, with two wheels.'

JJ pulled a face to say she understood. 'And the plan, apart from a slow, uncertain escape?'

'Have you scoped out the building?'

JJ rolled the riflescope round her fingers. 'Quite literally.'

'Did you see Butakhan?'

'Yes.'

Luca placed his flight bag on a table, unzipped the bottom section, and pulled out a slim metallic briefcase. 'Excellent. Well, now I want you to shoot him.'

'Where the hell is he? How could you have let him get away when you have so many men at your disposal?'

Jean Picardie took the dressing-down without complaint, knowing it was deserved. His hope of proving that the Chinese mercenaries were poor substitutes for recruits of his own had backfired; any ambition to head up the organisation's military operations had been delivered a debilitating blow by his failure in Shanghai.

The room in which he stood was large and, contrary to the faded exterior of the building, would not have been out of place in the headquarters of a New York hedge fund. Oak flooring, Italian furniture, an expansive desk, empty but for a telephone, laptop, and small metal globe. Across from this were sleek, high-backed leather chairs, minimalist sofas against the walls, objets d'art and several pieces by Jeff Koons.

Butakhan slammed the desk, the items on it jumping violently. 'I ask you again, how could you fuck it up so badly?'

Behind him, against the back of his chair, Scarlett was wearing an uncharacteristically sober outfit: a conservative white shirt and slim white skirt. Even her platinum hair was tied back for a more professional look. Only the crimson lipstick suggested her role in Butakhan's life, somehow undermining the best efforts of the business shirt to downplay her breasts.

The French-Algerian had seen conflict in every hellhole on Earth; while he did not fear his boss he knew that to work with people like Butakhan was to run the risk of incurring their ferocity, their venom, their psychosis.

'I promise that when I next see him next, only one of us will leave alive.'

Sitting next to Picardie was the only other person present, a young banker from one of New York's largest banks. He was also banker to Butakhan's organisation. McDaniel had no idea about the sort of business his client ran, although he suspected it was not all above board. He was quite happy to facilitate the organisation's banking needs, though, having grown exceedingly rich in the last decade by doing so. At Picardie's last words, he failed to stifle a dark snigger.

Butakhan's head turned slowly to look at the American. 'What was funny?'

McDaniel felt a certain familiarity with the Mongolian man, their scores of meetings giving rise to a sense of belonging to his inner circle. 'Just what he said.'

Butakhan looked from Picardie back to McDaniel. 'What did he say?'

The American gave a small sneer. '"Only one of us will leave alive." Well, it could be Luca Voss, that's all.'

Butakhan rose slowly behind his desk, looking from the slick-haired American to the casual, combat-styled French-Algerian. 'He's got a point. He's got a *point.*'

Picardie was sitting stock-still; he'd known enough killers in his time not to try to head off the rising anger.

Butakhan moved over to the other side of the desk, where the two men were sitting. He picked up a brass globe the size of a grapefruit from his desk and tossed it in his hand. 'Maybe you meant that you would let me down another time, that you couldn't be trusted, couldn't be *relied* upon.'

McDaniel was aware that Butakhan was passing the back of his chair and shot Picardie a stare to insinuate he was part of the management team, while Picardie was just one of the employees.

Butakhan's face began to twist into a snarl now as he spoke. 'You couldn't be relied upon to keep your fucking mouth *shut...*'

The Mongolian man brought the brass globe down hard on the crown of the banker's head. McDaniel gave a guttural cry as his skull cracked. Scarlett slapped her hand across her mouth, watching wide-eyed.

'Couldn't just shut the fuck up while I talked to my people.'

Butakhan slammed the globe once, twice, three times into the banker's skull, his head and torso slumped forward onto the desk. Each blow crushed more and more of his skull, causing blood to seep out of his ears and form a pool around his head.

Picardie watched impassively, not dumb enough to interfere, readying himself should the globe come in his direction.

Butakhan had not finished. As the banker lay dying across the edge of the desk, his body shaking with weak spasms, the Mongolian man brought the metal globe down on his head with both hands repeatedly, screaming a word with each blow as he did so: 'Where. Is. Luca. Voss? Where. Is. Luca. Voss?' Each blow disfigured the side of the American's face and more than once a spurt of blood spat across the room onto Scarlett's blouse as she looked away with as much composure as she could muster.

Then it stopped. As quickly and suddenly as it had started. Butakhan had exorcised the demon for the time being.

He stood upright, looked from Scarlett's red-flecked clothes to the unflinching blood-spattered face of Picardie. Then he considered his own hands, which were sticky with blood, hair, dark matter, maybe brain as well. He tried to locate the emotion he was feeling, but realised he was feeling nothing. He was calm.

'I'll ask again. Where—is—Luca—Voss?' He stared at the mercenary with eyes empty of humanity. He stared for so long that even the battle-hardened French-Algerian felt it would be wise to say something, anything.

The phone on the desk rang, but Butakhan didn't react. It continued to ring and ring. He wagged a finger at it. Scarlett reached a tentative hand, lifting the receiver slowly, speaking quietly when she did.

'Yes?' She listened, her expression switching from wariness to puzzlement. She put the phone to her chest. 'Buty? It's the front desk.'

Butakhan sighed heavily, blinking impatiently.

'Luca Voss is waiting to see you.'

Now Butakhan did look round. It was the last thing he had expected to hear, but pleasing news all the same.

He looked from Scarlett to Picardie and smiled. 'I'd better wash my hands.'

Luca was shown into the room by an attractive Burmese female. He found Butakhan seated behind his desk, Scarlett standing next to him with one hand draped across his shoulder and, seated on a sofa against the right-hand wall, Picardie, who he failed to recognise at first. Outwardly, Luca was relaxed, but he tensed at the sight of the red flecks spotting Scarlett's shirt.

Butakhan was in a buoyant mood. 'Take a seat, Mr Voss.'

Luca approached, the reason for Scarlett's tainted clothes becoming clearer when he caught sight of the dead man slumped against the edge of the desk, still sitting in one of the chairs, a pool of fresh red blood around his smashed head.

The Mongolian man laughed, as if it were a spilt cup of tea that might spoil the finish on the desk rather than coagulating blood. 'As you can see, one of the seats is taken, but please do take the other one.'

Butakhan smiled and gestured to the vacant seat. Luca did nothing more than raise an eyebrow at the sight of the bludgeoned murder victim as he sat down next to the corpse.

'Apologies for the untidiness Mr Voss, it's nothing more than a small employer–employee dispute.'

Luca smiled genially, knowing that whatever had taken place the body had been left there for effect, and therefore it was crucial to deny his host the satisfaction of just that. 'Well, I hope you managed to settle it amicably. How was Davos? I had to leave after our skijoring.'

Butakhan smiled waspishly. 'I believe I won that race, didn't I?'

Luca met his smile with a blank, and pointed at the corpse beside him. 'Yes, just like you doubtless won the argument with that chap through sheer force of reason alone.' He didn't pause at the icy look that met his comment. 'However, I was less than straight with you when we last met.'

Butakhan raised an enquiring eyebrow.

'I said I was in hedge funds. The truth is I'm—'

Luca reached inside his jacket, but before he could even begin to withdraw anything from it, Picardie was out of his chair and pointing a Sig Sauer P226 automatic pistol at the Swiss man's head. Scarlett punctuated the action with a loud gasp of alarm. Not flinching or cowering, the visitor merely looked from the gun to the French-Algerian's fierce face to Butakhan, and then continued slowly to withdraw his hand from his pocket to reveal a business card.

'I'm a United Nations inspector.' He put the card on the table and gave it a shove such that it skidded to where the Mongolian man's hands were resting on the surface. They had not noticed Luca switch on a cigarette-box-sized device in his pocket. A scanner was now copying any digital data stored within five metres of where Luca was sitting. He was particularly interested in the contents of Butakhan's laptop.

Butakhan remained unruffled throughout and smiled indulgently at Picardie's expert protection. He nodded for the mercenary to stand down and then turned his gaze to Luca.

'Are you under the impression I have weapons of mass destruction? What propaganda have the Americans been spreading about me this time?' He smiled at his own joke.

Luca met his smile with one of his own. 'I don't doubt that a man of your nature has his fingers in all kinds of pies, but I'm more interested in the boat you have moored outside.'

'*Charon*, what about it?' Butakhan would have Luca killed at any moment, but intelligence was intelligence. If there was something to glean from him he would be happy to learn it.

'Is it yours?'

Butakhan was intrigued. 'Are you head of the UN Yacht Club?'

'I work for the International Embargoes Inspectorate. As you may or may not know, under Security Council Resolution 1718 it is a crime to supply the North Korean regime with luxury goods.'

'I wasn't aware of that, but OK. So what?'

'*Charon* is a luxury yacht and we have reason to believe it may have been supplied to a citizen of North Korea.'

Butakhan was torn between interest and confusion. 'Who says I own *Charon*?'

'Nobody, yet, but the company that does own it is registered to this building.'

'There are no companies registered to this building.'

Luca gave a wide, deliberately charmless smile. 'Trust me, there are. I can show you on that laptop if you like, I saved it all in an email in my "Drafts" folder.'

Butakhan squinted, enough to acknowledge the reference to the draft email folder, but privately he was near to boiling over with rage that the building in which they were now sitting was linked in any way to anything he was doing. His secret ire was directed firmly at the dead man present, who would have overseen corporate matters of this sort. With a small shake of his head, he dismissed the matter from his mind.

'OK, everything you say aside, *Charon* is outside the building. So what's the problem?'

'But it was in North Korea.'

'Was it? I don't always know where it is.'

Luca flashed a cold smile. 'The burden of the wealthy. Anyhow, if I could see the ownership papers we could put the matter to rest.'

Now Butakhan looked at him for the longest time. 'I think the only thing we'll be putting to rest today, Mr Voss, is you.'

'I don't quite follow you.'

'No, just as I believe you don't follow the orders of the Seven Families.'

He waited a moment to see the effect his words had on Luca and detected a glimmer of recognition as his inside information sunk in.

'You see, Mr Voss, yours is not the only organisation with global reach, nor with a history spanning centuries.'

Luca's brow creased, the scale of Butakhan's intelligence stark. He hoped against hope that the snooping device had hoovered up enough data; his time was well and truly up. He raised a finger to interject. 'Butakhan, if I might—'

'Die? Be my guest, Mr Voss. Mr Picardie, if you would.'

Picardie rose slowly, lifting his hand so that the barrel of the gun was planted firmly on Luca's temple. Scarlett felt her breath shortening.

'Buty—'

Butakhan didn't take his eyes from Luca as he spoke. 'Say another word, my darling, and it won't be somebody else's blood on your clothes.' He was enjoying himself and he wasn't about to let this moment be spoiled by the spinelessness of a Californian drifter. He felt like Caesar, an Emperor, able to direct a life with the down or upward motion of a thumb. 'Any last words, Mr Voss?'

Luca looked at him, resigned to his fate, wearing the smile a gambler wears when the last horse fails to win back money lost on the previous seven.

And then, in that moment, the silence was broken by the sound of Luca's phone ringing.

'Do you mind if I get that?' Luca partly opened the side of his jacket where the phone was ringing.

Butakhan did not like it, liked the timing even less. 'Jean, you answer it.'

Without moving his gun from Luca's skull, the mercenary reached carefully inside Luca's jacket and pulled out a simple flip phone purchased an hour previously. He carefully opened the cover, put it to his ear, and listened. He looked at Butakhan with concern, which earned him a critical one in return.

'Well?' Butakhan said.

The French-Algerian was unsure how to start. 'Whatever you do, do not move.'

'What do you mean?'

Picardie rose his voice. 'I mean there's a rifle trained on you, sir, from a building across the street, and if you or anybody except for Mr Voss moves, she will shoot you.'

In a basement room of the building, a security guard sprang up in her seat, not believing what she was seeing on the monitor in front of her. It showed events upstairs in Butakhan's office, the camera hidden in one of the sculptures inside that room. It was standard procedure to monitor any meetings with outside parties and now Picardie had alerted her to the fact a shooter was positioned in the building opposite. She picked up a phone beside her.

'I need a team of men *now*.'

Upstairs in the office a tiny red laser dot was trained steadily on Butakhan's temple. From the bodyguard's position, it seemed Butakhan did not feel inclined to treat the matter lightly, but nor would he surrender too willingly.

'Where is it coming from, Jean?'

Picardie kept still, the gun at his victim's head. He turned his own head to the window, looking at the factory across the four-lane highway.

'A building opposite.'

'And have they got a shot?'

Picardie looked back at him. 'A clear one.'

Butakhan, knowing his fate was in his own hands, fought to quell the rage, the sense of impotence the situation made him feel. 'I'm surprised you could get your hands on a weapon like that at such short notice, Mr Voss.'

Luca thought the remark an odd one, strangely insightful. 'Well you know what they say: a man without a backup plan is a man without a plan.'

Butakhan had to resist the temptation to nod his agreement. 'Seems odd to assume that I wouldn't be tempted to move out of the way quickly, though, don't you think?'

Luca gave him a sceptical smile. 'Somehow I don't think you will.' He stared at Butakhan, remembering the skijoring, how they had raced to the last corner together—with room for only one horse—and how Butakhan had blinked first.

After a considerable pause Butakhan smiled as if beaten. 'And now what happens, Mr Voss?'

'Now I leave.'

Butakhan closed his eyes, the pain of defeat, however fleeting, stabbing him fiercely in his stomach. He opened his hooded eyes with a poorly concealed snarl. 'Till next time.' He looked at Picardie to signal he should remove the gun from Luca's head, which he did.

Luca rose, offered a warm smile to Butakhan and Scarlett, and then looked at Picardie who still had his gun pointed at him. 'You can keep the phone. It's still got a hundred minutes left on it.'

And with that, he left.

Luca took the stairs down as fast as he could, holding the handrail for good measure, knowing that the moment he left the room Picardie would be scrambling to stop him and JJ. He began to descend the last flight to the ground floor sensing that all bets might well be off, that his luck might be running out.

★　　★　　★

A group of six Burmese mercenaries were sprinting up the dilapidated staircase of the clothes factory as fast and as quietly as they could. They were dressed like a SWAT team and each carried an Uzi sub-machine gun, the bright laser sights casting a criss-cross of red beams on the space ahead as they reached the third floor.

With practised stealth, they approached the door to the sewing room. They knew the drill and didn't even need to swap glances let alone words.

One mercenary pulled a pneumatic door hammer from a strap on his back. He positioned it silently before the door.

Their commander counted down with his fingers. *Three, two, one.*

The door gave way in a split second, thumping off its hinges into the room, five mercenaries charging after it, drilling the space before them with hundreds of bullets a second. They were spread out across the width of the building, meaning that their bullets penetrated everything. Eventually their commander lifted a hand to halt proceedings.

There was nobody there they could see. And clearly, nobody would be hiding.

The lead mercenary ran to the tripod and realised they'd been set up. He pressed a comms device on his shoulder and spoke into it. 'Sir, it's just a rifle sight—there is no rifle.'

★　　★　　★

Picardie heard the news and his eyes snapped open at the deception. 'The *salaud* bluffed us.'

Butakhan felt a shooting pain down his neck from the effort to stay still. He finally dared to look to his right out of the window, where he could see six men wearing balaclavas through the window opposite. 'What the fuck is happening?'

Picardie decided in that second to risk his boss's wrath. He grabbed the phone on the desk and, after a moment, barked into it.

'Do *not* let Voss escape—shoot to kill.'

Luca took a breath and then pushed open the door to the ground-floor lobby. He calmly scanned the room: two heavies stood by the wide glass frontage while the receptionist, who had taken Luca up in the elevator earlier, was replacing the phone with a look of pure terror on her face.

Though she looked like she was about to scream, Luca figured that as a civilian in a military situation she might just let him get through that door. He gave her a winning smile and walked forward, watched warily by the two guards.

Outside, JJ pulled up on a pitiful off-road motorbike and threw him a look that told him to hurry up.

As Luca neared the two heavies, he could see they were concerned with the alarmed secretary behind him.

Just as he approached, she finally spoke: 'We have to stop—'

He didn't wait for her to finish, slamming a fist into the solar plexus of the man on his left, using the same arm to elbow the other in the windpipe causing him to collapse backwards; but the first of the men had put out a hand as he fell, grabbing Luca. Held at bay, Luca looked from the agitated JJ to the view across the road, where six mercenaries were emerging from the building.

He wasn't going to make it out.

'Go JJ! *Go*,' Luca screamed at her.

She dashed off on the bike while Luca twisted the arm of the man who had hold of him, rendering him helpless before kneeing him in a kidney for good measure. Then, with the mercenaries sprinting across the highway towards him, he ran.

Luca raced back inside the building, past the receptionist, kicking through a door that led to a long corridor with a door at the end. Pausing only to knock over a filing cabinet so as to block the door he'd just come through, he dashed to the exit.

Hitting the bar on the emergency exit door, it burst open. JJ was on the bike between the building and the quay where the *Charon* was moored, while in the distance police cars could be heard wailing their way towards them. Luca's backup plan was coming to life; telling the police that drugs and guns could be found at Butakhan's headquarters had introduced an element of confusion to help them in their escape.

Luca leapt onto the back of the bike and JJ accelerated as fast as she could, the underpowered machine doing its best to pick up speed along the quayside. Butakhan's SWAT team rounded the far corner behind them, some running and some dropping into a kneeling position to free their weapons. JJ and Luca were less than a hundred metres away, well within range.

Then police cars began barrelling into view and blocked the mercenaries' line of sight, the motorbike obstructed by the cordon they formed around the building, brakes screeching as they were hit with a wave of gunfire in the initial confusion.

JJ looked into the juddering wing mirrors and saw that police cars were swarming around Butakhan's headquarters. She shook her head at the madness, at the odds they had played. She glanced at Luca watching her in the mirror.

'Did you get what we needed?'

He nodded. 'We needed to get away, so yeah.'

14
Northern Myanmar

Luca knew that once Butakhan's men had untangled themselves from the police they would be on the hunt for him and
JJ, but by that time, they were already on a flight to Mandalay. They had arrived at the private airstrip outside Yangon
where the pilot, on a $500 retainer and a promise that he'd
get $500 at the other end, ushered them onto the four-seat
aircraft: a 1964 Beagle Airedale. It would be dark in a few
hours and all the money in the world wouldn't buy the pilot's
co-operation to fly over Myanmar at night; his fear of the
military authorities running too deep. Mandalay was as far
north as he would take them until the following morning.

The high-winged monoplane looked every bit its half-
century age and sounded it too; the engine noise making
conversation instantly exhausting. The only conversation
that did take place occurred just after take-off when JJ tapped
the pilot on the shoulder from the rear passenger seat and
pointed to the smoke intermittently piping out of the engine,
obscuring the windscreen.

'What's that?'

The pilot had smiled and waved a hand at it. 'It's oil. Is
good, is good.'

JJ had shot Luca a wary look where he was sitting up
front, but he'd met the look with a shrug before returning to
his tablet, which he had wired up to the surveillance device
used in Butakhan's office. JJ sat back in her seat, deciding
that thinking too much about the plane's mechanics would

finish her off. Instead she took in the view of a country that stretched from the warmth of the Andaman Sea to the cold southern tip of the Himalayas; there was no lack of wonders to observe.

After a touch-and-go flight and a very dubious landing, owing to the broken landing gear, Luca and JJ found their way to Mandalay train station in a micro taxi-van, arriving after sunset. The station, a forward-looking construction in a city of long-neglected colonial buildings, resembled a Buddhist temple crossed with a modernist 1950s Miami hotel and ended up being neither one thing nor the other.

As they stood among the low-watt bulbs that lit the wares of hawkers at the ever-present market stalls, JJ felt the closeness of the warm night air. It had that smell, so prevalent across the developing continent, of sticky food waste, bins, and poor sanitation, the odours she'd known as a child in a small backwater town in China.

Luca nodded towards the train terminal. 'There's a hotel above it, want to camp down here for the night?'

JJ looked at the people milling around, the military police lazily patrolling the streets. Everybody seemed to be casting discreet glances in their direction, probably because they stood out as the only tourists, but possibly for reasons more ominous.

'Where are we heading?'

'Up north, beyond Myitkyina.'

'Which translates as?'

'Very north.'

'Then I'd rather keep moving. Our Mongolian friend looks like a pretty bad loser; I've known his type from the poker tables.'

Luca cast a glance at his watch. 'There's an overnight train if we hurry.'

JJ looked about the compartment as the rickety train pulled out of the station. She pulled a face that said she was impressed.

'I'll be honest, I expected a lot worse.'

Luca dropped their bags onto one of the two bench-beds facing each other across a small wooden locker, which was meant for their belongings. 'This country exports gas, oil, and precious gems. Some of the money has to be spent on infrastructure. Which bunk would you like?'

JJ slid the door closed behind her, locked it, and dropped the cloth blind before returning to face him. 'Whichever one you're planning on taking.'

Luca looked at each of the bunks in turn. 'They're barely fit for one person as it is.'

JJ took a step towards him, looked up into his face, and ran her hands down his arms to his fingers, which she took in hers. 'That's half the fun.'

She planted a kiss on his lips.

'JJ, we need to talk about Butakhan's plans.'

'How long did you say this journey was?'

'Sixteen hours.'

'And do you expect that chat to take a full sixteen hours?'

He shook his head, unable to believe her lust for life and lust for lust's sake. He moved his hands round her back and down to her buttocks, squeezing them, pulling her into him. 'We really need to have a talk about your priorities.'

'My priorities? You're the one taking us to Myitkyina.'

'What's wrong with that?'

'What's *wrong* with that? What's romantic about making love to somebody on the road to Myitkyina?' She was almost purring as she spoke now, her lips an inch from his. 'The road to Mandalay, on the other hand, has such an erotic ring to it, don't you think?'

Luca looked down into her green eyes that seemed to him, impossibly, to sparkle at moments like this. 'My dear JJ, you could find something erotic in the bottom of a coal mine.'

JJ pursed her lips and whimpered as if Luca had just described what he wanted to do to her once he had tied her up. 'Coal mines are so dark and wet.' Then she seemed struck by a new and interesting idea. '*Talking* of dark and wet...' She put her hands on his shoulders and hopped up, wrapping her legs around his waist, Luca helpfully pulling her into his crotch. She kissed him languidly, long kisses that started gently, becoming hungrier as she felt his tongue inside her mouth.

'Actually, JJ, talking of mines,' Luca said between kisses.

'Luca, we *really* need to work on your dirty talk.'

Maybe it was the train braking or their lack of balance or maybe it was because Luca threw her there, but JJ found herself landing softly on one of the bunks and both began to work at each other's belts, their trousers soon kicked off. JJ pushed herself against Luca while he pulled her panties to one side and thrust inside her, the lights above them flickering. As the train rocked and rattled, the Chinese woman did her best not to express too loudly her pleasure as she was transported by the sensation of Luca taking her, devouring her, as only he could.

15
Kachin State, Myanmar

Lying next to the window, JJ gazed out at the lush, verdant countryside, then stretched an arm slowly across Luca's chest as he worked on his tablet. She attempted to move, only to find herself pinned between her companion and the wall.

'There's hardly room for *one* person in one of these.'

Luca raised his eyebrows in reply. 'Sleep well?'

She was half-asleep still and not in any rush to wake up yet. 'Hmmm. I'll tell you once I'm up.'

Out in one of the fields a solitary elderly woman was walking through rows of sugar cane, a large woven basket on her back. JJ felt a curious muted nervousness grip her, which subsided when she gave it a name and realised she had seen herself, or what she could have been, had she not been adopted. Her English adoptive parents, who she felt she had disappointed from the earliest days, had plucked her from a path that would have seen her traipsing through paddy fields each day, or moving to a polluted city to toil in factories manufacturing electronic goods and toys for Western markets. She felt a rush of guilt, a sense of loss that she could no longer tell her parents that, for that much at least, she was grateful. A Christmas holiday on the island of Sumatra in 2004 had put paid to that: the tsunami that struck the island took her parents and tens of thousands of other locals and tourists with them. That was JJ's first ever Christmas without them.

Somehow, all these twists of fate had led her to the Swiss man beside her. Now her mood seemed to change. She felt a profound gratitude for the unpredictable course her life had taken, was still taking, now that she and Luca had struck out on this perilous road together. She felt alive. Her life was held in the balance and she knew it, but she felt no need to shy from the realisation that time spent with Luca was somehow essential to her feeling of being alive. She put her head on his chest.

'You said something about mines.'

'What?'

'Last night, before you had your wicked way with me, you said something about mines.'

'I did, didn't I? Well, I was referring to this one in particular.'

Luca tilted the tablet so that JJ could see the enormous opencast mine with titanic earthmovers descending its tiered levels.

'Where is that?'

'Nowhere.'

'Nowhere?'

'It's not shown on any government records, maps, on any company's books, but somehow it happens to be on Butakhan's personal laptop, with map references showing exactly where this non-existent mine can be found.'

'Does it show up on satellite images?'

He smiled at her quick mind and switched apps. Google Earth threw up an image of a vast green mountainous landscape, which Luca zoomed in on until a brown patch grew and grew; a spartan town—linked by a road to an opencast mine populated by small blocks—became visible. JJ pointed at them.

'What are they?'

'They're the earthmovers, the vehicles used to move whatever it is they're mining.'

'You can see them on satellite images?'

'Those trucks are as big as houses.'

'OK, wow. Why do you think the mines are important?'

'Because they don't officially exist, and because Butakhan cares about them, and—'

'And what?'

Luca went quiet, he was troubled and might as well admit it: 'Because we haven't got much to go on.'

She looked at him sympathetically. 'So it could be a dead end?'

'Or it could be everything.'

'But it could be a dead end?' He conceded her point with a shrug. 'Did you find anything else on the laptop?'

Luca could not hide the dissatisfaction on his face. 'There's a cargo flight from Yangon to Pyongyang tomorrow night.'

'Is a flight from Myanmar to North Korea suspicious, apart from the fact that anything to do with Butakhan merits suspicion automatically?'

'Maybe, when it's unscheduled, and when North Korea is sabre-rattling against Japan, and when the US deploys both its Third and Seventh Fleets to the region and begins flying reconnaissance flights along its borders.'

Luca switched apps to the BBC News website and JJ read the story. There was a question she wanted answered. She propped herself on one elbow to look at her partner properly.

'Do you really think Butakhan is working with the North Koreans? What could he be delivering to them that would help them?'

'No, I think he's working for himself. I'm not assuming he's trying to help them. What I'm trying to figure out is what he's got to gain by this whole episode, I need to...' He trailed off, in two minds about the logic of his thinking.

'You need to what?'

'I need to speak to my godfather.'

She smiled crookedly at him, unsure what he meant.
'Spiritual doubts?'
  'Political uncertainties.'

16
The Apostolic Palace, Vatican City

Sir Stephen Devereux worked at an ornate antique desk, surrounded by exquisite decor, in a room overlooking St Peter's Square. For many years, he had argued to have the grandiose room, with its grandiose scale, converted to a more communal use, his office moved somewhere more modest, but other forces at work in the office of the Papacy were concerned about the precedent that would set and found reasons to defer any consideration of such matters.

At present, he was writing to the American ambassador to the UN over a stance the Americans had taken that had made him decidedly unhappy. He found himself increasingly unhappy with the American empire's determination these days to show off to the world that its reach was greater even than that of God. He wrote with a fountain pen, deciding long ago not to allow himself to be swept up in technology. Recent revelations concerning the scale of snooping by America and the UK into online communications made his preference for the relative security of the handwritten word the more satisfying.

The window was open and a mild winter breeze could occasionally be felt, his papers lifting at the corner. He looked up, thinking he should close the window, when his mobile phone began to beep. As he picked it up Devereux realised it wasn't the ringtone of an incoming voice call but a video call. This caused him to stiffen, alert to a problem he had yet to discover. Only one person could contact him this way, the person who had set up the application for him. He followed the instruction to swipe the screen, handling the action like the Luddite he was.

'Stephen, how are you?'

The cardinal seldom displayed pleasure but he did so now, secretly relieved. 'Worried, Luca, my boy.'

'Oh, what about?'

'About *you*.'

'In which way?'

'In *every* way. Is it true you disregarded the direct orders of our General Counsel to return after your trip to Russia?'

'Well—'

'Is it true that you attracted *attention* by your activities in Shanghai?'

'When you say attention—?'

'And is it true that you did not board the plane that was sent to Yangon to collect you?'

'That was for me?'

Sir Stephen felt himself relax now that he had issued his wayward godson with a ticking off. It seemed to have become a ritual greeting between them in recent years.

'All of that aside, Stephen, how are you?'

The cardinal sighed; aware that to pursue his grievances now would be an indulgence given the plight Luca was probably in. Seeing the Swiss man's face on the screen of his phone was, he could not deny it, a blessed relief. 'No, Luca, how are you? Or perhaps I might ask *where* are you?'

'I'm good, but are you asking my location in confidence or for the rest of the Families?'

Sir Stephen's brow furrowed to hear his caution, but he knew that his godson had said it for a reason, which was an explanation in itself. 'Assume my confidence until I say otherwise.'

'Your godson is travelling in Thailand.'

The cardinal's chest heaved. They had a code only used in times of trouble, to alert the other to danger. If either of them used the third person to refer to himself, it signalled that they were unable to talk freely. Sir Stephen wanted to know why, but knew he couldn't ask openly.

'Are you safe, Luca?'

'As long as nobody knows my whereabouts, but that's not why I rang. Butakhan has a cargo plane travelling from Yangon to Pyongyang tomorrow evening and I was wondering if you might know why?'

The cardinal shook his head. 'There has been no discussion about this matter as far as I'm aware.'

'What's the real situation in North Korea?'

'Not good, my boy, not good: Butakhan is offering to bring about regime change and has offered it up to the Americans in exchange for cutting their ties with the Seven Families.'

Luca was rocked by the news.

'So the deaths of Franz and Raoul, and the attacks on me, were all part of a bigger plan then. But why, why does he want to isolate us?'

'We don't know. Herr Hesse is looking into it as we speak.'

Luca was shaking his head. 'But North Korea hasn't got any natural resources to speak of, how would America profit from a war on that scale?'

'On the contrary, Luca, we hear from our sources within the Council on Foreign Relations that Butakhan has proof that North Korea owns huge deposits of rare earth minerals.'

Luca's eyes widened. 'The kidnapped geologists—'

'Exactly. It must have been Butakhan, and he must have learned what they had discovered.'

'And apart from the sheer value I assume the US is keen to break China's monopoly on this market?'

'I fear you have identified the exact issue. It will be a terrible war, Luca, and I hesitate to guess at the number of North Koreans that will die in the process.'

They looked at each other, Luca thinking it over. 'So perhaps, for now, Butakhan's just flying hard cash over to buy everything North Korea is willing to produce?' He nodded to himself, the pieces dropping into place. 'How are the Families?'

'Concerned. They fear a period of retreat.'

'Because of Butakhan? Are the Americans really thinking of turning on us?'

'Let's just say that sometimes discretion is the better part of valour. One way or another, our Mongolian friend is proving an existential threat to our kin; survival is our priority. Why don't you come back, Luca? There are people, governments, we can talk to about this. Nobody is asking you to put yourself at risk.'

Luca felt odd even as he answered. 'You said it yourself, Stephen, the Families are in trouble.'

'And is it up to you to save them Luca?'

The Swiss man felt the sharpness of the question and his voice rang cold as he spoke. 'Who said I could save them?' Then he was almost regretful. 'I'd better go.'

'Your godfather has a question for you, Luca.'

The young man paused, alive to their collusion.

'Do you intend to intercept the cargo bound for Pyongyang?'

Luca paused before replying, carefully choosing his words. 'I think, given recent experiences that would be unwise. So, no, I will not.'

Sir Stephen nodded. 'Goodbye, Luca.'

'Goodbye Stephen.'

They watched each other for a moment before Luca killed the call.

JJ watched Luca as he stared at his phone's blank screen. 'You lied to him about where we were.'

Luca turned to her as if he had forgotten she was there. 'He knew.' He tapped a thoughtful finger on the phone's screen and hoped the second lie had worked.

★　　★　　★

Back in Yangon, Scarlett was working her way around Butakhan's body; gently placing kisses with her pillow-soft lips around his neck and down his chest and torso, exposed by the open silk dressing gown he wore, as he lay on the bed in the presidential suite on board *Charon*. Scarlett's generous breasts threatened to burst out of the low-cut bra at any moment. Butakhan focused on her breasts hoping, but failing, to become aroused. The Californian considered his physical state and pulled a sympathetic and patient face.

'Don't worry, Buty, there's no rush. You relax.'

He turned his head from side to side, distractions flooding to the fore of his mind. 'It's not that.' On the table by the bed, his phone rang. He saw the name and snatched it up. 'Yes?'

The robotic voice was as emotionless as ever. 'Voss is in Thailand.'

Butakhan sat upright. 'Thailand? Why?'

'I don't know yet. You shouldn't expect him back any time soon.'

'Tomorrow evening?'

'No, apparently not. I will revert when I know more.'

'Good, good, you've done well.' The Mongolian man was conscious that he was overpraising because the news was so welcome to him.

Butakhan set the phone aside and considered the erotic vision on all fours at the end of his bed, her breasts brushing his knees. He felt a wave of arousal wash over him and moved forward while Scarlett raised a naughty eyebrow in response. 'Somebody's come out to play.'

17
Myitkyina, Myanmar

The city of Myitkyina had a population the size of a town and the mongrel feel of so many former colonial locations. The defining characteristic of Myanmar's most northerly conurbation was that it was fought over, but never held. This had never been truer than during World War II, when it was captured by the Japanese only to be taken by Allied Forces due to its strategic value. When the war was over, Myitkyina was abandoned overnight, the subsequent rebuild slow and low-key. It was a trading post, mostly jade, gemstones and heroin, but none of the money found its way into the city itself. Despite being three hundred kilometres from the most northern tip of Myanmar, Myitkyina was the end of the line: no trains travelled north of there. The only reasonable transport link was the road to China in the east; the road west to India was as neglected as the heroin addicts seen lingering in the cafés and on the street corners. But Luca wanted to travel north, on the worst road of all.

The bus station was next to the train terminal and JJ found her Mandarin useful in establishing that there was a bus to Putao, the last officially inhabited town, and the northernmost. The bus was full of miners returning from leave and Luca and JJ joined them, boarding warily. An emulsion paint had been used to cover the vehicle in the colours of the Myanmar flag: green, yellow, red and white. The bus looked like a pre-World War II hangover, from the days of British colonial rule.

As it spluttered out of the city, across a wooden bridge of questionable construction, JJ was surprised that Luca seemed not to share at least some of her concerns.

'You know, we'll be lucky to make Putao by sunset.'

Luca rolled up his jacket and positioned it as a pillow against the window. 'No. We'll be lucky to get there at all.'

JJ watched with mild incredulity at his insouciance as he made himself comfortable and shut his eyes for the journey ahead. She looked about her. To the other passengers they were objects of curiosity, but the men didn't eye her with the prurience she expected everywhere west of here. She met their smiles with a tight one of her own, then, feeling the fatigue from the journey, realised the wisdom of her travelling companion's decision. She nestled up against him and, having relaxed her body against the rhythmic thump of the poor road beneath, fell asleep.

Putao turned out to be a tiny airstrip with a village attached to it, but it also proved magnificent. To the north and to the west, the Himalayas reared up on the horizon and nothing but green rainforests surrounded them.

Half a day later, as the bus coughed its way out of the town without them, Luca and JJ disembarked to find themselves being watched by a small group of villagers looking after their roadside stalls.

'I thought we were travelling north?' JJ said.

Luca offered a warm smile to the growing crowd gathering about them. 'We are, but I'd rather arrive unannounced, just in case the alternative isn't too wise.'

'And we do that how?'

'It's not far, somebody will give us a ride.'

JJ looked around. There was little evidence of any houses beyond thatched roofs nestled into the hills. There was no lack of life, though, she could hear strange birds cawing all around them, the simian cries from hidden monkeys.

'Do you really think there are any cars in this village?'

'There's a road, isn't there?'

'Yeah, you said the road would be a nightmare, but it turned out to be fine once we left Myitkyina.'

'That's because it's new. I didn't even expect the bus to be taking people this far north, the old road used to be inaccessible except in summer.'

'So? Roads get built, don't they?'

'Around here, only when there's an economic reason to do so.'

'What do you mean?'

'I mean that whatever mine those men were travelling to will be producing enough valuable raw materials to build a brand new highway. And I think they're producing them for Butakhan.'

'Do you know what they are?'

'No, but I know a way to find out.'

The jeep that picked them up made the bus they had ridden in look like a Rolls Royce fresh off the production line. A World War II model, anything non-essential to its running was missing or adapted for other purposes elsewhere. The jeep's tyres were from a more modern model and its seats had been re-covered over time with a variety of national flags: a red British Burma flag, a blue one, a peacock-dominated State of Burma flag, and a mostly red Union of Burma flag.

'Colourful,' JJ said, amused, and quite taken with the exotic nature of the jeep's interior. What with there being no windscreen, she was grateful it could not exceed fifty kilometres per hour.

As the recently constructed road began to ascend into a valley and the colour of the landscape started to fade, the wildlife seemed to thin out and the green lustre of the natural habitat began to take on ashen shades.

JJ looked from the front passenger seat to her partner in the rear. 'The countryside looks sick, Luca.'

Luca didn't say anything at first. He was watching a malnourished stray dog down by the river they were driving alongside.

'Ask him if he knows why,' Luca said.

JJ asked the driver, but the man's body language told Luca he was dismissing their concerns even before JJ had begun to translate the exact reply. Luca shook his head, he got the gist, he said, and sat quietly looking out of the window at the increasingly withered plants, the dying trees, and the sheer soullessness of the landscape that was sunk into the bowl of greenery high above.

As they travelled over the crest of a hill, a small town emerged about a kilometre away before it quickly dropped out of sight again behind the landscape. Luca leaned forward and tapped the driver on the shoulder.

'Tíngzhǐ.'

The driver repeated the request to stop as a question, which Luca confirmed, and the man pulled over to the side of the road. Luca retrieved a fifty-dollar bill to pay him, but the driver waved it away, protesting vociferously. Luca was unable to understand his hybrid of Mandarin and Burmese.

'He's saying you've already paid him, you had an agreement.'

Luca went to put the money away and the driver nodded vigorously, almost offended. The passengers got out and the driver wasted no time in swinging the car round and heading back towards Putao.

JJ looked down at the two travelling bags. 'Not exactly going to carry off the backpacker look are we.' She smiled nervously at Luca.

'You OK?' he said.

'Is it alright to be nervous? I mean, here we are in the middle of nowhere, and nowhere turns out to be the world's end. If things go wrong how do we escape?'

Luca considered her with something close to admiration and affection, all rolled into one. 'You wouldn't be human if you weren't a bit nervous.' He leaned forward and kissed her, his friend growing two inches taller as he did so.

She looked into his warm eyes. 'So, are you nervous?'

'Let's not approach by the road until we know what we're walking into.'

He headed to the shallow river babbling past them.

JJ shook her head, not because he hadn't answered her question, but because he emphatically had.

The shallow mountain river rushed noisily over the rocks in an off-white froth. It was clear that a misstep when hopping from rock to rock would result in a very wet ending. Luca and JJ made the leap to the other side. The Chinese woman looked at the river, following its downstream course, the banks lifeless on both sides.

'Shouldn't that water be making the villagers in Putao sick?'

Luca looked along its southward trail. 'They must get their water from another source, or they would all be as dead as those trees. But all these rivers eventually run down through the main cities to the sea, so a lot of people are going to get pretty sick sometime soon, if they're not already.'

JJ stayed watching the river for some moments more before she dismissed her thoughts about it for another time. It was then that she noticed her partner had struck out in a new direction.

'Hey, the town's that way.'

'Yeah, but something's happening over there.'

No sooner had they left the rushing river than they could hear another sound coming from the other side of a low ridge.

As they walked closer, the sounds became clearer—heavy, industrial; machines, trucks. They had to scrabble between boulders to reach the lip of the ridge itself, approaching it cautiously, peering over together, both greeting what they saw with awestruck silence. Together they scanned the vast expanse rolling out beneath them, both staggered by the scale, both needing time to assimilate their discovery.

'So we found the mine then.'

Luca merely nodded in return. Not only was he astounded at finding an anonymous engineering project of this magnitude in such a remote part of the world, he was mesmerised by the scale of it compared to what he had seen before—even what he'd seen on the outdated satellite images.

The opencast mine was circular with a diameter of approximately three kilometres. Within this landscape, it stepped down in circles of ever-decreasing size, yet even the crater at the bottom was roughly half a kilometre wide. The steps, or levels, were also the haulage routes used by the leviathan-sized trucks, each step connected by a ramp.

Everything mechanical they could see was enormous. The dumper trucks, whose cabins were dwarfed by the vehicle itself, needed an access ladder. There were excavators with shovels like monstrous jaws that gorged the land. Outsized articulated trucks on impossibly large wheels trundled beetle-like between levels. Then there were dragline excavators, and mobile cranes with car-sized buckets swinging beneath. And on each step was the largest vehicle of all—the bucket-wheel excavators, superstructures that were stand-alone mining operations in themselves. As tall as a 30-storey building and longer than two football fields, these machines consisted of a series of booms: a bucket-wheel dug away at the wall of each level of the mine and sent the earth's minerals back along its own conveyor belts, into a discharge boom above a dumper truck. The effect was like one end of a suspension bridge with a wheel at the front.

'I'm going to say it if you don't—Wow!'

Luca nodded at that sentiment. 'Quite the operation.'

'How deep must that be?'

'I'd guess about a kilometre.'

'A *kilometre*?'

'If not more. I had to make a trip to Bingham Canyon just outside Salt Lake City once, which is the deepest opencast mine in the world. This isn't far off that. Bingham Canyon has been operating since 1906, but this can't be more than twenty years old. Somebody has been mining in a hurry.'

JJ looked at him incredulously. It took a while but eventually Luca noticed.

'What?'

'How do you know all this stuff?'

'What do you mean?'

'How can you just rattle off all this data, it's not normal.'

The Swiss man gave no clue as to his feelings about her observation, thinking for a moment.

'Where did you learn geography?' she asked.

'When I was studying glaciers I went to the Antarctic; when studying volcanoes I went to Vesuvius. I learned physics at CERN, I learned linguistics at MIT, and I learned every language I can speak in the country of origin.'

JJ was dumbfounded, not just at what she was hearing, but that Luca had opened up at all. It was the most he had volunteered since they'd met and it went part way—*part way*—to understanding him.

'That's some remarkable school. What were the other students like?'

'I wouldn't know—there weren't any.'

He gave her a cold smile and climbed back down the ridge to the river.

188

Dusk was falling as they approached the outskirts of town. They crouched down as two pickup trucks and a bus drove south on the road to Putao; then secured a position behind a raised boulder. First Luca, then JJ, scoured about for danger.

'What do you see?'

JJ, with the eyepiece of the telescopic rifle lens to her eye, scanned every street, door, and window. 'Grey people in a grey town.' She inspected the area some more before letting out a low, sad whistle. 'I've never seen such a colourless place.' She could see miners shuffling listlessly along in monochrome, the odd pick-up truck slowing as they crossed the street.

'What about soldiers? Anybody look like security?'

JJ shook her head. 'Not really, just all these lifeless people. They all look like zombies, Luca.' She pulled her eye from the lens. 'And that smell, what is that?'

'Look over to the left of the town.'

She did, uncertainly. 'You mean the warehouse?'

'Next to it.'

'Oh, Jesus, Luca. There are ponds full of… What colour is that?'

'Let's just call it puce. Some of the water from the river is being diverted for use in the hydro-metallurgical processing of the minerals in that warehouse, then collecting in those tailing ponds before overflowing back into the river. Somebody thinks they're diluting it enough to mean it doesn't matter, but I bet a quick analysis of medical records downstream would show an increase in lung and pancreatic cancer. Leukaemia too.'

JJ gave him a sly sideways look. 'Don't tell me, you studied a primer in medicine at Harvard?'

Luca slid off the rock to the ground. 'University College London.'

189

JJ followed suit, unsure if he was joking or not, before concluding—correctly—that he was not. 'Now what?'

'Now we see if we can book a room for the night.'

'Excuse me? And just how would that work?'

'The people back in Putao were running roadside stalls. That means they must get enough passing trade to sustain them, which in turn means plenty of people come and go up here. I suspect we could blend in well enough.'

'But haven't we seen enough?'

'What do you mean?'

'You saw details of the mine on Butakhan's laptop, you've seen the mine for yourself, why don't we just go back and report it?'

'I'm not interested in *what*, I want to know *why*, JJ. Why is he doing this? Why is he doing it in secret? Why is there no record of where these minerals end up? Why is there only this, and the details of tomorrow night's cargo flight on his laptop?'

'So what's your plan? To go into that hotel and ask if anybody can tell us what Butakhan's plans are for all this?'

Luca seemed to weigh it up for a moment. 'After we've booked a room yes, why not?'

'And what if we don't get to book a room; what if we walk into a trap? Who's going to come to our rescue all the way out here?'

Luca seemed to snap to, as if receiving a glass of water in the face. 'That's brilliant?'

'What is?'

'Your idea.'

'My idea?'

'Yes. It's going to stop us walking into a trap.'

'Really?'

Luca pulled a face.

Twenty minutes later Luca and JJ entered the town and felt that all eyes were on them. Every local they met was grey, it was hard to say where their clothes ended and their skin began. Each of them wore a mask and rag around their face, hanging like a neckerchief above their heavy shoulders; all of them appeared exhausted and some had toothless gums and bloodshot eyes. Clearly, everyone was sick.

The town comprised one main street with a barrack-style complex at the far end. There were no pavements and the road appeared to have been built cheaply, showing cracks and potholes. The only two-storey building in town was the hotel, while every other building was a cement-block affair that looked like it had been built in one day; any exterior decoration was limited to advertising, the shop name, or a thin coat of paint. There was only one building that had been given any attention so as to distinguish it and that was the local bar. The building had been painted bright yellow with a series of smiling Buddhas along one wall. Even here the noise was subdued.

To JJ's relief they reached the hotel. It was simple but acceptable, clean where the rest of the town was dirty, a notch above the rest of the vapid, rust-coloured, dust-covered buildings. Its fixtures and furnishings were curiously western, like a soulless roadside motel, and it took Luca a moment to realise that at some level this might be used for international customer meetings; perhaps even Butakhan himself would occasionally need to stay here, albeit in an emergency.

They were greeted by the first clean person they had seen since arriving in town. He was an old man wearing a dark purple suit. He looked at them with curiosity, his gaze falling on the crosses hastily made from sticks around their necks.

'Can I help you?'

Luca, who was surprised when the old man greeted him in English, spoke to him in a soft tone and gentle manner.

191

'We're from the Saint Peter's Missionary in Rome, and I believe you have a room for us?'

The hotel manager who had been wrong-footed by the novelty of their appearance, continued to smile. 'We haven't had any bookings.'

'Are you sure, our clerk said it was all done?'

'Really? We haven't had a booking. I would remember, they're quite rare.' The proprietor signalled around the empty lobby where they were standing.

'Oh dear, this is awkward. Do you have a room?'

'Yes. I have eight rooms.'

'Could we book one?'

The manager looked confused. 'Just one?'

'We're married.'

JJ hid her left hand in her right to cover her bare finger.

'Certainly, our biggest suite is free tonight.'

The manager placed their bags on the pleasingly large bed and walked over to a door on the far side of the room.

'You have an en suite with a shower and bath and there is the mini-bar. I am sorry to say the satellite television is not working. Can I bring you anything to eat, a bowl of fish soup, pork noodles, lamb curry?'

Luca and JJ gratefully chose the curry and the manager left with a smile, his mood enhanced by the 10,000 kyat note Luca had handed him.

Luca leaned his back against the door and looked at JJ on the bed.

'So, *husband*, what now, should we ask the manager if he can tell us Butakhan's master plan or see if anybody in the local bar knows?'

Luca dropped his head onto his chest, feeling the fatigue of the past few days, tired of the implications of JJ's analysis: they'd arrived at a dead end. Maybe this really was a false flag;

maybe while they were up in the north of Myanmar all the real action was taking place in the south. He wasn't sure of anything beyond the knowledge that he wanted to sleep.

'How about we eat and go to bed?'

JJ could see that his exhaustion matched her own, and felt a rush of protective affection for him. She stood up from the bed and approached him. Looking up into his tired face, she smiled, taking the cross he had fashioned from sticks on the edge of town between her fingers, eyeing it before looking back at him.

'I think that's the best idea you've had in a while.'

★   ★   ★

Downstairs, the manager stepped into the compact office behind the reception area and sat at a small computer. He considered something, agonised over it, and then finally decided to do it.

He pulled out his mobile phone and hit a number on speed dial.

★   ★   ★

Butakhan was enjoying a cocktail in the lounge area on the top deck of *Charon* with Scarlett, when Jean Picardie approached them.

'Sir?'

The Mongolian man was slightly drunk and wished business would stay at bay tonight. 'What is it, Jean?'

'I've just had a call from the hotel manager near the mine in Kachin State; he says a man and woman have just checked in.'

Butakhan waited for more.

'I think it could be Voss.'

The Mongolian man was bothered by this. 'I've been told by my best source that he's in Thailand.'

'Can we risk that, sir? If he discovers what—'

'OK, OK.' Butakhan could feel his irritation and stress rising. 'What are you proposing?'

Jean flicked his head in the direction of the helipad at the rear of the boat. 'I'll take the helicopter up at first light, just to be sure.'

'But I need you for the flight tomorrow night—'

'It only takes three hours to get there. If it is Voss, there is nowhere to hide, and no way of escaping. Either way, I'll be back by sunset tomorrow.'

Butakhan knew it was the right thing to do, but decided to take his time considering it to remind Jean that he, Butakhan, held the wisdom between them; he was the architect of his organisation's success. Nevertheless, he liked Jean, admired his ambition and hunger to rise as high as he could. He needed people like him—so long as they could be managed.

'OK. First thing, but come right back, there's a lot to do. What will you do if it is him?'

Jean shrugged. 'Kill him, of course.'

★　　★　　★

The light of the full moon was gently diffused by the red dust from the nearby mine. It was a twenty-four-hour operation and when occasional pickup trucks had ceased to travel along the main street, work on the site could be heard with surprising clarity: the grind of the bucket-wheel excavators gorging at the earth, the occasional clank of vehicles trundling along the spiral of roadways. One of these sounds, a dream, or the absence of anybody in the bed next to her, woke JJ from a deep sleep. She patted the blankets on the empty side of the bed then sat up with disorientated alarm to see somebody sitting on a chair by the table in front of the window. It was Luca, wearing a dressing gown, sitting in the cold glow of the red moon, staring out of the window.

'You OK?'

Luca looked back at her. 'Couldn't sleep, sorry.'

She rolled her neck loose as she roused herself. 'Everything alright?'

'Fine, go back to sleep.'

JJ was awake now and got up, using the sheet as a make-shift dressing gown. She crossed the room to sit opposite Luca whose computer tablet was before him on the table. She was silent, but followed his eyes out of the window to see lines of men walking listlessly to work in the predawn hour, tired before they had even begun. It seemed to JJ that the people started the day as they would end it, grey, and she was struck by the scene's resemblance to some nightmarish regime; men marching, reduced to ghouls, living to work, owned by a private mine.

'What if everything we're doing doesn't matter?' Luca seemed far away when he spoke, almost as if speaking to himself.

'What do you mean?'

'I mean what if instead of trying to save the world, what if we should be trying to save one small part of it? What if we just cleaned up this town; just shut down the mine and gave the people something else to do? Gave them the chance to work on a modern farm, build things, or just do anything other than digging up poisonous earth for the rest of their lives.'

She watched him watching the men tramp by and wondered what his childhood had been like. Hers was one of rebellion, but his had been one of endless schooling and training—conformity.

'You couldn't,' JJ said.

When JJ didn't continue, he looked up at her. 'Couldn't what?'

'You couldn't stop your life.'

'Why, because it's the only life I know?'

'No, but if you worried about every person you ever met you'd go mad.'

'Maybe not caring about anyone at all is what's driving me mad.'

JJ felt a stab of pain. 'Don't you? Don't you care about anyone?'

Luca caught the meaning of her words, the look on her face, and almost laughed. He reached a hand across the small table and took JJ's in his. 'Next time I get maudlin smash something over my head will you?'

JJ was cheered by his show of affection, rewarding him with a mischievous grin. 'You kidding me? We wouldn't have any furniture left.' Luca smiled, but JJ could see he was forcing himself not to look out of the window. 'What's bothering you, really?'

'I don't know.'

'Honest?'

'No, I mean, really, I don't know. I don't know why I came all the way up here.'

'Because of Butakhan—'

'What of Butakhan? I've been told not to deal with Butakhan but I'm still dealing with Butakhan.'

'Because you care.'

'But about what?'

'Would you like me to smash the chair or the table over your head?'

Luca smiled fleetingly. 'I've dragged you all the way here, but for what? I've just spent the last two hours going over everything: Franz's pictures of the dock, the details of the mine, Shanghai, Russia, all the news coming out of North Korea, and nothing. Nothing more than a gut instinct.'

'Gut instincts are OK.'

'No they're not, JJ. They are exactly what I was trained to ignore. I was trained to follow the facts, follow a process.'

'Maybe you're better than that.' She stared at him, challenging him to challenge himself.

'Or maybe I'm worse.'

'Worried you're not as exact as a Swiss watch, is that it?'

He wiped his face with his hands and sighed. Then a resigned smile of sorts worked its way across his face. 'Let's get breakfast and then go.'

'Go where?'

'Go back to Ticino.'

'But they'll crucify you.'

The look he wore was one of resignation. 'Only if I want to be the Broker.'

Either breakfast was surprisingly good or Luca and JJ were very hungry; they devoured the fried chapatis and naan bread with fervour. The dining room was just off the lobby with half a dozen tables. Like the rest of the hotel, it felt like an American motel right down to the Formica furniture. It was pleasant enough, though, and to their relief did not face the street. As he reached for yet more naan bread, Luca shook his head at the flavours he was enjoying.

'Noodles last night, chapatis this morning, I could get used to this.'

'Well, squeezed between India and China, this part of Myanmar gets the best of both.'

'Switzerland is squeezed between Italy and France, and all we've managed is Emmental cheese.'

JJ grinned at his light mood; while she was sad that they had reached the end of the road, she felt glad that he felt unburdened, even if he had loaded the burden on himself in the first place. She resisted the urge to start planning their post-Switzerland trip even though, privately, her mind was working overtime on the well-earned break they would surely be enjoying.

The door opened and a trio of Burmese men entered, aiming for a table in the far corner. They were slightly less unwashed looking than the army of miners they had seen so far and wore faded t-shirts and jeans; Luca thought the two wearing baseball caps were probably management. JJ, being the first woman they had seen in weeks and a jaw-droppingly beautiful one at that, received many discreet looks from them; she sensed their eyes, but it didn't bother her; she had ogled men herself, and so long as they left it at ogling she didn't consider it a crime. The men nodded respectfully at Luca, which seemed like typical patriarchal behaviour until Luca and JJ remembered they were wearing crucifixes. Luca smiled genially at them in his best imitation of a benign minister.

They took their seats. Then everything stopped. Everything.

Luca looked at the wall beside them, his peripheral vision telling him that he had seen what he had seen. And JJ knew enough to know that something had punched the air out of him.

'What?'

'Don't look now, but check out the one with the Elvis t-shirt and baseball cap.'

JJ had spent too many years playing poker against crooks and spotting their accomplices around casinos to require a lesson in reading a room, and registered him without being seen.

'Yeah?'

'The baseball cap.'

She stole a look at it, emblazoned USS *Missouri BB-63*. She searched for the design in her memory. She knew she had seen it somewhere, but she couldn't place where.

'Explain.'

'It's the cap worn by one of the geologists kidnapped from the cargo ship on their way to Japan a week ago.'

'I can't believe it.'

'Neither did I at first, but you can't buy those things; you get them for serving on the ship.'

'No, I mean I can't believe that was just a week ago.'

She wasn't joking; she was shocked, astounded by how much had happened without her realising she was even on a journey. She felt curiously lost, adrift. Only now—when it was about to begin again—did JJ realise how much she wanted it to stop. The ride was over for her—Luca had said so himself—and she wanted time out. Time with Luca, but time out all the same. It would have to wait.

'So what do we do?'

'I need to follow them, see if I can find the geologists.'

'Please don't, Luca.'

He looked at her calmly, but unemotionally, and she recognised the silent resolve.

'OK. And me?'

'You need to cause a distraction.'

She eyed him sceptically. 'What sort of a distraction?'

'Well…' It was delicate and his face showed it. 'You might want to take that cross off for a start.'

Luca stopped by the store, made a purchase, and then headed for the town's watering hole. He was not surprised to find that not only was it open 24/7, but that it was populated by a group of men fresh off their shift and treating 7 a.m. as the start of their night's drinking.

He stood at the bar nursing the strongest beer his lips had ever tasted, dreading to think what toxin went into it to give it that kick. The room was full, every table and stool occupied by an exhausted worker, many drinking in preparation for the shift ahead. The Swiss man was first the subject of much interest and then mild amusement when people saw his cross and heard the rumour about missionaries pitching up in their godforsaken town. One table in earshot erupted into dark laughter when one of the party quipped: 'Maybe he does miracles, maybe he'll make our water drinkable.'

He had to wait at the bar for ten minutes, dishing out unassuming smiles, but eventually it happened. A miner, covered in rust-coloured dust, entered the bar and made for the toilet. Luca gave it fifteen seconds then followed.

The toilet was out back, through a door opening into a freestanding cement-block building that housed a row of cubicles and a metal communal urinal. No women's toilet was needed. The miner was just finishing urinating when Luca entered. Met with a beatific smile from the fake minister he hastily zipped up his fly with a coy and rather uncomfortable look. He passed the stranger and made for the safety helmet and goggles he had left on a coat hook by the door, but never reached them – the chop to the back of his neck made sure of that.

Luca caught him as he slumped forward and dragged him back into one of the cubicles. Satisfied that the miner still had a pulse, he slid a hundred dollar bill into his pocket. By Luca's estimation, the Burmese would be out cold for around four hours, by which time his discovery would prove academic. Luca closed the door on the cubicle and used a multi-tool screwdriver to lock the door from the outside before removing his cross and shirt to reveal the cheap white t-shirt bought from the store. He folded his shirt twice and employed it as a facemask, then grabbed the miner's helmet and goggles and left.

Behind the toilet block, Luca covered himself in dust from head to toe until he and his clothes were the colour of the greyish-red earth. Then he headed down the road to the mine a kilometre outside town.

More than once, as Luca walked the road to the mine, another miner skipped past him, in a hurry to reach the site. This was wildly at odds with the lifeless display he had witnessed so far and he began to wonder what could possibly be causing the excitement. His first—and major—fear was that JJ had messed up and that his plan was no good. Perhaps, she had gone ahead only to fumble the plan, putting herself at risk; she may even have been dragged off for questioning. Then, suddenly, he wondered how different this would be to the experience in Russia: sex-starved men suddenly in possession of a beautiful woman cut off from any contact; JJ helpless in the face of whatever they wanted to do. He could not believe he had let her take the risk—had *asked* her to take the risk. There were so many other ways to achieve what he needed, if only he had been patient. The idea he had come up with may have exposed her to absolute danger.

He heard voices. Shouts. Cries. He began to trot, turning a corner. There she was, on the back of a pickup truck, surrounded by almost a hundred miners railing their fists at her. Luca sprinted, nearing the back of the group. It was—

Better than he could have imagined.

'So I ask you all again, if I come here with my girls and we set up a nice comfortable house, you come visit us?'

Congregated next to the main entrance to the mine the men cheered at her suggestion, the mood brighter than it had ever been. JJ continued in her deliberately simple mix of Mandarin and Burmese.

'If we get lonely we leave.'

This brought an almighty—if good-natured—protest from the excited group. From her position on the back of the

201

pickup truck, JJ thought she recognised Luca in his disguise and inwardly relaxed; she could only keep them hooked for so long. She was certain it was Luca when he ignored her and the crowd, and went round to the back of the group instead, making his way into the opencast mine.

'Perhaps we give the first ten visits for free. Who want to be one of our first ten visitors?'

The clamouring became a roar as every man held up his hand to claim a place, many laughing, others more anxious.

But as Luca walked unchallenged through the gate, something happened. One by one, in quick succession, everybody looked back to the town, and the good mood fell away in an instant.

A helicopter was coming in, and something about it made the men uncertain, a collective look of nervousness dampening the good mood. JJ could not understand how the mood had switched; she still aimed to execute her side of the plan.

'Maybe we give first twenty men a free visit?'

The men were walking away as Luca came back through the gate to warn JJ. She cast a worried look at him, which he acknowledged by flicking his head in the direction of the town. She took the hint and stepped down to the road.

Luca watched the helicopter swoop round the edge of the mine. He noted the model, an MD 600N, and then the colour: black. It was the helicopter from Butakhan's mega-yacht.

Which meant it was trouble.

Luca picked up his pace and made his way back through the gates to the mine.

The mine had at least twelve levels leading steeply down the crater, a metallic-blue lake at the bottom. The haulage roads leading up and down were the width of a six-lane motorway but still only wide enough for two scaled-up vehicles to pass side by side.

The men were flooding back to their posts and machinery, which made Luca's hope of a relatively uninterrupted inspection of the site impossible. On the top four steps, where mining was in progress, a gargantuan bucket-wheel excavator worked away at the seams while dumper trucks with wheels the size of double-decker buses ferried rocks back to the entrance. Clouds of dust were everywhere, touching everything.

Luca, his face covered by his impromptu mask, goggles, and helmet was not worried about being spotted straight away but he knew he had to look busy, or risk looking conspicuous as he interrogated the cavernous hole about him. There were several portakabins near the entrance, many stacked on top of each other, but each seemed to be busy with people coming and going. His instinct told him that the geologists—if, indeed, they were here—would not be hidden somewhere so public. He fell back to his earlier plan: he would follow the miner wearing the USS *Missouri* baseball cap. Once the mob had disbanded, he saw his target jump into a Land Rover Defender and scoot off to the far side of the mine. Then Luca saw something else: two portakabins, one on top of the other, with two guards stationed outside.

Luca calculated that half the distance round the top of the mine was over four and a half kilometres. He asked himself the next question: even if he found the geologists, how would he get them out? Then he asked himself the question he had been putting off asking: if that was Butakhan's helicopter just landing, who was in it?

He looked along the dirt road arcing round in a wide circle to the far side. Halfway round a titanic dumper truck was being loaded by a bucket-wheel excavator, a dozer parked up beside them. Then, further round, just before the portakabins another, smaller bucket-wheel excavator, this one only the length of a football pitch, stood parallel to the road, clawing away at the mine face. The occasional pickup truck ferried between these sites and when Luca saw them he had an idea.

As one of these trucks approached him, coming up from the level below, Luca held up a hand to halt it.

Jean Picardie's black Toyota pickup stopped at the main gate in a swirl of dust and the guards on duty ran to the driver's door. The hairless French-Algerian looked at them with dark suspicion, doubting their competency, as well as half-believing, half-hoping to find Luca present.

'Have you seen either a European man or a Chinese woman here today?'

The skinny Burmese sentry tripped over his words with fear. 'No, I mean, yes.'

'Yes or no?'

'There was a woman here this morning, Chinese, trying to sell... to the men.'

'What about the man?'

'I, I don't know.'

'What do you mean *you don't know?*' said Picardie, furious that the security practices he instilled had been abandoned.

'Well, the men all came in together today.'

The French-Algerian could not begin to comprehend how the number-one rule had been broken. *Every person is to show ID on entry on every single shift.* He repeatedly banged his steering wheel at the news, shredding the nerves of even the mercenary beside him in the passenger seat.

Picardie closed his eyes to calm himself. When he opened them again, he looked with unnerving directness at the shaking sentry.

'Could he have entered the site this morning?'

'Well—'

'*Could he...?*'

'Yes. Yes, he could have.'

Picardie nodded once, emphatically, to let the guard see this was all he had wanted to ascertain in the first place. Then he shot him.

The bullet, like the gun, seemed to come out of nowhere, the back of the guard's head exploding as the force of the impact lifted him back off his feet and into the sentry hut itself.

The half-dozen mine workers nearby immediately froze with fear. Picardie spoke with a restrained scream.

'*Nobody* is to come in or out of this mine until *I* say so, do you understand?'

The Burmese men all nodded vigorously, immediately coming together as a team of sentries at his command.

He turned to his sidekick. 'Get out, commandeer a car, and search the left-hand side, I'll take the right. Find him, kill him.'

'Yes sir.'

'If he escapes you…' His junior was already out of the car, he did not need to hear the rest and the look said it all.

Picardie drove off into the violent cloud of dust thrown up by the wheel-spinning truck. Once he reached the top step of the mine he eased the Sig Sauer P226 pistol back into his thigh holster. He was set on making his way to the portaka-bins, on the far side. As he drove he reached behind the passenger seat and lifted up an Uzi sub-machine gun, hungry to use it. Picardie knew that to kill Luca, in spite of Butakhan's intelligence that he was in Thailand, would be a resounding feather in his cap. He also knew that he deeply disliked his victim. By escaping Picardie in Shanghai and Yangon, the Swiss man had humiliated him. Picardie struggled to fight down his excitement and impatience.

Luca pulled what he could from the seats behind him as he drove the white pickup truck to the far side of the mine. The high visibility jacket he found came as something of a surprise to him in this apparently health-and-safety-free mine, but he gratefully yanked it out and spread it across his co-matose passenger. He drove as quickly as he could without attracting attention.

Attention.

That was the problem nagging at him. There were hundreds of men here, and he did not expect their loyalties to rest with him if it was to kick off. In his rear-view mirror, Luca spied a black Toyota a kilometre back and could not help feeling concerned that Butakhan or one of his men was on his trail.

As he approached the trio of mining vehicles, Luca had a brainwave which he was certain would draw all the miners away. He slowed as he weaved between the behemoth of a dumper and its dozer counterpart. Then he stopped beside the dozer next to the mine face and got out of his borrowed vehicle. The dumper truck was sitting across from the bulldozer in the middle of the haulage road waiting for another load from the bucket excavator. The dozer looked like a steampunk locomotive engine with an improbably large eight-metre-wide blade at the front.

Without missing a beat, Luca clambered up the caterpillar tracks of the stationary dozer then onto the side of the cab itself. The driver, who was sitting back enjoying a cigarette with the door wide open, was too surprised by the appearance of a man at his cab door to register that anything untoward was happening. Luca grabbed him a second later, taking him by the front of his shirt and deftly tossed him from the cabin as if he weighed the equivalent of a bag of shopping.

Before the man had hit the ground, Luca was in the driving seat. He thrust forward the two levers that controlled the caterpillar tracks, guiding the blade with the joystick on his right. For a 340-tonne vehicle, it was surprisingly responsive,

Luca thought, as he directed it at the stationary dumper truck opposite. Moving at about three times the speed of walking pace, the dozer continued inexorably towards the rear of the truck; the driver, not having noticed the dozer coming at him, did not know what had hit him until it hit—*smack*—with the blade and began to nudge the massive dumper towards the edge of the kilometre-deep hole.

Jean could not believe his eyes: ahead, he could see a bulldozer pushing a dumper truck towards the edge of the road, forcing it over the edge. The driver, panicking against the superior power of the vehicle behind him had no time to attempt to reverse into it; instead, clambering out of his cab he performed a fire fighter's slide down the ladder. The truck driver hit the ground just as the wheels of the vehicle rolled over the edge of the precipice. The dozer paused as the rear of the dumper rose into the air and then the dozer rammed it again, the bottom of the dumper scraping the edge of the road until the sheer force of gravity caused it to tip over the edge of its own accord. The French-Algerian mercenary drove as fast as he could towards the incident. An electrifying excitement animated him, he had his man now, and a bloodlust, the permission to kill, spurred him on. Lifting the Uzi into his hand and swinging it out of the window, he watched with macabre fascination as the 200-tonne dumper tipped over the edge. It went crashing down to the next level, where it rolled over in strange, lumbering, slow motion, before rolling down to the next level, a process it would repeat all the way down, to the inky lake a kilometre down below.

From where he sat in the cab, Luca saw the Toyota bearing down on him and the miners abandoning their posts to gape at the tumbling truck. Chaos and confusion were Luca's friends right now.

The Toyota was approaching Luca fast from the left; bullets from an Uzi sprayed at his vehicle as the driver leaned out of the window. The Swiss man had been ready for this: he span the dozer on the spot as fast as he could so that the blade faced the oncoming car; the bullets pinging off it harmlessly. The car slowed to a halt, kicking up a cloud of dust. When it cleared, Luca recognised the driver straight away as the bald mercenary from Butakhan's office.

As the haulage road was wide enough for the dozer and three normal car widths, Luca had guessed at his antagonist's next manoeuvre. The Toyota backed up and tried to pass between the dozer and the face of the mine, but as it did so, Luca was already reversing. He veered into the wall, almost catching the pickup truck. The Toyota braked and the dozer continued back on the road that would lead round to the bucket-wheel excavator, past which nothing would be able to pass.

Picardie let the Toyota fall back, twenty metres short of the reversing blade, keeping pace with it. The French-Algerian guessed that his opponent's plan was to get to the portakabins—presumably by foot at some stage, given the roadblock caused by the bucket-wheel excavator ahead. He cast a look back over his shoulder and saw miners swarming down to the stricken vehicle, all work suspended by the drama. Picardie pulled a walkie-talkie from between the seats.

'Nicolas?'

After a pause and a burst of static, his accomplice broke through. 'Sir?'

'Make your way clockwise to the bucket-wheel excavator on the top level and meet me there.'

'Yes sir.'

Picardie dropped the comms unit back down between the seats. A glance to his left showed a red Toyota kicking up dust as it raced round the far side of the mine.

He decided it was time: he dropped the car's gears and made a dash round the left side, between the dozer and the edge of the road. Luca, though, was alert to the move and veered the dozer backwards recklessly towards the edge, the gap narrowing as the car sprinted past. The Toyota scraped along the caterpillar wheels, sparks flying, as Picardie tried to navigate the shrinking gap. Then, sensing the space was too small, he hit the brakes. The dozer continued and slammed itself into the space where Picardie would have been, the French-Algerian spooked by the near-death escape.

'*Lunatic.*'

He watched, as the dozer lost no momentum, nearing the bucket-wheel excavator where even it would have to stop: the mighty dozer was no match for the networks of beams atop the caterpillar-mounted powerhouse, itself the size of a large hotel.

One thing was clear—Luca Voss had almost reached this behemoth of a machine and once he got there he would be trapped between Picardie and his associate. From his desperate measures to outwit them, Picardie guessed Luca was unarmed and out of ideas. Picardie was in agony: should he kill him outright or torture him to death as a punishment for evading him; perhaps he should torture him in front of the miners to focus their minds and demonstrate his leadership skills to Butakhan.

The agony.

The agony of choice.

Luca looked back and saw he'd reached a dead end. The bucket-wheel excavator blocked his path. He had hoped a plan would suggest itself, but, on the evidence, it had not. He weighed up his options: an immoveable force behind him, a deadly one in front.

He reached the leviathan of a vehicle behind him and stopped. It had happened. He had finally run out of road.

The world's largest bucket-wheel excavators are the length of two football pitches. The one blocking Luca's path was more modest, merely the size of one. It rested on two enormous sets of caterpillar tracks that supported a power plant the length of a tennis court and half as tall again; this powered the excavator and received materials mined by the enormous wheel comprising a dozen digger-buckets. These buckets fed a conveyor belt, which then sent the materials back towards a jaw-crusher above the power plant that pummelled the rock to nothing. These products were then taken along another conveyor belt at the rear where they were discharged to piles for collection in the machine's wake. The two booms jutting from the power plant—the bucket-excavator at the front and the discharge boom at the back—were suspended, like a bridge, by thick steel cables from a superstructure above the plant housing. Around all this was a network of ladders, steps, and gangways. The machine was specially modified to accelerate Butakhan's mining operation, his own plans extending far beyond maximum profitability. This mine's purpose was more than just to collect raw materials, it was intended to change the course of history.

Luca stopped reversing the dozer a few metres from the excavator and saw Picardie's Toyota come to a stop ten metres in front of him. For a fleeting moment, he had been tempted to drive towards the French-Algerian but saw the foolhardiness of it immediately.

So instead he bolted.

The Swiss man threw the door of the cab open, ran along the side of the vehicle, and then leapt off the rear onto the railings of one of the excavator's gangways. Picardie was immediately out of his car and running round the huge blade of the dozer. He saw Luca running to his right and sprayed bullets after him sending sparks flying near the Swiss man just as he dipped into a recess in the superstructure. Picardie strapped the Uzi over his shoulder before mounting the side of the dozer in pursuit. What had been a guess before, he now knew for certain: his enemy was unarmed.

Reaching the recess, Picardie discovered his prey had disappeared up a ladder. Leaping up two rungs at a time, he found himself halfway up the plant that powered the monstrosity he had boarded. Luca was nowhere to be seen. He paused to listen but hearing anything proved impossible above the sound of the engines. Then Picardie caught a glimpse of Luca leaping over a gap above him. He raced after him.

The operator's cabin, though minuscule by the standards of the vehicle, was considerably spacious. Apart from the relatively generous driver's hub, there was a wall covered with computer monitors that fed back with millimetre-accuracy the actions of the bucket-wheel up ahead, including the load it was under, degree of mine face penetration, and the volume mined per hour. It was these readings and others the Burmese operator was scrutinising when the door was pulled open, and a European man's face loomed large before him in the split-second before he blacked out.

Luca kept his claw-like grip on the man's shoulder as he guided him to the floor. Then he flicked his eyes from controller to controller, lever to joystick. He pulled some levers back from their neutral position as far as they would go then slapped a joystick to the left. The power plant fired up with a deep rumble as a warning horn began to sound like an ominous, hellish chime. This was a warning that the enormous vehicle was about to start moving—albeit at one kilometre per hour. At the same moment, only slightly more quickly, the counterweighted beams, each jutting out forty metres in front and behind of the bucket-wheel excavator, began to rotate anticlockwise.

Then Luca started to get the hell out.

His plan was as desperate as it was simple: avoid confrontation on the grounds that his enemy was armed and creep back to the Toyota; then drive to the portakabins through the gap created by the moving leviathan from which he was trying to escape. He needed to find out if the hostages were being held there; then he needed to head back to town, get out, and call for help. Simple, or as he reminded himself, simple and desperate.

The facts of this endeavour were underlined for him the moment he emerged from the excavator's cabin to see Picardie leaping through the air from another section of the power plant, before landing gracefully a metre in front of him. Luca paused. He was a long way from escaping; he had walked directly into the path of his pursuer. He waited for Picardie to reach for the Uzi, planning to use the moment his enemy's hands were engaged to make a move, but he was wrong-footed again. Picardie wanted to play.

Luca barely blocked the first punch and the second found his face, forcing him to swing away with its momentum to avoid a third. The Swiss man stepped back, moving to find a surer footing, but aware that if he moved too far the temptation to shoot him might prove too great for Picardie. Thus, as Picardie approached he backed up at the same rate. Twice he threw feints and both times Picardie parried them without engaging fully. It was then Luca realised Picardie was relishing this. He didn't just want to kill him—he wanted to punish and dominate him in such a way that his superiority was established. The French-Algerian was bringing not just his mission to bear but his ego as well. With the expert martial arts moves and lightning reflexes Picardie had hinted at so far, Luca felt he might just be right to think this way.

As he stepped backwards, both of them watching for the next blow, Luca tried to remember what was behind him. A gangway for sure, but leading where? Was he about to find himself pinned down by his opponent? What did Picardie know that he did not? From the corner of his right eye, he saw the aperture of the jaw-crusher in the middle of the plant housing, large rocks being fed into it. Then, as he backed up farther, he found himself alongside the conveyor belt that travelled from the bucket-wheel way up front, the rocks thinning out now since the wheel itself had slowly rotated away from the face of the mine. All the while the deep horn sounded, warning that the vehicle was imperceptibly crawling.

Luca was aching to look back, aching to get a visual idea of the options open to him. Picardie, meanwhile, was confidence personified, enjoying his opponent's discomfort, enjoying every second of a kill he had clearly wanted since Shanghai, vengeance writ large across his face. All the time, Luca was aware that should he get any distance between himself and the man opposite, his attacker had recourse to a sub-machine gun.

Luca's peripheral vision on the left told him the option in that direction was no option at all: a twenty-five-metre drop to the ground below, a distance which was about to double as the beam they were on began to slowly arc out across the road below.

The two of them shuffled along the length of the gangway that ran parallel to the now empty conveyor belt. Occasionally, Picardie would throw punches or kicks, but never commit to engage fully in fight. Luca knew why: Picardie was gauging the quality of his adversary, wanting to delay committing just in case he lost his edge—and his chance to kill. Luca considered the bald dark-skinned man before him, toned like the war machine he evidently was; there was muscle where others had fat and the scars on his face were a testament to the battles he had seen. To Luca, though, his unwillingness to commit to a fight was something, he was confident, but not *supremely* confident.

Luca struck with a series of tight punches and kicks, elbows and knees flying at Picardie, who blocked everything. He managed to stop every punch before aiming a blow of his own at Luca, Picardie outmanoeuvring him with furious speed until, after ten seconds of blurred action, Luca jumped back from the fight.

It had been a trap. Picardie was a formidable fighter and had been luring him into the fray. Now Luca had done exactly what had been desired of him and displayed the limits of his fighting abilities.

Picardie grinned maliciously. 'If I'd known, I wouldn't have bothered bringing the gun.'

Luca pulled a less-than-happy face. 'If I'd known, I would have.'

This confession seemed to please the French-Algerian. 'You can have mine.'

'With pleasure.'

'If you manage to get it off me.'

Luca smiled in a way that suggested he was less than amused by his antagonist's wit. At that moment Luca's back came up against the rail; he had reached the end of the gangway. Backing off was no longer an option, and if Luca needed it, the malevolent glint in Picardie's eye was assurance that both of them were fully aware of the fact.

It seemed like a good time to react.

Again, Luca flew at Picardie with tight punches and kicks, slamming him with elbows and knees; this time faster, closer and harder. Each blow came faster than Picardie could block it, one strike after another finding his torso, face, legs, arms, head. Picardie realised that he had been played.

Finding a surer footing, Picardie leapt back and pulled out his Uzi only to be headbutted by Luca. As they both grappled with the gun Luca managed to rip it out of the French-Algerian's hands, but neither managed to keep hold of it as Luca succeeded in tossing it away onto the conveyor belt beside them. Picardie immediately fell back again.

The transformation of Luca from underdog to superior foe had infuriated Picardie, but he was even angrier with himself. He wished now that he had cut Luca down when he had the chance, drilled him full of bullets when he had a gun to hand. Now, his nose flowing with blood, he shuffled back quickly to create some space and reached around behind him to pull out a hunting knife, wasting no time in slicing the air with its serrated edge. The knife tipped the balance back to evens at least and Luca was forced to halt his advance.

With Luca a few steps back, Picardie had the opportunity he had been looking for. He grabbed a railing beside the conveyor belt and hopped up and over onto the moving machinery. Luca saw Picardie scrabbling to stand upright and get to the disappearing sub-machine gun, and felt he had no choice but to follow.

By the time Luca had leapt on to the two-metre-wide conveyor belt, Picardie was already ten paces ahead. Luca sprang towards him forgetting all sense of the danger at hand, his only goal to stop Picardie before he reached the gun. As Picardie dropped his knife on the walkway running parallel to the conveyor belt and lunged for the Uzi, Luca dived to tackle him. Bullets rebounded off the metal, as Luca bowled into Picardie and both of them crashed down to the conveyor belt, his assailant's back slamming the rollers beneath hard. Losing his hold, feeling his gun-hand being slammed down on the conveyor belt by Luca, Picardie refused to release his grip, knowing that Luca's focus on it represented his edge to win.

Looking up, Luca could see that the conveyor belt was twenty metres from the jaw-crusher; a gaping hole with two industrial-strength corrugated sheets in a vertical V-shape, one fixed, the other pneumatically pounding against it, anything falling into them mercilessly reduced to tiny pieces of rubble that fell into a small slot at the bottom.

Luca slammed his assailant's hand down three times to break the hold, the third his dumbest move all day: Picardie used the shifting of his weight to throw Luca over and pin him down. This was how they found themselves as they edged ever closer to the jaw-crusher banging away in front of them. Luca bucked, trying to shift the judo pin he was under, but Picardie had him fast. The French-Algerian looked up with glee at the machine coming ever nearer, calculating how late he could leave it to escape, the jaw-crusher his destination of choice for Luca.

Luca shifted, one way then another, trying to dislodge his assailant, who had him fixed fast, pinning down his arms with his body, the Uzi gripped between them.

The beam they were on had almost completely swept out across the lower level of the mine and back again. Meanwhile the miners, who had run to attend the dumper's tumble down into the pit lake became aware of the bucket-wheel excavator's huge, long caterpillar wheels beginning to appear over the edge of the haulage road it was on. Very slowly, it reached out over the step below.

The only hand Luca had any room to move was the one on the Uzi. To remove it was to give Picardie free reign to use the gun—or his hand. He could see the mercenary calculating the moment to escape the jaw-crusher. Luca seized his chance, releasing his grip on the Uzi and slapping his hand onto the automatic pistol on Picardie's thigh. Picardie raised the Uzi and brought it down on Luca's head. He did not feel Luca pull the trigger of his gun with his thumb, but he did feel the bullet blow off his kneecap. Luca launched his assailant up and over with his own bodyweight, hooking a foot on a railing, the conveyor belt scraping under him as he grabbed at another rail with his hands. Picardie landed by the mouth of the jaw-crusher, but grasped at Luca. Luca's foot gave way, forcing him to swing helplessly round, his legs hanging over the edge of the industrial crusher as he held the railing with one hand. Picardie managed to wrap his arms round Luca's shins, the pneumatically pumped panel of the jaw-crusher slamming the French-Algerian's shoes, but not smashing them; he was still high enough to escape, and Luca looked down at Picardie's imploring face.

'*Please.*'

Luca was holding on to the rail above him with both hands now, the conveyor dragging at him as it passed underneath and Picardie was threatening to pull him into the pit ahead. Luca tugged at his leg, pulled it back repeatedly, until it came free of Picardie's arms. He stared down at his enemy.

'Please? Is that what Franz said?'

Luca stamped his foot on the mercenary's face with all his strength but Picardie grabbed his foot again as he inched further along the conveyor. Then the crusher had Picardie in its teeth, his feet pounded, the pain blinding, all consuming, as he screamed like a beast possessed. Luca wriggled farther away, Picardie still holding on as his shoes caught and his feet were crushed, the machine dragging him down. Luca wrenched his foot from the hands of the twisting body.

Even with all the noisy machinery on site, everybody within half a kilometre had heard the cry. Luca had to take a look, but then looked away; Picardie's body was being consumed by the jaws of the machine, blood erupting from his mouth. The mercenary's hands clawed uselessly at the conveyor belt, before he lost the ability to fight it and sank out of view.

Then the entire machine seemed to lurch—*downwards*.

Luca was still trying to regain his strength when he remembered he had pointed the machine over the edge of the step.

He got to his feet and sprinted along the conveyor belt as it began to rise and tilt, grabbing Picardie's hunting knife on his way, the colossal vehicle riding over the edge. Luca ran the fifty metres to the enormous bucket-wheel at the end as the beam he was on began to rise above 45 degrees. Yells seemed to fill the mine's every corner while Luca dashed forward, the wheel in his way, sensing the ground beneath his feet was falling away as the vehicle tipped over the side. He leapt up to one of the buckets, using them in sequence as stepping stones, but running out of steps and bounding into mid-air. Luca found himself travelling through nothing; he adopted the best landing position he could but floundered. As he hit the ground hard, the impact shocked his body and he rolled to one side, inches from the edge, just in time to see the bucket-wheel follow the excavator down over the side, where it landed cacophonously on the level below.

As pandemonium broke out across the mine, Luca wanted nothing more than to crawl into a hole and rest. He lay where he was, spent, the crisis erupting around him seeming more than he could deal with.

'You bastard.'

Luca looked round to see another mercenary standing over him, an automatic pistol in his hand. He wore a look of murderous fury.

'What did you do with Picardie?'

Luca realised he had no defence, the game was up.

He pointed over the edge, then dropped his hand and sighed, totally spent.

'Then this is where it ends for you too.'

The mercenary chambered a bullet and pointed the pistol at Luca's head.

A horn sounded.

The mercenary looked round.

A Land Rover Discovery hit him at sixty kilometres per hour, braking in a cloud of dust as the lifeless body flew up and over the edge where it joined the bucket-wheel excavator down below.

Luca rolled slowly onto his side, peering through the cloud of dust engulfing the stationary car.

The door opened and JJ ran to him. She helped Luca to his feet, but could not stop herself from looking at the spot where the man had stood, nausea rising inside her. 'I'm going to have nightmares about that,' she said. 'Come on, they're waiting for you.'

Luca was starting make sense of what had just happened, his brain clearing like the dispersing dust cloud kicked up by the car.

'They?'

JJ floored the Land Rover Discovery's accelerator as she headed for the main gate on the far side of the mine. In the seat next to her, Luca looked round. Three distraught Americans were sitting on the rear bench, two more on the flip-down seats in the back. He nodded gravely at them and received confused, frightened nods in return. As Luca was aware from his training, if there was one thing more terrifying than being held captive it was being rescued.

'What are you doing here?'

JJ flinched at his critical tone. 'What? What do you mean?'

'You were meant to be back at the hotel.'

'I just saved your behind.'

'But you were meant to be back at the hotel.'

JJ was almost speechless. When she did speak, she lashed out. 'Is this your idea of a thank you?'

'It's my idea of sticking to a plan.'

'Well, you're welcome.'

Outside in the confusion, the Land Rover dashing from one side of the mine to the other was barely noticed due to the main drama of two large plant vehicles plunging off the haulage roads.

'So?' Luca said.

JJ shot Luca a look as she drove. 'So what?'

'So, what happened?'

'Do you mean the bit just before I saved your life?'

Luca rolled his eyes, still angry she had put herself at risk and aware that he was a stubborn mule for not being quicker to appreciate the fact she'd saved him.

'Well, I was walking back to the hotel when I heard a gunshot.'

'That is exactly why I asked you to go back to the hotel—'

'Says the man who would be a corpse now if I had. Anyhow, I crept up to the top of the mine to see what was happening and saw a dozer pushing a dumper truck over the edge.'

'Because I had it under control.'

It was JJ's turn to roll her eyes. 'And I noticed that when the dumper truck was delicately shoved over the edge the only people who didn't react were the guards standing by some of the portakabins on the far side.'

Luca glared at her.

'So I ran round the outside of the top of the mine then crept up behind the guards, and, you know.'

'They could have been armed, JJ.'

'Oh they were armed. But, they were also not expecting me and they were slow, and distracted, by the subtle entrance you had made.'

The young man on the rear bench was in mortal terror of the crowd of miners through which they were driving at speed, the checkpoint at the entrance to the mine fast approaching.

'Excuse me, but are you with the American Government?'

JJ looked at him briefly in the rear-view mirror. 'Yeah, we're Seal Team 6.'

Luca was annoyed, but mostly at himself. 'So what happened to the guy with the USS *Missouri* baseball cap?'

JJ didn't answer, but pulled the cap out of the door storage compartment, dropping it between them. Luca looked at it, and thought about the fact that there were five people not six in the back.

'Its owner?'

A gaunt-looking middle-aged woman spoke with surprising firmness from the back seat. 'He died shortly after we arrived. He had been struck by the Mongolian guy on the boat and he suffered complications.'

Luca nodded at her, but JJ interrupted him.

'Luca, what do I do here?'

JJ was indicating the checkpoint immediately ahead. On Luca's side, an uncertain helmeted guard was waving them down, a Kalashnikov hanging from his left hand.

'*Keep* going.'

As the Land Rover roared to the exit the security guard lifted his assault rifle and made ready to fire just as Luca opened his door wide. The door hit the guard so hard it slammed shut again, the window shattered.

With the car bouncing along the road back to town, Luca turned in his seat and spoke to the middle-aged woman, concluding she was the least shell-shocked of the group.

'What's happening here?'

The young man burst in. 'We were meant to be on a cultural exchange. We were meant to be guests of the University of Pyongyang, then we were woken by our guides in the middle of the night and smuggled onto a boat—'

Luca gave him a stern if not unkind look. The young man was traumatised, it wasn't his fault, but the Swiss man didn't have time. He looked back at the woman beside him.

'We were working with North Korean geologists, looking for rare earth minerals,' she said. 'Then, after a week of field trips we were woken up and taken to a speedboat, which took us to a cargo ship. Then we were kidnapped and brought here by the Mongolian. We didn't know we were part of something.'

Luca nodded. 'It was most likely the CIA. They were using you to gather information about the country's resources, that's why they allowed it.'

'Why would they put our lives at risk like that?'

Luca shrugged. 'Since you didn't have any knowledge of their real agenda, at least you weren't doing anything wrong. Clearly, they hoped the North Koreans would feel the same—clearly, at some point, they didn't. What rare earth minerals did you find?'

The spokeswoman shook her head. 'None from North Korea.'

Luca was amazed. 'What does that mean?'

'We took a lot of samples and found many rare earths, but they all came from the mine we were being held at.'

Luca glanced at the mine from the window, the road they were on running alongside it.

'Hang on, they took minerals from *that* mine, dumped them in a mine in North Korea, and let you think they came from there?'

'Yes.'

Luca's mind began to work overtime as he tried to understand the angle. 'Could you be wrong?'

She shook her head. 'Everywhere is unique, and if you have enough information everywhere has its own fingerprint. We were fooled for a while, but as soon as they made us analyse what they were finding in the mine here, we knew that all the samples originated from it.'

Luca needed time to process this information. 'Did you learn anything else?'

She pulled an uncertain face. 'The Mongolian wanted to know how long after a radiation leak you could safely mine an area. He talked about Chernobyl. Why would he do that?'

Luca nodded and turned back to face the road ahead. JJ watched him for a moment.

'Yeah, why would he do that?' JJ asked.

But her companion was lost in thought.

★   ★   ★

The manager of the hotel had JJ's travel bag on the reception desk and was taking his time going through its contents. He held up a short black dress, admiring its potential resale value and sexiness, feeling pleased about both.

Grinning at his windfall, he lowered the dress only to be hit square in the face by a fist; his head smacked off the cabinet behind him and he was unconscious before he hit the floor.

Luca stepped behind the desk, put JJ's items back in her bag, zipped it closed, and took it back to the Land Rover with his own bag.

★   ★   ★

JJ knew, from the way Luca was standing at the passenger door of the Land Rover that he didn't intend on getting back in.

'You've got India or China 150 kilometres east or west, but the road to China is quicker, and your Mandarin better than your Urdu,' he said to her.

'Aren't you coming with us?'

'No, there's one more thing I need to do.'

'Don't, Luca, don't do this. It's not your battle.'

He held her look of concern with his own, feeling her pull, aware of the danger of giving into those feelings.

'I'll phone Sir Stephen, he'll arrange safe passage for all of you at the border.'

'No, no, no. I want to come with you, I want to help you.'

'You can help me by getting these people to safety.'

'OK, forget the help bit. I want to come with you.'

'JJ…'

She knew from the look he was giving her that he wasn't just asking.

'But, Luca, it's not your battle. Why are you doing this? Ask yourself, please.'

He nodded, but not in agreement. 'I'll call Sir Stephen. Once I've learned what's in the cargo going from Yangon to Pyongyang tonight, I'll call you.'

'Don't do anything else, Luca.'

'Like what?'

'Like something brave or something stupid.'

They swapped concerned smiles.

'I thought they were the same thing?'

He closed the car door. JJ looked at him with ill-disguised affection. She shook her head and sped off, Luca watching the car until it turned a corner and was out of sight.

As soon as he stepped into the bar Luca saw who he was looking for, the sole out-of-towner, the only person who wasn't covered in dirt and dust. Sitting in a corner by a dusty window, the well-turned-out Burmese pilot was nursing a cup of coffee while he read the newspaper.

He looked up when a chair was pulled up in front of him, Luca sitting astride it. The man looked up slowly, but was unable to hide the mild look of surprise at seeing a European face.

'Can I help you?'

Luca spoke without excitement or fuss. 'The two men you brought here this morning are dead. If you don't give

224

me the keys to the helicopter and your phone you'll be dead too.'

The pilot navigated life with a swagger. He earned good money, had an exotic job by local standards and was good-looking to boot. But the man in front of him sent a cold chill through him; his eyes were lifeless and hard. The pilot went to answer, but his mouth was dry and in that moment, out of the corner of his eye, he noticed the European's hand twitch. When he looked down he saw Luca gripping a sharply serrated blade.

To fail his employer meant extreme consequences and, even though every part of his brain screamed at him to co-operate, the pilot felt he had to do something. He reached inside his pocket, reading correctly a warning from Luca's stare about doing anything stupid. He pulled out his keys and his phone and put them on the table between them. Then he spoke as defiantly as he could: 'They'll find you and you know what they'll do.'

Luca scooped up the objects and gave a curt smile; both men knew how desperately the pilot wanted to get to a phone to warn Butakhan of what was happening. The Swiss man stood up and addressed the half-filled room in the best Mandarin he could muster.

'Excuse me everybody.'

One by one the drunk miners looked up.

'People will be coming here to ask about the incident at the mine where machines have been destroyed and men died. I want you to know that I did it. And this is my partner.'

The pilot switched from looking bewildered to mortified. 'No.'

'He told me where to find his employers and how to kill them.'

'*It's not true...*'

The pilot made the mistake of grabbing at Luca in desperation, so terrified was he by the consequences of what the stranger was saying. Luca instantly snatched the hand that took hold of his shirt and twisted it, the pilot crumbling; he slammed the joint against the edge of the wooden table and the room heard a clean sound of bones snapping before the man wailed in blinding pain. Luca let him fall to the floor.

'But, as you can see, we have had a disagreement. It was all his idea. He wants to kill a man called Butakhan. The man he wants to kill is Butakhan, do you understand?'

'No, no, it's not true—*please...*'

Luca walked out knowing the pilot would have to run for the rest of his life, that he would not dare to contact his former boss and that he, Luca, had avoided killing him needlessly.

The helicopter lifted into the sky, its blades drumming up red dust in every direction. Luca was relieved to see that the MD 600N was not dissimilar to aircraft he had flown in the Swiss Air Force. Having established his route to Yangon, Luca decided to stay at two hundred feet above ground for the duration of the three hour flight; he wanted to come in under the radar, in every sense.

Having patched his phone through the aircraft's headset he tried to call Devereux's mobile, but reached his voicemail. He tried the Vatican's main switchboard, but was told the cardinal was in a meeting and could not be interrupted. Luca tried to explain that it was a matter of exceptional urgency, but the woman remained adamant. The best Luca could do was leave a message. He told her that JJ needed help getting though passport control with five Americans without papers on the Myanmar–Chinese border and that Sir Stephen was to call him *immediately*.

Luca skimmed the eight-seat luxury helicopter south, across the tree tops, mountains rising up on both sides. With an unusually heavy heart, Luca now called Herr Hesse.

The call was answered with typical terseness. 'Hesse.'

'It's Voss,' Luca said.

There was a pause and then a voice spoke with something close to concern. 'Are you OK, Voss?'

'I'm fine. Look, I took a detour and ended up in northern Myanmar.'

'Did you?' The question was asked in a tone of surprised intrigue.

'Yes, Butakhan's got a rare earth mine. He's shipping mineral resources out of there, and dumping them in a mine in North Korea.'

The news was met initially with silence. 'Are you certain?'

'My sources are good. I think Franz was onto it, and that's why they cut off his fingers, so that no one could trace the minerals he had been handling.'

Another briefer pause. 'Yes, yes, that makes sense. But faking mineral resources doesn't.'

Luca swooped, the helicopter tracing a bending river, wide-open plains beyond.

'But it would make sense if somebody had sold the idea of invading North Korea as financially viable, because there was money to make selling its rare earth minerals on the open market.'

'Oh my God, Luca.'

Luca was stunned by the General Counsel's unguarded tone, the frigid mask slipping in a way Luca had never seen before.

'Luca, have you been following the news? North Korea is like a tinderbox right now. The US has slapped so many sanctions on it that it's virtually cut off from the world.'

'So presumably North Korea is testing cruise missiles as a reminder of its trump card?'

'Exactly.'

'How bad is it?'

'Our sources are telling us it's worse than the Cuban Missile Crisis.'

Luca shook his head in grim wonder. 'It's what Butakhan wants—it's what he's been planning for.'

'But nuclear war, Luca?'

Luca realised he felt uncomfortable at Hesse's unusually familiar tone. 'A nuclear war means it will take years to realise that there are no rare earth minerals to be found in North Korea, by which time Butakhan will have ousted the Seven Families and replaced them with allies such as America.'

Another silence followed, the longest of all.

'Luca… I apologise.'

The Swiss man was stunned at what he had heard—an apology—from *Hesse*. 'Why are you apologising?'

'For doubting you. This is the sort of information only a Broker could have discovered.'

Now Luca went from stunned to disbelieving. Was he being told he was to be the next Broker? Had he disobeyed direct orders, done everything his own way, but still won the day? He was confused. He should have felt delighted, but somehow, the promise felt more like a prison sentence.

'Well, thank you, Herr Hesse. But we need to tell the North Koreans not to take the bait following any attacks; we need to tell them they're being set up.'

Another silence followed, until it was broken eventually in Switzerland. 'Tell them yourself, Luca. Come back, report to the Families.'

'I can't, Herr Hesse. I have one more thing to do.'

'Luca, I have indulged you to date but, please, now is not the time.'

'I have to. Promise me, that you'll speak with the North Korean ambassador in Geneva?'

A sigh preceded the next words. 'OK. You know best. Where can I send a plane to pick you up once you're done?'

Luca hesitated before he spoke, wrestling with his feelings about the phone call, but he really did only have one more thing he felt he could do. 'Yangon, I should be able to catch it back tonight.'

'I'll have it waiting for you. Will you be arriving with your friend?'

'No, she's gone another way.' Luca had choked on the truth, uncomfortable about revealing anything more.

'Well, she has clearly done a good job. We can track her down another time.'

'Sure.'

'Until this evening then. You're five and a half hours ahead of us, so I'll greet you when you return tonight.'

'OK. Sure.'

Luca killed the call, then tried to pinpoint the source of the bad feeling he felt. *Track her down another time.* He did not like the sound of that.

★   ★   ★

Herr Hesse pulled out a mobile phone that had only ever called one number. He paused to smile at how well it was all going. Even if it hadn't all gone exactly to plan it was certainly close enough. His thumb hovered over the speed dial as he prepared his message.

18

50 kilometres South-West of Yangon, Andaman Sea

Stretching out on a sunlounger in a white bikini, Scarlett drank a preposterously large cocktail through a straw, studiously ignoring events.

Butakhan was by the swimming pool in which he had just been swimming lengths. As he wrapped a gown round himself, two nervous aides trembled in front of him. Both were bodyguards, both had seen colleagues killed for less than the news they had just imparted.

'When did this happen?'

The stockier of the two men looked at Butakhan's feet while he spoke. 'This morning, we've only just been told the news.'

'What has Picardie said about this?'

'Jean is...'

'Jean is what?'

'Jean Picardie is dead sir.'

Butakhan looked as if the guard had just slapped his face. After a moment, he asked with unnerving calm. 'And we're sure it was Luca Voss?'

The aide nodded vigorously. 'Mr Voss and a woman, a Chinese woman.'

'And how exactly did he escape?'

The smaller of the two guards mumbled his reply. 'In your helicopter.'

Butakhan twitched. He looked away, his face contorting with silent rage. 'I want him brought to me. I want Luca Voss brought before me. I want him punished. I want to punish him myself. Tell everybody—*everybody*—that *this is what I want.*'

Now both the aides nodded vigorously, keen to comply and just as keen to get away.

A phone on the lounger beside Scarlett started ringing. Both she and Butakhan looked at it sharply, the rising trill of the ringtone telling them who it would be. Butakhan waved the men away and stalked towards the phone.

'Yes?'

'I've just spoken to Voss.'

Butakhan's eyes popped wide open at the revelation delivered by the robotic voice. 'Where is he?'

'On his way to Yangon.'

'Why?'

'I can only assume it is something to do with the cargo flying out tonight.'

Butakhan's eyes searched the sky as if his thoughts were projected onto it. 'Does he know what it is?'

'No, not at all. He knows what we were doing with the rare earth minerals, but he thinks the nuclear strike will come from America. I'm sending a plane for him this evening; you can be waiting for him if you like.'

'This evening?' Butakhan smiled maliciously. 'No, I've a better idea. I'm afraid he won't be making that plane so don't worry about sending it.'

He killed the call and looked out to sea thoughtfully. Would there be time? Would it complicate things? Was it a risk too far? But, no, the answers were all good and the solution satisfying. He nodded to himself. He knew what to do with Luca Voss.

Scarlett had returned to her cocktail and was nonchalantly sucking at the straw, hoping her enormous sunshades and sun hat concealed the worried look on her face. She knew her phone would have no signal. When, she wondered, would she be within range to send this latest development to her spymaster, Herr Hesse.

19
Sea of Japan,
150 kilometres East of North Korea

The Japanese Maritime Self-Defense Force was dispersed across the Sea of Japan: twenty-six destroyers, four aircraft carriers, eleven frigates, six destroyer escorts and thirty minesweepers, as well as patrol vehicles and tank landing ships. Below the surface were sixteen attack submarines while the skies above buzzed with reconnaissance planes and fighter jets. Every piece of intelligence told the Japanese that North Korea was about to fire a missile; the entire Navy and the attack arm of the Air Force had been gathered there to blast such a missile out of the sky.

Alongside them was the United States Third Fleet, an armed force larger than the entire Japanese Navy and Air Force combined. It included four carrier-strike groups, each containing an aircraft carrier with approximately sixty-five aircraft, at least one cruiser, as well as a destroyer squadron. In addition to all of these, a fleet of submarines with both anti-missile and nuclear-missile capabilities stalked the seas. Never had so many ships gathered in one sea mass since World War II. What had started out as war games had turned nasty, the pretence had been dropped when the president of America had personally called the Glorious Leader of the world's most volatile country to tell him why America was there in force and what it would do if provoked.

In case the presence of the Third Fleet in the Sea of Japan was not enough, the United States Seventh Fleet was stationed south-west in the South China Sea with the same military capability and the same task: to protect America and its allies by all means possible.

The presence of the two American fleets saw the considerably smaller, but nonetheless dangerous, Chinese Navy deployed alongside the Seventh Fleet, and Russia's alongside the Third, each demanding that America stay out of whatever hostilities broke out between Japan and North Korea for the sake of world peace. The president made it clear both privately and publicly that America would contain North Korea by every means necessary.

If America, China, and Russia became engaged in conflict, it would mean that first the region and then the whole world would have to take sides. Such were the tensions that every major military power on every continent found itself on the highest state of alert. The very event that the doctrine of mutually assured destruction was meant to prevent was becoming more likely by the minute.

20
Naypyidaw International Airport, Yangon, Myanmar

Three large airliners were parked by the terminal at Naypyidaw International. They were due to remain there until morning, such was the airport's low-volume air traffic. With the last flight of the day already departed, a quiet calm had descended. A solitary cargo plane was sitting at one end of the only runway, ground crew readying it for flight. It was a C-27J Spartan freight transporter, waiting, Luca thought sceptically, for its cargo of humanitarian aid. A bloated, stubby twin-prop plane painted in military grey, there were windows around the cockpit and two more on the cargo deck. Luca recalled it had been the go-to plane for the American military in the Afghan war until, quite suddenly, the entire fleet had been sold off. He wondered if the one he was looking at was an actual ex-US Army model. The irony would have been too much.

The Swiss man's plan was simple: to find out the exact nature of Butakhan's cargo on the flight from Yangon to Pyongyang and then broadcast the news via the Families. If it was the shipment of more minerals, he did not want the embarrassment and wasted time of alerting Sir Stephen, Herr Hesse, and possibly his own military contacts to the fact. If it was more than that, he still felt it could prove crucial to the events currently playing out on the world stage. He had listened to the major news networks during the rest of his flight to Yangon, all of which had suspended regular programming to bring rolling news of the events taking place off the coast of South East Asia. Luca's gut instinct told him Butakhan was behind it all. Instinct, once again overriding his Teutonic training; whether that was a good or a bad thing he hadn't decided. Something else was playing on his mind: there had been no confirmation text to say that JJ had arrived safely at the border. Crouched near the cargo warehouses, he felt compelled to push the thought to one side.

He had been waiting in a narrow gap behind a wall of pallets for over an hour watching the row of warehouses. The occasional airport vehicle had passed by, but now even these had ceased. With the end of daylight all business activity seemed to have stopped for the night, except at one warehouse where a Burmese man walked up and down, his hand resting on the pistol in his holster. For the first thirty minutes of his shift, Luca had witnessed an alert, vigilant security guard who walked the length of the warehouse before turning and walking back again, his eyes scouring the airport about him. His initial good intentions had waned, however, and he had found a pattern of pausing more often, at one time even lighting a cigarette. Twenty minutes later, he had another cigarette, nicotine clearly his crutch for the night shift. Fifteen minutes after the second cigarette, Luca made his move.

With barely a sound, Luca eased out of the space between the pallets and crept over to the corner of the warehouse. He allowed almost a minute of inactivity and quiet to prevail, checking to see if the security guard had become suspicious. The man was as indifferent as he had been when he'd lit his first cigarette; now he was holding the packet in his hand about to light another one.

The warehouse wall was in shadow and, as long as he kept close to it as he approached the security guard, Luca was almost invisible. He waited until the man placed a cigarette in his mouth and bent down into his hand to use his lighter. Then he pounced.

The pinched nerves of his neck sent a lightning bolt through the Burmese man's head half a second before he lost consciousness. Luca dragged his body back to the alley by the warehouse, silently cursing the inevitable skidding noise of the comatose man's heels. The man would not wake for a few hours, but for good measure Luca tied the man's hands behind his back with his belt and used the cravat from his uniform as a gag to silence him. It would not buy him much time, but the commotion might just save him in a fix.

Taking the guard's pistol and slipping it into the back of his belt, Luca rose and made his way back to the front of the warehouse. Halfway along, there was a regular-sized door within the huge cargo door. As carefully as he could he opened it, wincing at the minute clunks that accompanied it, but immediately gratified at the darkness that greeted him. Taking nothing for granted, he closed the door with the same caution with which he had opened it.

The only lighting was from two rows of dim, red emergency lights running the length of the huge loading bay. He waited for his eyes to adjust to the light and gradually the physical objects came into focus. The cavernous space in the centre was easy enough to pick out. It contained row after row of pallets, with enough room to drive a forklift truck between them. He knew he would have to move fast to find the cargo he was looking for.

Luca checked the details of the flight on his phone and then used its light to examine the delivery label on each piece of cargo. He examined the first two rows of goods and found nothing. There appeared to be no third row, not immediately. There was a gap—six empty rows—before the rows started again farther inside the warehouse. In this gap was one lone pallet. Luca looked about him, pausing for the slightest sound. Nothing.

He moved over to the lone cargo stand. The silence was total, his movements like that of a ghost; Luca knew from experience, from training, how to walk immediately behind a sentry without announcing his presence. His breathing was paced, his footfall relaxed, the weight rolling gently onto each foot at a constant speed. Listening, watching, as he neared the pallet, he switched on the faint light from the phone screen—

Then he froze.

Outside an electric vehicle was humming towards the warehouse. In the darkness, Luca looked back, remembering where the door was as the vehicle came closer and closer until...

It went past without slowing down.

Luca let out a silent sigh, relieved, and returned to the cargo. From what he had seen so far this was the only load not wrapped in swathes of plastic and the first to have a delivery note whose details were written in Korean Hangul script. It was also the only one to have a large, yellow-and-black hazardous waste symbol emblazoned across it. Luca's heart began to race as he scanned the length of the cargo with his phone to make out its shape. It was a blue metal tube, six feet in length and three feet wide. It was, without any doubt in his mind, enriched uranium or something equally dangerous. Whatever Butakhan's plans were, they appeared to fit perfectly with the events now gripping the world. Luca still had questions, dozens of them, but at least he now had one piece of the answer.

For the first time since arriving at the airport, he allowed himself to make a noise, one word spoken softly to himself: 'Bingo.'

At that exact moment, as if the word had triggered it, floodlights exploded into life and Luca was instantly bleached white by their overbearing brilliance. Blinded, he closed and covered his eyes; but he had seen something, silhouettes of armed men, revealed by the light for a second.

Then a booming spoke voice over a Tannoy. 'Looking for something Mr Voss?'

At the sound of Butakhan, Luca opened his eyes and shaded them with his hands. It was still too bright. In desperation, he pulled the gun from the back of his belt and held it in front of him.

Laughter rang out over the Tannoy. Real laughter, Butakhan genuinely amused by the Swiss man's wretched state. That was the last thing Luca remembered before the impact at the back of his skull put all the lights out; then blackness, all sound ceasing.

21
Chinese Airspace

Luca could hear a mighty propeller whirring away. He tried to move his head, but his muscles did not respond. Then a nausea rose in him. He could not fight it, but he didn't need to; it subsided, along with his consciousness.

A slap, as if delivered at the end of a long, white corridor. The sound—the sensation—distant, so that it seemed it was happening to someone else. Then he heard something else, a voice coming in and out of range, a man's voice. Then the propeller again. Louder now or clearer... Then another slap.

Luca came round.

'I wondered if perhaps you wouldn't be joining me after all.'

Luca was in the co-pilot's seat in the cockpit of the C-27J cargo plane. On his left Butakhan was sitting in a flight suit complete with pilot's helmet. He was smiling, as if he was taking a friend for a novelty flight rather than carrying out a kidnap. The Swiss man knew immediately that he was unable to move and a quick, restrained wriggle of his body confirmed he was bound tightly by a lot of rope. Butakhan tut-tutted, mocking the prisoner and his limited investigation of his bonds.

'Forgive me, Voss, but I was worried about the effects of turbulence on you as you slept, and may have got carried away.'

His humour was wasted on Luca who was then scanning the cockpit, trying to see what information he could garner.

Both men had control wheels in front of them and a bank of tablet-sized screens made up the main instrument panel, offering them identical flight and navigation displays—direction, height, speed, elevation, and countless other metrics. Between them ran a wide console packed with controls, keypads, and small digital screens pertaining to the non-flight functions of the craft—defence systems and other military requirements absent in a cargo plane.

'I don't know what you think you're doing, Butakhan, but—'

'Do you know, Voss, if you left it right there it might be the most intelligent thing you've ever said.' Butakhan flashed a smile, part gloating, part amusement. 'Are you aware of the Battle of the Thirteen Sides, Voss?'

Luca suddenly rebelled against the ropes that bound him, using all his strength. It was futile. Butakhan laughed, mocking him.

'Really, Voss? Do you think I had boy scouts tie you up?'

Butakhan was sitting quite comfortably in his chair while the plane cruised at an altitude of 10,000 feet on a course that had been set hours earlier.

'Let me ask you again, Voss. Are you aware of the Battle of the Thirteen Sides?'

Luca made no effort to hide his anger and refused to answer his captor's question.

Butakhan pulled a face that acknowledged that Voss did not want to play. 'Well, the Seven Families and their predecessors, the Thirteen Families, cannot claim to own all history for themselves. Old as the Families are and ancient as their history is, other tribes have come and gone around them. The Battle of the Thirteen Sides took place in 1201. The Great Khan was uniting the many nomadic tribes of north-east Asia before the great expansion that, to this day, created the largest single continuous empire the world has ever seen. But, he almost didn't, you see. During this battle Genghis Khan was—'

'Shot in the neck with an arrow.'

The Mongolian man paused, equally impressed and irritated by Luca's knowledge. 'Very good. And he asked the defeated soldiers who had done this to him. And the warrior Jebe confessed, saying: "If you kill me right here I'll fertilise a bit of dirt the size of your hand. But if the Khan will allow me to live, I'll ride out in his service and cut the deepest waters in two, split the brightest diamond." And not only did he do as much, but through loyalty and good work he rose through the ranks to the position of general.'

Luca stared at him, refusing to go along with this showmanship. Butakhan did not seem to mind, time seemingly his friend.

'So, the question I have to ask of the man who eluded me first in Russia, then Shanghai, then Yangon, and even at my own mine, is this: would a warrior such as yourself prefer to end up as a meal for the fishes of the sea, or join me, and cut the deepest waters in two?'

His prisoner squinted at him then looked away, puzzled by the offer. 'When Emperor Khan addressed the defeated warriors he asked them who had shot his horse: he was too proud to admit that it was him who had been wounded, not his horse. Jebe announced that the arrow had struck his neck. Proud man that Genghis.'

Butakhan did his best to hide the sting he felt from Luca's observation, not missing the intended meaning. 'But Jebe still followed him.'

'Do you really think you could ever command the loyalty that would require?'

Butakhan smiled, privy to something Luca was not. He glanced at the instrument panel and saw that before long they would be entering North Korean airspace. He weighed something up in his mind then nodded to himself.

'You know your history well, Voss. You know that the Seven Families were once thirteen.' He watched for Luca's reaction. 'You know the Six tore at each other—tore each other apart into non-existence—ceding power to the Seven.'

Now Luca was watching him closely.

'But you're wrong.'

Luca was confused. 'What do you mean, wrong?'

'I mean that after we tore each other apart we didn't go away—we went quiet.'

Luca felt his stomach drop, his head throbbing, from more than just the blow earlier. 'No.'

'Very much "Yes", Herr Voss.'

'No, there's no way—'

'And we have bided our time, waited out generations and wars for just the right moment.'

Luca was still sceptical, yet something told him what Butakhan was saying was true—it made sense.

'And what moment would that be?'

'The moment to take control.'

Luca looked at him in disbelief. 'You can't take control of the Seven Families.'

'Really? Because when they read the airport paperwork and discover that you were the pilot of this plane, and when I tell the authorities you were acting on the orders of the Seven Families—along with considerable supporting evidence for good measure—none of you will have anywhere to hide. Especially not after the war that is about to break out. People will want revenge. The Seven Families will be to blame.'

'War? I'm not so sure flying hazardous waste to Pyongyang will start a war, Butakhan.'

'Oh, I agree, but then once I've bailed out of here, this plane isn't landing at the airport—it will be landing in the palace of the Glorious Leader after officials at air traffic control are sent a message in Japanese.'

Luca received the news like a kick to the solar plexus. He instantly knew the implications: after such a message, North Korea would shoot the plane out of the sky and then, more than likely, launch missiles at Japan. The war would escalate from there; nuclear conflict inevitable.

'The hazardous waste?'

Butakhan smiled smugly. 'That would be enriched uranium.'

'A dirty bomb over Pyongyang?' Now the nausea returned. North Korea's response would most definitely be nuclear.

'As per the message in Japanese, it's only fair that we warn them.'

'Don't you mean, provoke them?'

'Warn. Provoke—it's down to them.'

'And what if North Korea shows restraint? What if it doesn't bite?'

'Well, first of all, with their capital city uninhabitable due to a dirty bomb, that isn't going to happen. Secondly, it's win-win, Voss: either there's a war and we move our own government in, or we precipitate regime change from within and become America's new best friend—and you get crossed off their Christmas card list. And then, after the fireworks, I will gather the heads of the Seven Families and offer them a choice: either oblivion or a return to the Thirteen. Thirteen Families, wielding not just influence but real power.'

The plane started to bounce slightly as it hit a patch of turbulence. The Mongolian man glanced at the screens but was satisfied with the readings.

'I think you overestimate your organisation's reach, Butakhan. If the Seven Families don't want to be found they can quite easily disappear.'

'Really, Voss? We have not had much trouble tracing them for the past half-century. Your Brokers have had very short life expectancies, haven't they?'

Luca stared hard at him, daring him to say anything more on the matter.

'You see, where some people had fairy tales at bedtime I had my father's tales of the Seven Families' Brokers, almost always with a bloody, but happy, ending.'

'Well, I guess that would explain some of your psychosis.'

The plane rocked again, the turbulence more severe now. Butakhan checked the instrument screens and turned back to Luca with a wry smile.

'And not just stories of dead Brokers, Voss.' Butakhan had a sadistic look in his eye now, which presaged something else, something that was already chilling Voss's blood. 'The Seven Families never seem to have much luck at all, do they Voss? I mean, even *your* parents died when you were young.'

The plane suddenly dropped for a second before continuing on its way, turbulence nothing for a warhorse like this. Luca barely registered it, his mind racing over the possibility of there being any truth in Butakhan's hinted involvement in his parents' death.

'You're making it up.'

'Am I, Voss? Did nice Herr Hesse show you the pictures of the crash?'

'I didn't need to see pictures of the crash, they were dead; it was an accident. Their plane crashed over Kenya.'

'Did it Voss? Then why have I seen the pictures?'

'The pictures made the press.'

'Of a crashed plane, Voss? The pictures I saw were from before the flight, before your parents' bodies were put on the plane. The pictures where your mother begs your father not to tell my organisation where you were. The pictures in which your father has been shot and your mother kneels over his body. The pictures of your mother lying dead across your father's body, a hole where her brains used to be. Are these the pictures you mean?'

'It's bullshit. It's all bullshit.' Inside, Luca knew every word of it was true; Butakhan had nothing to gain by lying. And now that he thought about it, there had always been a kind of strange, silent void surrounding the subject. After the news had been broken to him, it was never mentioned again; even Sir Stephen had stayed silent. *Could they have kept the truth hidden*, he wondered.

'I think the picture I liked most was when your mother saw the bullets entering—'

'Shut up. Shut up you son of a bitch, you goddamn son of bitch.'

The sound of a third voice in the cockpit made Butakhan and Luca suddenly turn their heads. Scarlett was standing in the doorway with a gun in her hand. It was pointed at Butakhan.

The Mongolian man was stunned by Scarlett's presence— and the fact she was holding a gun.

'What... What are you doing here?'

'I'm stopping you. That's what I am doing.'

Luca had as much of an idea about what was going on as Butakhan, but one thing was certain, she was no fool. Dressed in a black jumpsuit with a slim parachute attached to her back, Scarlett was an actor playing a part, though he did not know the nature of her role. Seeing her with the gun gave him hope, but the way she held it made him wonder about her experience. Moreover, Butakhan was not giving up just yet.

'You mustn't worry about what is happening here, Scarlett. You don't understand.'

She pulled a face. It wasn't like any expression Butakhan had ever seen her show before; it was the impatience of an intelligent person believed to be dumb. 'How about if I am worried and how about if I do understand?'

'No, no, your Buty knows what he is doing.'

The plane rocked with a brief spell of turbulence before settling.

'Good. Then you can explain it to the North Korean authorities when we land. Move and I promise I will shoot you.'

She opened a flick-knife and carefully sidled up to Luca's seat, not taking her eyes off Butakhan for a second.

'Is it money you want, or the yacht? You love the yacht—'

'I *hate* the yacht. I hate everything you have ever given me. You bought it all with blood money.'

She began to saw at one of the ropes holding Luca, who felt now was an appropriate time to understand more—and quickly. 'What's going on, Scarlett?'

'I work for the Seven Families.'

Butakhan's eyes opened wide, but Luca had no time to savour his reaction.

'The Families? Why wasn't I told?'

'I don't know. I was waiting for you to say something, but just thought you were being careful.'

'No, I was being kept in the dark. To whom do you report?'

'Herr Hesse.'

One by one, the ropes loosened, but Scarlett moved slowly, keen as she was to keep an eye on Butakhan.

'But he never mentioned it to me. What was your mission?'

'To watch the Six Families by watching Butakhan. I've informed him about everything I've seen—the geologists being sent to the mine, Butakhan's plans to kill you in Russia and then in Shanghai. I even told him about *Charon* shipping enriched uranium from North Korea. Didn't he say anything to you?'

Butakhan was grinning nastily at Luca. 'Nice touch don't you think, using their own materials to make a dirty bomb against them? I can't wait to see that tinderbox go up in approximately...' he glanced at the instrument panel '... twenty-five minutes.'

Luca was able to wriggle his arms out of the ropes and began to unthread himself. His arms, however, deadened by lack of blood supply, were not just painful to move, but restricted and in need of exercise, bolts of pain fired up towards his shoulders. 'They'll shoot you down the moment you deviate from the agreed flight path.'

'And the bomb will be just as effective and you know it. It will start my war.'

Scarlett was highly wired, uncomfortable with the gun, uncomfortable with the situation, but more distressed at the idea of doing nothing. Butakhan's voice was shredding her nerves; she had heard it call for so many deaths already.

'Shut up,' she said.

Butakhan smiled. He was getting to her and he knew it. He was looking for an edge and would take anything he could use, 'Or what, my darling?'

'Or, so help me God—'

The plane dropped like a stone. In the space of a couple of seconds, it lost altitude of almost a hundred feet, a drop so sudden even gravity seemed suspended. Luca and Scarlett saw the same thing—Butakhan springing like a coiled snake, striking at the American woman with venomous speed. Scarlett tried to get her hand back down towards her assailant, while Luca, nearly free of all the rope now, thrust his arms up at Butakhan, but his limbs would not obey, offering only a feeble response. The gun exploded, a bullet smashed through the windscreen on the pilot's side and Butakhan grabbed the gun from Scarlett before leaping back and pulling the trigger. This time it was pointing at her.

Luca froze where he was, half out of his chair, the gun pointed at him from across the cockpit. The hole in the windshield hoovered up loose papers noisily while an alarm began to sound and lights flashed, warning of the depressurisation of the cockpit. The workhorse of a plane, however, automatically adjusted for the effects of the damage and powered through.

Scarlett hovered between the two men, a red stain spreading from the torso of her jumpsuit. She seemed unable to talk, dumbly touching a hand to the seeping blood, and then examining it as if unable to believe her eyes. Butakhan felt fraught, a boundless fury directed at both her and Luca.

'Why did you make me do that, Scarlett? You could have had anything.'

She shook her head and dropped to her knees before crashing face down on the floor.

Butakhan spat with rage as he addressed her corpse. '*You whore—you stupid whore.*'

While reluctant to return to his seat, Luca did not think it wise to move towards his adversary either. He stayed still and waited to see what would happen next.

With an angry squint of his eyes, Butakhan reminded him not to do anything stupid and waved him back to his seat with a motion of the gun. Luca slowly slid back down in his seat wondering what lay in store. He did not have long to wait to find out. Butakhan looked around the cockpit almost nostalgically.

'The word is that America might not be about to retaliate, that they have enough of an alliance to make the first strike.' He suddenly considered Luca with a cold smile, almost as if he felt regretful. 'And to think you'll have played your part, your name, the name of Luca Voss, infamous. Bin Laden will have nothing on you.'

They stared at each other.

'The symmetry, you and your parents both ending up like this in aeroplanes—'

'What of it?'

'It's nice.'

Luca gave him nothing, no reaction, no insight to how he felt. Butakhan looked from Luca to the punctured window and back again.

'When I leave you're going to try to escape. You can use her parachute if you like. But I should warn you...'

Butakhan fired three bullets into Scarlett's back where she lay dying.

'It's got holes in it.' Butakhan smiled a final time. 'Enjoy the rest of the flight—the rest of your life.'

He left, closing the door behind him. A moment later Luca jumped out of his seat and threw his weight against the door just as something heavy was moved to block it on the other side. When he tried kicking the door open, it wouldn't budge.

Just as Luca was looking around for something to smash the door down with, he felt the aircraft juddering. This time, he knew it wasn't turbulence. The instrument panel showed a simple schematic of the plane, its rear cargo door flashing red, accompanied by the words 'Loading Bay Opening'.

Luca jumped back into his seat and switched the screens on the instrument panel to a navigation update. He was two hundred kilometres west of the North Korean coast, another sixty kilometres farther to the capital Pyongyang. At the plane's current cruising speed of 555 kilometres per hour, he had about twenty minutes before he reached the coast. If he stayed any longer the plane would be blown out of the sky by the DPRK's Air Force. Luca thought of the pre-recorded Japanese declaration of war Butakhan had prepared and knew it had to be stopped. Safer still would be to turn the plane round and fly it as far away as possible.

The Swiss man began the procedure to switch from autopilot to manual, flicking the necessary switches on the console between the two pilots' seats to take back control, but there was no response. He flicked them all in sequence again. There was nothing.

'What the—?'

Luca had flown a C-27J Spartan many times before; it was the Special Forces' heavy-lifting beast of choice during his years in service. He had flown them in every type of weather, and in and out of Peshawar, Pakistan under Taliban fire. He knew, therefore, that switching from autopilot to manual was as easy as counting to ten, but he could get no response from the control panel in front of him.

He had been locked out. Butakhan's last surprise was to seal him in a prison hurtling towards the North Korean capital with a dirty bomb in the back. He knew he couldn't override the autopilot but all might not be lost if he could adjust it.

Luca turned the dial that varied the autopilot altitude—no response. That was not supposed to happen and he knew even before he turned the airspeed dial, that it would be the same. He looked at the analogue clock between the two halves of the windscreen: eighteen minutes before he hit the coast. He was running out of time.

Then, from a source he could not place, a radio transmission began to broadcast over a speaker in the cockpit. His Japanese was proficient enough to understand the majority of what was being said.

'*Citizens of the Democratic People's Republic of Korea –* '

Luca knew that eighteen minutes had suddenly shrunk to any-moment-now.

'*... This is a message from the Japanese Armed Services.*'

'God dammit.'

As the opening line was repeated in a different Asian language, which Luca guessed was Korean, he started

251

flipping through every switch, dial and lever at his disposal—anything to change the course of the aircraft. He ran through every mechanism on the console then reached up and did the same on the ceiling control panels. Try as he might, not one aspect of the aircraft—not the engines, flight controls, or electronics—could be influenced. To all intents and purposes, the controls were dead. Even the cargo bay door had been opened from outside the cockpit.

'OK, OK, so it's autopilot all the way,' Luca said to himself.

'*We wish that you begin the immediate evacuation of the Palace of your Glorious Leader and the surrounding areas …*'

As the radio transmission switched to Korean Luca was out of his seat and standing in the cockpit. He lunged at the door with all the strength he could muster, kicking it hard with the flat sole of his shoe. The door didn't budge and he felt a lightning bolt of pain surge up his leg. He looked around the room for something, anything, to assault the door with, but nothing presented itself.

'*With immediate effect the nation of Japan is at war with DPRK. We consider all North Korean citizens our enemies and will destroy you by any means possible…*'

As the transmission flipped to Korean, the radar screen began to flash red; four triangles were racing toward the C-27J transporter in which Luca was trapped. He reached down and removed the parachute from Scarlett's corpse as quickly as possible. Even riddled with bullet holes it was better than nothing.

Luca had a suicidal plan for escape, but if the plane was destroyed and nuclear materials were detected over North Korea—and they would be—Japan's so-called intention to bomb the Korean capital would be believed and war would follow as surely as night follows day.

'*After this first bomb an endless wave of missiles will strike your country as Japan and its ally the United States of America wipes North Korea from the map of the world once and for all.*'

A MiG-21 appeared exactly parallel to the cockpit, barely twenty metres away. Luca and the pilot looked directly at each other. The fighter pilot pointed downwards.

Luca did his best to mime a helpless shrug but decided he could waste no time on such theatrics. The North Korean pilot tilted left then levelled the aircraft again, signalling for Luca to do the same. The Swiss man looked to his right— another MiG-21 was doing the same, but there was no time to respond.

'*Citizens of the Democratic People's Republic of Korea this is a message from the Japanese Armed Services...*'

The transmission had looped back to the beginning. Luca doubted that it would be played a third time. He turned back to the barricaded door of the cabin. This was it. He took a deep breath then charged at it with all his might, smashing the full weight of his body into it with his shoulder. To his amazement it gave way, just a few inches. After that he stepped back and aimed several hard kicks at it with the sole of his shoe, eventually pushing the metal crate that had been used to keep it in place far back enough to edge out.

The cargo bay was large enough to house two armoured personnel carriers but all it played host to now was a pallet with a long blue tube on it.

Luca ran to where it lay strapped down to the decking. He pulled out Scarlett's flick-knife and began to saw through the polypropylene strapping. Through the porthole windows that ran the length of the aircraft, he saw the MiG-21 roll to the left and veer away from the plane.

He knew what that meant. They were abandoning the escort. They were about to strike.

Luca furiously cut the last two straps and bent down to lift the container from the pallet. A couple of minutes later he looked up and saw two distinct flashes coming from the

MiGs far behind the Spartan. They had already fired their missiles; he had seconds left. Luca's mind raged at the prospect of being beaten now.

He grabbed the pallet and lifted it as fast as he could. The cylinder rolled off the front, towards the open cargo door and Luca ran after it. He pushed it to the top of the ramp and gave it one last shove, aware that the lives of millions depended upon it.

As the missile slammed into the rear of the plane, it erupted in a fireball.

The squadron leader watched everything from the side, only understanding the sacrifice the European had made in the very last moment.

22
Ticino, Switzerland
1 Month Later

'I have accepted failure and offered my resignation; you have not accepted my resignation, therefore, as ongoing General Counsel, may I remind you of the fact that brave though Herr Voss was, had he obeyed orders, we could have garnered this information without the loss of life—his life specifically.'

The seven holographic figures were sitting in sullen silence, everybody angry, but nobody angrier than Sir Stephen Devereux. Stalking up and down the room, he did not attempt to present his mood as anything other than it was.

'Why didn't you report Luca's intelligence earlier, as soon as you had it?'

Herr Hesse was in an unusually passionate mood; several of those present thought the news of Voss's death had affected him more deeply than perhaps he would admit. 'Either we applaud Herr Voss's initiative—in which case we all agree I should have done nothing until after his last visit to Yangon as I agreed with him, or we disapprove of it—in which case he is the master of his own demise for his litany of disobedience. Which one is it?'

The cardinal swirled round, his red cassock flowing with him in a symphony of hot-blooded wrath. 'Why do you keep coming back to those two facile options when we all know that as Luca was carrying out his mission in Yangon you could have updated the various ambassadors and they could have adjusted their reaction accordingly? His death is on your hands, Gustav.'

Hesse was out of his chair. 'How *dare* you? Are you seriously suggesting that with a dirty bomb flying towards Pyongyang, North Korea would have acted *any* differently? Your affection for your godson makes you an unreliable participant in this matter.'

'How dare you suggest—'

'Can I suggest you both just shut up?'

It was Ulla Thord-Gray, shimmering with irritation not only at the men's perennial spat but also at the loss of a favoured son. Both men went quiet; not only was she right, the hierarchy of the group had been in place for centuries and nobody had ever questioned it.

'He is dead. We have grieved these past few weeks, we have argued, but we have not yet agreed on a next step. A bomb that was totally unaccounted for exploded in the sea. It has not gone unnoticed.'

The room was silent. Hesse lowered himself back into his chair, wanting to boil over at Devereux, but also aware that he needed to reassert control.

'What is the wisest path now?' continued Ulla Thord-Gray. 'What of that woman, JJ? I understand that she has tried to contact you Herr Hesse?'

'Yes, she even went so far as to turn up here unannounced,' said Hesse. 'Her knowledge of this location is yet another indiscretion on Herr Voss's part.'

Sir Stephen would not let that pass. 'A Broker's facilitator is allowed to know certain facts about the Families.'

'He was not the Broker and she was *not* a facilitator.'

Ulla Thord-Gray reasserted order: 'So what do we intend to do with her? Pension her off?'

'Kill her off.'

Everyone present was aghast at the General Counsel's suggestion.

'She knows too much. She is not one of us, we have no reason to trust her, and even if we could, the risk would be too great. It is unfortunate, I know, but we need to clean house.'

The cardinal shook his head unhappily. 'No, no, no. She is an innocent bystander in this—'

'She is far from innocent; she has seen everything and knows everything. Are you telling me that the account she gave you when she arrived at the Chinese border suggested otherwise?'

'That does not mean we should execute her. It's a barbaric suggestion.'

'It is a practical suggestion. Are you forgetting how close the world came to the brink of nuclear conflict? Are you forgetting how we were shunned from the very talks that could have averted such a crisis? Have you forgotten how our influence was ousted by Butakhan and his organisation? Have you?'

'But murder—'

'We would have stopped that war—a war that almost cost unimaginable loss of human life. Recent events have taken influence away from us. If, in any way, she was to play a part in us losing influence again who, here, would answer for the deaths we could have avoided?'

The silence was eventually broken by Devereux. 'We cannot take a life because of a small risk in the future.'

'Yes we can, Sir Stephen. And we have done so on numerous occasions in the past millennia and averted numerous wars, and you know it.'

'Times change, Gustav.'

'But not the forces of history. I suggest a vote.'

The cardinal had not expected such swift action and appealed to the assembled members. 'No, no, there is no need to do this now.'

The Texan, Mr Furst, coughed significantly. 'Actually, Stephen, I believe there is, I vote aye.'

Stephen swirled round to Ulla Thord-Gray. 'Surely no—?'

'Stephen, the vote has begun and there can be no more talk.'

She looked from him, now silenced, to each member in turn. The head of each dynasty spoke clearly and sadly. Each repeated Mr Furst's 'aye'. It remained only for the Nordic head herself to vote, but she could have no real affect now that the majority had spoken.

'No.'

Everybody looked at the person who had spoken, not at Ulla Thord-Gray but at the figure now emerging from the shadows: Luca Voss.

Stephen's face was at once incredulous. 'Luca!' he exclaimed.

Luca shook his hand as he passed him, making his way to where Herr Hesse stood in the centre. Hesse rose to greet him, startled not just by his appearance, but by the gun hanging from his hand.

'Luca…' he stammered. 'You're back.'

'Did you tell them?'

The General Counsel could not gauge Luca's manner: menacing when it should have been obedient, happy even. 'Tell them what?'

Luca was two metres from Hesse now. 'Everything.'

'Yes, yes. They know you wanted me to wait until you had been to Yangon before bringing you back, but you disappeared. You boarded the plane without telling us, so there was nothing we could do. But you're alive, it's fantastic.'

'That's very… effusive of you, Herr Hesse.'

The General Counsel hovered uncertainly, unsure how to read his former student. 'I'm pleased to see you, Luca. We all thought you were dead.'

'Like Franz? Like Raoul? I'm sorry, tell me again, how was Raoul killed?'

Herr Hesse sensed something was very much askew. He felt dumb in the face of Luca's fierce confidence. 'I gave Franz your addresses. You know I made that mistake.'

'Did you give them to Franz—or did you give them to Butakhan?'

Now Herr Hesse spoke as much to the room as to the Swiss man, 'The Mongolian? That is insane. Whoever cut Franz's fingers off, they tortured him for that information, that's how they knew.'

'But as I told you Herr Hesse, his fingers had been cut off to hide the rare earth metals that would have been found on them. You did tell everybody that didn't you?'

There was disquiet in the room. Devereux spoke up. 'You never mentioned this, Gustav?'

'I do not tend to repeat every piece of intelligence I hear.'

'You never said anything about Butakhan shipping rare earth minerals out to North Korea to fake the geologists' results?'

'I did not think that was proven—'

'Did you tell them Scarlett's intelligence about Butakhan shipping enriched uranium back from North Korea?' Luca asked.

The room looked at Herr Hesse now, a discomfort growing among them. For a moment, he was lost for words.

'You know Herr Hesse, North Korea is like a tinderbox, right?'

The General Counsel nodded carefully, not sure what was meant by the last remark.

'Is that your phrase or Butakhan's?' Luca asked.

'What do you mean, Luca?'

'Do not call me by my first name. Whose phrase was it?'

'It's a common phrase Herr Voss.'

'Yes, but both of you happened to say it to me on the same day.'

'Did we? But you haven't told us where you've been?'

'I've been a guest of the North Korean people, Herr Hesse.'

Hesse feigned concern, which fooled no one. 'What did they do to you?'

'They nursed me back to health and sent me on my way. Lying in bed in hospital, you get to thinking. Scarlett, she was telling you everything all along. You knew all along about Butakhan and his plans. You didn't tell me, you didn't tell the Families and you didn't tell Butakhan either, did you?'

'What are you talking about?'

'I'm talking about how you almost allowed a war to break out for your own petty agenda.'

'Nonsense,' Hesse said, appealing to the wider room. 'This is nonsense.'

'He knew at the end, Herr Hesse. He knew you had betrayed him. And he's out there.'

'No, no, he died.'

Luca shook his head. 'He got away and he'll come looking for you. I'm guessing he's feeling like a tinderbox right now…'

Herr Hesse felt everybody's eyes on him. He knew he had lost the room, but still hoped to explain. 'We had a chance to unite the Thirteen Families again, Luca. We had a chance to move from influence to power as it once was—as it should be again.'

'I know. Butakhan told me.'

'Did he tell you he wanted to destroy the Seven? Did he tell you that I turned his revenge into ambition?'

'You never thought to share that with us, though. Why is that?'

Now Hesse threw caution to the wind; he had nothing to lose, a pent up moral outrage brimming over. 'Because the Seven Pyramids of Power are no longer powers, they are shadows of themselves, mere foot soldiers when they should be generals. They have accepted the decline of their dynasties as surely as a weak emperor does the decline of his empire.'

'Or perhaps the world has moved on, Herr Hesse. Perhaps absolute monarchies with absolute power were consigned to the trash can of history for a reason.'

'You think small like the rest of them, Luca.'

'But Butakhan thinks big, is that it?'

Herr Hesse looked at him spitefully, a look that soon turned to defiance. 'Who among us would have the stomach to start a war these days? A nuclear conflict would have been our opportunity to seize the reins once again. People would have bent their knee to us, not the other way round.'

Luca raised a weary, ironic eyebrow. 'Damn those sovereign states.'

Stephen looked on as the two stared at each other in silence. Like the heads of the Families, he wanted to spew forth a torrent of rage at the General Counsel but he was so in thrall to Luca's return that he wanted to allow his godson to play out his own hand first.

Herr Hesse puffed out his chest as a physical reminder of his status, and eyed Luca scornfully. 'Now what?'

Luca looked down at the gun. 'What, after the deaths of Franz and Raoul and Scarlett and also after your dealings with Butakhan?' The Swiss man lifted the gun and pointed it at his former teacher.

Herr Hesse hesitated then stiffened. A curious smile seemed to crawl over his face. 'I heard about your exploits, Herr Voss. About Russia, Shanghai, Yangon—the mines, even. Rumour has it you never did kill a man with your own hands; you did not have the stomach for it. It takes a lot to murder somebody in cold blood.' He flashed a condescending smile at Luca. 'You haven't finished your training. Luca Voss could not shoot me if he tried.'

Slowly Luca lowered his gun, a blank expression on his face. 'You're right. Luca Voss couldn't... but the Broker could.'

Raising the weapon, Luca fired at Hesse with a sudden, abrupt bang. The bullet that entered Hesse's forehead made any reaction on his part impossible.

The room was silent as Luca returned the gun to a holster inside his jacket and walked back into the darkness.

23
Ticino, Switzerland

Luca crossed the gravel to the Bentley Continental Zagato parked outside the chateau and climbed into the passenger seat. He stared out across the lake that surrounded the property on three sides.

From the driver's seat, JJ considered him, letting him take his time. After a period of silence she followed his stare, letting her own drift to the ancient stone bridge that crossed from the road to the chateau. It made her think about leaving.

'So...'

Eventually Luca looked at her, but said nothing.

'Did you do everything you needed to?'

He stared at her with a look that was somewhere between affection and resolve.

'Yes. Yes, we did.'

She smiled at his choice of pronoun, fired up the engine with no idea where she was meant to be taking them and felt all the happier for it.

As they sped through the Swiss countryside, JJ's mind buzzed with questions. The adventure had only just begun and now she was wondering what might happen next. *Had the Seven Families hired Luca as the Broker? Had she been accepted as the Broker's equal?*

And then there was the world around them, catastrophe looming large in every direction. JJ thought of the Middle East, the situation there becoming more and more complicated by the day. She thought of the drugs war developing along the length of America's east coast, cyber terrorism and the fragility of the world's banks. With China, Russia, Japan and North Korea all flexing their muscles, could any previous Broker have faced so many threats?

As these thoughts and a thousand others tangled together in her mind, one issue never needed a moment's consideration: if Luca wanted her, she would be his confidante and partner.

All she knew for sure was that she had fallen deeply in love with the man now nodding off next to her. She wanted to surprise him and play some very grown-up games but now was not the time for wicked thoughts.

He had used the term 'we'. In her mind, JJ was suddenly weighing up the prospect of becoming the Broker's partner. As she steered the Bentley through the lush countryside she pictured them out there together, side by side, tackling one international incident after another on behalf of the Seven Families.